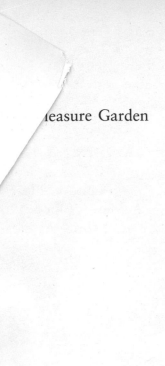

easure Garden

THE LAST PLEASURE GARDEN

by

Lee Jackson

William Heinemann: London

Published in the United Kingdom in 2006 by William Heinemann

3 5 7 9 10 8 6 4 2

William Heinemann
The Random House Group Limited
20 Vauxhall Bridge Road, London SW1V 2SA

Random House Australia (Pty) Limited
20 Alfred Street, Milsons Point, Sydney,
New South Wales 2061, Australia

Random House New Zealand Limited
18 Poland Road, Glenfield,
Auckland 10, New Zealand

Random House (Pty) Limited
Isle of Houghton, Corner of Boundary Road & Carse O'Gowrie,
Houghton 2198 South Africa

The Random House Group Limited Reg. No. 954009
www.randomhouse.co.uk

A CIP catalogue record for this book
is available from the British Library

Papers used by Random House are natural, recyclable products made
from wood grown in sustainable forests. The manufacturing processes
conform to the environmental regulations of the country of origin

ISBN 0 434 01249 1

Typeset by Palimpsest Book Production Limited,
Polmont, Stirlingshire
Printed and bound in the United Kingdom by
Clays Ltd, St Ives plc

PART ONE

CHAPTER ONE

'Who's for Cremorne?'

The young man's cry rings out along the paved embankment, echoing beneath the girders of Hungerford Bridge.

'How about you, sir? Care to go down to Cremorne tonight, sir?'

The gentleman in question is a rather whiskery man in his sixties, on an evening stroll along the river terrace. He merely shakes his head and offers a regretful smile, as if to say, 'No, no, I am too old for that – far too old.'

The young tout grins sympathetically. He looks down and rubs the brass buttons of his uniform. The tout's coat is an eye-catching red, a deep crimson, upon which is embroidered a capital C, the mark of the Citizen Boat Company. He raises his voice once more.

'Cree-morne! Departin' on the hour!'

The cry carries far in the evening air. It is not long before it finds more receptive ears. For the tree-lined Thames Embankment is busy with promenaders and West End pleasure-seekers; the young man will not have to work too hard. Indeed, for every dissenter, there are two enthusiasts directed towards the wooden huts that serve as the company's ticket booths, quite prepared to pay the fourpenny fare to Cremorne Gardens. And they do tend to come in pairs, two by two, much like the inhabitants of a certain famous vessel of ancient times, a good mixture of every breed of Londoner: the prosperous costermonger and his Poll; the shop-boy and his Sarah; the up-and-coming City clerk in sparkling white turnover collar, who walks in company with his Angelina, a muslin-clad creature, a zephyr shawl draped over her arm, a white rose pinned to her dress. And if there is no bona fide aristocrat amongst the steamboat crowd, there are at least a few swells, men who polish jewelled tie-pins and stroke their extravagantly long side-whiskers.

One couple, however, strike the tout as peculiar: a gentleman in his fifties, in a billycock hat and brown tweed jacket, and a younger man, no more than twenty-five, black-suited, with a fulsome white cravat. They seem an oddly formal pair for the Cremorne boat.

In fact, if the tout thinks anything, as he turns away, and resumes his vociferous entreaties to passing pedestrians, it is merely one word: 'Coppers.'

———

'Have you ever wondered, sir,' says Sergeant Bartleby, unconsciously straightening his cravat as he completes his business at the ticket booth, 'why we get all the queer cases?'

'Stop your preening, man.'

'Sorry, sir. I just thought, if we're supposed to be out on the spree, I'd dress the part.'

Inspector Decimus Webb looks rather brutally at the cravat. 'I fear it would take more than that.'

4

There is no time to reply. A nearby chain is removed and the crowd jostles forward along the wooden pier. Knots of impatient customers begin to form, as the more delicate women in the assembled company cautiously negotiate the wooden bridge that leads to the waiting steamer.

'Take it slow, your highness,' says a raucous female towards the front. Several of the costers break out in hearty laughter. Others merely tut to themselves. Meanwhile, behind Decimus Webb, a pair of men raise their voices.

'Stop that scrouging, won't you?'

'Well, perhaps you'd be so polite as to mind where you put your bleedin' hoofs?'

Most of the people nearby raise a smile at this debate. But Webb frowns. He is familiar with metropolitan crowds and possesses a sixth sense in such matters. He turns slightly towards Bartleby, raising his eyebrows significantly, giving a slight nod.

The sergeant, to his credit, unobtrusively glances down and responds instantly, placing a firm hand on the shoulder of the first 'scrouger'.

'And perhaps you would be so kind,' says Bartleby, whispering in the man's ear, 'as to remove your hand from the detective inspector's pocket, and hook it – the pair of you.'

The scrouger turns a shade of white and his friendship with his neighbour is abruptly renewed. The two men hastily push back through the throng under Bartleby's watchful gaze. The crowd, quite oblivious, moves forward.

'We should have taken them down to Bow Street, sir,' says Bartleby, as they finally reach the steamer.

'And spend half the night at the police court? Don't you want to get to Cremorne, Sergeant?'

'Me, sir? I'm quite looking forward to it.'

The two policemen find a spot up on deck and it takes only a matter of minutes for the steamer to receive its full complement of passengers. The ropes are loosed from the moorings and the sound of the boat's engine, already rumbling below, changes its pitch. The machinery emits a reverberating rattle and, with a puff of steam from its tall funnel, the vessel moves off. Twin paddle-wheels direct it beneath the iron railway bridge that spans the river, linking Charing Cross Station with the south bank.

'Not going below, sir?' asks Bartleby, gesturing towards the trap-door and steps that descend into the lower deck, where liquid refreshment is on sale.

Webb shakes his head. 'It will be far too cramped for my liking and I much prefer to see where I'm going, even on this fool's errand. Besides, it's a good while since I've been down to Chelsea; I expect it has changed a great deal.'

Bartleby casts a longing glance to below decks, but stays beside his superior. 'You think we are wasting our time?'

'The whole business is quite ridiculous. It is not a detective matter; not for Scotland Yard, at least.'

'You think this fellow's harmless?'

'I do not think he is a modern Sweeney Todd, put it that way, Sergeant.'

Webb's gaze returns to the river and, as the boat passes by, the breweries that line the south bank. The tall smoking chimney of Barclay, Perkins & Co.'s famous establishment wafts the faint smell of hops towards the Palace of Westminster. Webb looks back at his sergeant.

'Very well, you may go below. Nothing more than

a half of stout. Make a few casual inquiries. Doubtless many of them make it a regular night out.'

'Thank you, sir,' says Bartleby with a grin.

The journey upstream takes little more than forty minutes, the boat stopping briefly at Nine Elms and Battersea, though few come on board at either location. It is only when the steamer approaches the old wooden supports of Battersea Bridge, passing the giant black tub of the local gasometer upon the southern shore, that a perceptible change of spirits occurs amongst its passengers. Gaily-coloured shawls are gathered up, drinks are downed, hats and bonnets returned to their rightful places. Sergeant Bartleby takes the opportunity to return to the deck, where he finds Decimus Webb watching the sun set, its final rays dissolving into the murky brown silt of the Thames.

'Well? Anything of interest?' asks Webb.

'Not much. They've all read the papers. No-one's seen the fellow themselves but a friend of a friend swears they know someone – you know the sort of thing.'

'Worthless,' mutters Webb. 'Ah, well, here we are, at least.'

As Webb speaks, the pilot guides their vessel towards the pier upon the north bank of the river, the wheels slowing to a leisurely speed, then stopping entirely. The pier is a wooden structure, illuminated in the dimming twilight by a row of gas-jets, mounted on a makeshift-looking iron rail along its length. Each light burns brightly within a large glass globe, casting a fiery glow over the waiting attendants who grasp at the mooring ropes flung out to the shore. The steamer is soon pulled in, its hull banging noisily into the timber piles, until it settles, bobbing gently upon the water.

'Cremorne!' shouts the man on shore, as the boarding plank is secured, the guide-ropes pulled tight. 'Everybody off!'

The announcement, of course, is a mere formality. Nobody can doubt their location, even though the river esplanade that runs along the south of the pleasure gardens is not marked by any signpost. The signature of Cremorne is its aura of gas-light. It is not from any individual flame, though there are a dozen more lamps along the riverside path. Rather, it is the omnipresent radiance of the Gardens themselves: a garish, cheerful glow that, from the Thames, suggests a magical kingdom hidden from view behind the trees.

The passengers of the steamer all but run into the little riverside ticket hall.

'Shall we make ourselves known to the management, sir?' asks Bartleby, as the two policemen quit the boat, being amongst the last to alight. 'I've met with the lads from T Division already, mind you. I know them on sight.'

'I think,' says Webb, 'we merely watch and wait. If he is here, he will make a move. Now, Sergeant,' he continues, peering at the queue for the box office, 'tell me, do you happen to have two bob?'

———

It is gone half-past nine when the two policemen reach the heart of the pleasure gardens, the famous dancing platform. Its wooden boards are already thronged with people, enjoying the warm summer air. From the outside, the area is almost hidden from view; for it nestles amid a grove of ancient elms, and is surrounded on two sides by twin tiers of supper-boxes, which resemble the boxes in a theatre. But the stage that the boxes overlook is not of the regular variety. It is the Crystal Platform, a great circular rostrum in the open air, raised a foot or so off the ground, railed around by wrought iron. The railings are interrupted at intervals by tall triple-crowned lamps and, between them, above the crowd, arched iron festoons dripping with tear-drops of coloured cut-glass, sparkling in the gaslight. At the heart of it all is the hexagonal Chinese Pagoda, its upturned eaves and exotic fret-work painted rainbow colours. It contains a 'Refreshment Room' devoted to the sale of 'Choice Wines and Sprits' but, more importantly, upon the top storey, a thirty-piece orchestra, providing a noisy accompaniment to the couples gaily waltzing below.

'They say it's the place for loose women, now the Casino's closed,' remarks Bartleby, gazing at the platform as the waltz comes to an end, and the M.C. calls for a quadrille. 'And those supper-boxes too. You can imagine, can't you?'

Webb looks around at the boxes. Indeed, in a couple there is merely a hint of candlelight and indistinct movement behind a muslin curtain.

'I know what they say, Sergeant, and you can spare me your vivid imagination. We are not here to grub up dirt. Keep your eyes peeled for our man.'

'How do I spot him?'

'In the act.'

Bartleby looks round the exterior of the platform. White-aproned waiters move briskly around the tables set on the grass, accepting the 'refreshment tickets' that are the Gardens' particular currency. Men and women seem to lounge in an easy intimacy, listening to the resounding music, admiring the sets formed by the more proficient dancers. A blue-uniformed member of T Division strolls past, giving the two detectives a discreet nod. But no-one appears remotely suspicious. Plenty are inebriated; a good few may possess dubious morals, but nothing out of the ordinary, not on a summer's night in such a place.

Then Webb taps the sergeant's arm.

'There – that fellow in the heavy great-coat. A bit warm for that sort of article, is it not?'

Bartleby peers at the man, upon the opposite side of the platform, a good two or three hundred yards distant. He is about nineteen or twenty years of age, flitting behind the dancing couples, with something rather nervous and awkward in his movements.

'You go round on the left, I will take the right,' suggests Webb.

Bartleby nods, and the two policemen begin to work their way around the seated groups, in front of the lower tier of supper-boxes. It takes them a good couple of minutes to negotiate past Cremorne's revellers, but the man gives no indication that he notices them. Rather, he walks cautiously up to the queue for the sheltered 'Money Box' that lies just beyond the clearing, one of the small cabins where Cremorne's own bankers change cash into tokens. He stands just behind a young woman wearing a dress of dark blue poplin, and seems to hesitate for a moment.

Webb motions to Bartleby to get closer.

As the quadrille comes to a close, applause echoes round the platform. And the man in the great-coat reaches towards the woman's neck.

'Grab him!' shouts Webb.

Bartleby springs forward. The sergeant is both considerably taller and faster than the man in the great-coat; he tackles him to the ground even as the man's hand touches the woman's dress. The woman herself spins around in surprise. A chorus of exclamations break out from the nearby table; some express concern, but mostly they are words of encouragement, as if *al fresco* wrestling is suddenly upon the evening's bill. Webb, for his part, stands to one side. Bartleby looks up with an imploring glance, his captive squirming vigorously in his grip.

'I could do with a little—' says the sergeant, interrupted by the necessity of avoiding the man's fist.

'On its way, Sergeant,' replies Webb, as two men from T Division run round the platform. 'On its way.'

Sergeant Bartleby says nothing, otherwise occupied. He is only relieved when, at length, the strong arms of the two constables prove sufficient to render the struggling man quite prone.

'Sorry, Miss,' says Webb, at last, turning to address the victim, whilst peering rather strangely at her shoulders. 'I am a police inspector. Don't be alarmed. Are you quite all right? Did he harm you?'

'I think he took my necklace,' says the woman, a little shaken, anxiously touching her neck.

'Oh, damnation,' exclaims Webb, rather to her dismay. 'Is that all? Check the fellow's pockets, Sergeant. Is there anything?'

Bartleby obliges. A trawl through the coat quickly reveals two sovereigns, a gold fob watch, two necklaces, one silver, one gold, a purse, and a season ticket to the Gardens.

'Nothing. Is this your necklace, Miss?'

'Yes, that is mine,' replies the young woman, both shocked and bemused. 'But what did you expect to find?'

Inspector Webb sighs. 'A pair of scissors.'

Outside the gas-lit rockery of the Hermit's Cave, in the western portion of Cremorne Gardens, Sarah Jane Hockley, maid-of-all-work, quits the company of the Gardens' famed elderly prognosticator and walks back in the direction of the lawn. She dawdles behind her male companion, a young groom who is eager not to miss the fireworks at ten p.m., and who has, in his own words, 'waited all night'. In part, her slowness is a growing disinclination for the young man's company; in part, she is bent on reading the prophecy vouchsafed to her by the sage:

> Thalaba's Prophecy. The star of your nativity intimates a very good foreboding. Although not entirely unchequered, it promises much future prosperity. The conjunction of Mars with Venus in the square of your nativity offers tokens to show that energy will bring about your advancement and that your union will prove the token of your felicity. See her in the magic mirror. Many future blessings are shown towards the end of the year – many good results will arise, and profitable friendships spring up to your interest.

So fascinating is her destiny, written in a scratchy hand on the crumpled foolscap paper, that she hardly notices the sound of soft footsteps on the grass behind her. And it is far too late to run, once her dress is slashed and torn.

Far too late, when something pierces her side, colouring the ripped muslin bright red.

CHAPTER TWO

In Edith Grove, Brompton, the sound of a Haydn sonata fills the upstairs drawing-room. It is played rather competently by a pretty young woman of eighteen years of age. She sits alone, practising at the pianoforte, with her back to the door. She possesses an abundance of curled auburn hair, which trails down her neck in loose ringlets, and there is a certain grace and self-possession in her posture, not least in the delicate movement of her hands upon the keyboard.

The voice of her mother interrupts her.

'Rose!'

Rose Perfitt stumbles over her notes, stops, and turns her head. Her mother stands at the door.

'Rose, it is past two o'clock, please.'

'I am sorry, Mama,' she replies. 'I just wanted to finish . . .'

Mrs. Perfitt shakes her head. 'My dear, please, a little peace and quiet. You may play later.'

Rose obeys, removing the music and closing the piano lid. Her mother is a handsome woman, her face scarcely hinting at her forty years. It is not too fanciful to see in Mrs. Perfitt's well-bred features the source of her daughter's youthful beauty.

'Are you expecting anyone, Mama?'

13

'No, but Alice Watson may just call. I would simply like a little time to compose myself, if I may.'

Mrs. Perfitt smiles a tight-lipped smile, as if to express a sense of relief at the restoration of peace and quiet in the drawing-room. She settles herself on the ebonised chair that sits by the hearth.

'You might read, my dear,' she suggests to her daughter, who wanders idly to the window, peering through the lace curtains, down onto the street below.

'I think there's someone coming,' says Rose, teasing back the lace.

'Rose, the window! Don't be so vulgar!' exclaims Mrs. Perfitt. Her daughter instantly releases the fabric.

'It's Mrs. Featherstone.'

'Oh, heavens!' exclaims Mrs. Perfitt. 'That woman!'

Mrs. Perfitt pauses for thought, looking at her daughter. 'Rose, go and brush your hair.'

⚬

The social niceties of the 'morning-call', the illogically-named custom of paying afternoon visits to one's friends and neighbours, have never held much fascination for Rose Perfitt. The endless exchange of visiting cards, the polite refusals of cups of tea, the awkward discussions of the weather, have always seemed a terrible bore to her youthful mind. The only consolation she can take from Mrs. Bertha Featherstone's presence in the drawing-room, when she returns from arranging her coiffure, is that the latter carries her bonnet in her hand, and has her woollen shawl – a rather unnecessary article for the time of year – still wrapped about her shoulders. It is, thinks Rose to herself, intended to be a brief visit.

'Ah,' exclaims Mrs. Featherstone, a rather robust-looking broad-built woman, turning to face Rose

Perfitt, once she has settled in a chair, 'here she is, your youngest. I trust you are well, Miss Perfitt?'

'Yes, ma'am. Very well.'

'But you look a little pale, Miss Perfitt? Are you sure you are not ill? I generally notice such things. The Reverend says I am most sensitive to human frailty.'

'I don't believe so, ma'am,' replies Rose, politely. 'I am quite well.'

'Hmm. Perhaps,' says Mrs. Featherstone, seeming a little aggrieved by this contradiction of her infallibility. 'Still, never mind that. Mrs. Perfitt, now, how long has it been?'

'Oh, I could not say.'

'Well ma'am, forgive me for not calling sooner.'

'There is nothing to forgive,' says Mrs. Perfitt, with the utmost sincerity.

'Thank you, ma'am. Well, I have come today because, if I may be blunt – and knowing your charitable instincts, ma'am – I wondered if I might presume on your support for a worthy cause.'

Mrs. Perfitt waves her hand majestically in regal permission, though a rather glacial smile remains fixed upon her face.

'The Reverend—'

'And how is your dear husband?' interrupts Mrs. Perfitt.

'In good health, ma'am, thank you,' replies Mrs. Featherstone, not deflected from her purpose. 'And he is planning a charity bazaar at the College, in aid of the Society for the Suppression of Vice. That is what I came to tell you. Such a good cause! Lady Astbury has promised to do the penny ices, quite a coup, you know.'

'Has she really? Well, then, you must let us know

the date. We shall be sure to attend, won't we, Rose?'

'Oh!' replies Mrs. Featherstone, joyfully, before Rose can even answer. 'You are a rock, ma'am.'

Mrs. Perfitt nods. 'And I am sure Mr. Perfitt will be willing to contribute a little something.'

'Ma'am!' exclaims the clergyman's wife, her naturally stony expression melting into a warm smile. 'I confess, I knew we might rely on your goodwill. I said as much to the Reverend.'

Mrs. Perfitt merely gestures once more, this time a dismissive shake of her hand, indicative of her own unworthiness.

'No, no, you are too modest,' continues Mrs. Featherstone, reaching inside her handbag. 'Now, what was the other matter? Ah yes! I have the Reverend's latest pamphlet in here somewhere. Now, where is it? May I give you a copy?'

'I am sure we have it, thank you,' says Mrs. Perfitt, perhaps a little too hastily.

'Oh, that cannot be. It has only just arrived from the printer's.'

'Really?' says Mrs. Perfitt, her perfect smile creasing a little. 'The Reverend is so prolific.'

'With cause, ma'am, with good cause,' says Mrs. Featherstone, producing a folded pamphlet, which she hands to her hostess. 'There!'

Rose Perfitt, seated beside her mother, leans over to read the title:

CREMORNE : THE CURSE OF THE NEW SODOM

'You have heard what went on there last night?' asks Mrs. Featherstone.

'No, I do not believe so.'

16

'A servant-girl was stabbed in the Gardens. The act of some frenzied madman; and I understand it is not the first such incident. One wonders whatever the girl's mistress could have been thinking, giving her liberty to show herself in such a place? And yet, still, I'll warrant they will renew the licence, come November. The Reverend is quite at his wit's end, ma'am.'

'I am sorry to hear that.'

There is the sound of the door-bell ringing downstairs, but *politesse* demands that no-one should remark upon it.

'We must see the place closed for good,' continues Mrs. Featherstone. 'It is our duty.'

'It would improve the area, I am sure,' replies Mrs. Perfitt, with polite indifference in her voice. There is a hint of a yawn, stifled in her throat. 'It has rather gone downhill.'

The conversation is interrupted by a knock at the door.

'What is it, Richards?' asks Mrs. Perfitt of the young maid-servant, who stands timidly, half in the room, half upon the landing.

'Begging pardon, ma'am, Mrs. Watson presents her card.'

A fleeting look of relief passes over Mrs. Perfitt's face.

'Do have her come up.'

Rose Perfitt quits the drawing-room after the departure of Mrs. Bertha Featherstone and the arrival of her mother's more intimate friend, Mrs. Watson, complaining of a 'head'. Behind her, as she closes the door, the conversation is rather more animated.

'Alice, I swear, that woman is enough to make one turn Mahometan!'

'Caroline, really! Behave yourself!'

Rose ascends to her bedroom upon the second floor and closes the panelled door behind her. She walks over to her writing desk by the window, and sits down, feeling for one of its concealed compartments, the artifice of some long-forgotten master of the carpenter's art. Sliding the drawer open, she pulls out a careworn white envelope and unfolds the letter inside. The paper gives the impression of having been read and read again, even though it is written in her own hand.

My Dear Beloved,

All this day I have wished for one moment to kiss you, to have you in my embrace. Come tonight, sweetheart, and we shall be happy . . .

Rose stops reading, and looks to the window. It is a warm day, even for the time of year. She lifts up the sash, leans out and smells the afternoon air. In the distance, past the end of Edith Grove, across the King's Road, she can just make out the distant walls of Cremorne Gardens, plastered with the multi-coloured fly-posters that promise untold delights within.

CHAPTER THREE

OUTRAGE AT CREMORNE. A young woman is now lying at the Chelsea Union Infirmary having suffered a brutal assault at the hands of an unknown assailant. Sarah Hookey, a servant who resides at 23, Worthing Terrace, Pimlico, was in the Gardens on Saturday evening last when her person was attacked with a sharp instrument, which cut her dress, and penetrated her side. A number of men, attracted by her cries, hastened to the scene. The woman lapsed into an unconscious state and was carried by Constable 104 T to the King's-road, where she was conveyed in a cab to the infirmary. There is every hope of a recovery, but the perpetrator of this peculiar sanguinary outrage remains at large.

Decimus Webb puts down his copy of *The Times* and looks rather despondently out of the window of the cab, at the shops and houses of the King's Road. Bartleby, seated beside him, picks up the paper, and reads the brief article.

'They've got the name wrong,' says the sergeant.

'That is the least of our worries, Sergeant,' replies Webb, as the cab begins to slow. 'Just wait until the gutter rags put two and two together. I've already had a personal note from the Assistant Commissioner.'

The cab judders to a halt. As the two policeman alight, Bartleby spies a piece of paper trodden into the dirt by the side of the road. He picks it up.

'I think you're too late, sir. Look here – "Ballad of the Cremorne Cutter". Look's like a new one. Now, let's see—'

'Spare me the doggerel, Sergeant, I can quite imagine,' replies Webb.

The cab-man, overhearing the conversation, looks down from his perch atop the hansom. 'Saw a little 'un selling those yesterday. Selling like hot-cakes they were.'

'Yes, thank you,' says Webb, passing the man his fare. 'That will be all.'

'I'll wait if yer like.'

'I am sure there's no need,' replies Webb, rather sourly. The cab-driver shrugs, tugs on the reins, and swings the vehicle around, whilst the two policemen approach the pay-box that guards the iron gates to the pleasure ground. The clerk inside deliberately busies himself with other matters.

'Will you let us through?' asks Webb.

'We ain't open until three,' replies the clerk brusquely.

'My name is Webb. Mr. Boon is expecting us, I believe.'

'Ah,' says the clerk, eyeing the policemen up and down, then tapping his nose in the approved 'knowing' fashion, 'is he now? Well, why didn't you say so?'

The clerk takes up a set of keys, and steps out to the iron gates. 'Here, come through. You'll find him at the Circus, I reckon. Through the Fernery – you can't miss it.'

Webb and Bartleby follow the man's directions. The walk through Cremorne in daylight is not an unpleasant one. For, despite its man-made vistas, it possesses a certain rustic charm in the large oaks and elms that dominate the landscaped paths. But there is also something of going behind-the-scenes: the fountains have been turned off; the marble limbs of the Greek gods that adorn the park's arbours seem pale and wan in the daytime; it is, all in all, a little lifeless.

At length, the two policemen reach the Circus, though the area is obscured in part by the primeval foliage of the Fernery. The Circus itself is a large circular amphitheatre of wooden construction, surrounded on all sides by raised benches, gaily decorated with flags and streamers, with a canvas tent for a roof, rising to some forty or fifty feet above the ground. In the dirt-covered ring at its centre a dozen horses prance in circles, forming complex patterns around a moustachioed gentleman in riding costume, who directs them with the occasional flick of a long whip. There is no audience but for a solitary, rather portly middle-aged man in a fashionable silk suit, watching from the side. He gets up when he sees the two policemen.

'What do you make of that?' says the man, enthusiastically, before either Webb or Bartleby can introduce themselves. 'Twelve horses. Fine specimens, thoroughbreds, but is it a decent draw? Now, I've told him, put a posture-master on each one, have them juggle, and we're in business, eh? Now, am I right? I believe I am; one must always think of the public, eh? Always!'

'Yes, I suppose so, sir,' replies Webb.

'So, enough of that, what do you do, eh?'

'Mr. Boon?' says Webb.

21

'Of course, sir!'

'My name is Inspector Webb. This is my sergeant, Bartleby.'

'Ah,' replies Mr. Boon. His enthusiasm instantly ebbs. 'I see. You must excuse me. We have been holding auditions and . . . well, an honest mistake. Please, take a seat.'

'Then I can assume you know why we are here?' says Webb.

'I regret I do. That business last night. First, how is this unfortunate girl?'

'The surgeon says it was a lucky escape; a flesh wound,' says Bartleby.

'Well, that is something,' remarks Boon. 'I suppose it is the same man that attacked her – the same as the others?'

'More than likely,' replies Webb. 'But, I would like to be quite clear, he has never stabbed someone before?'

'I hope the police have all the facts, Inspector. There have been three incidents to my knowledge. In each case he only cut away some of the girl's hair. I must confess, when I first asked for help from Scotland Yard, I did not expect it to come to this. I thought the fellow was merely a nuisance.'

'I hardly think you can consider us responsible, sir,' says Bartleby.

'No, I did not mean that. But if the fellow . . . well, what if he does it again? Does this wretch have a thirst for blood?'

'Please, sir,' says Webb, 'if you'll forgive me, there is no need to be quite so dramatic. We've drafted in ten more men from Westminster. If he tries it again, we will catch him.'

'I see. You have no clue as to his identity?'

'I've spoken to all the women personally, sir,'

22

interjects Bartleby. 'Not one recalls anything of value. One thought he was a tall fellow; one thought he was short. I don't believe any of them even saw him, not to speak of. He picks his moment.'

Boon sighs, rather theatrically. 'You must realise, if this continues, I will be ruined. This could be the final straw for Cremorne.'

'Sir?' says Webb.

'You need not be coy, Inspector. You must have read a certain letter that appeared in *The Times* last month?'

Webb nods. 'I seem to recall something rather uncomplimentary.'

'Uncomplimentary! To say the least! I have suffered the grossest imputations upon my character that one can imagine – you might think I keep the Gardens open specifically for the ruin of young women. And now this!'

Webb says nothing.

Mr. Boon frowns. 'We do our utmost to maintain propriety – you may ask anyone.'

'I am sure we spied a few females of the unfortunate variety on Saturday night, sir,' suggests Bartleby.

'As with any public place of recreation. What theatre or concert-room would be any different? Come, you know how it is. We do not encourage any species of immorality. Quite the reverse.'

'That is not the Gardens' reputation, though, is it, sir?' suggests Bartleby.

'The result, Sergeant,' replies Boon, a note of anger in his voice, 'of the braying of half a dozen narrow-minded puritans, who have hounded me in the press. I've half a mind to sue, you know.'

'I am sure,' replies Webb with a rather disinterested tone to his voice. 'Tell me, are you the owner of the grounds, sir?'

'The lessee, Inspector. I hardly see what difference that makes.'

'No, quite. And we can assume you have no idea yourself as to the identity of the attacker?'

Boon shakes his head despairingly. 'You may as well call him "The Cutter", Inspector. Everyone else is.'

'I am not of a melodramatic disposition, Mr. Boon,' replies Webb. 'And I do not much believe in monsters or phantoms, not of any variety.'

<hr />

The two policemen return to the King's Road, but the wait for a cab is a considerable one, and Webb begins to regret his decision to dismiss the driver that brought them to Chelsea.

'What do you make of it, sir?' says the sergeant.

'There is no connection between the women that this "Cutter" attacks, Sergeant. I am sure of that much – except that they are in the first bloom of youth. He seems quite particular about that. They have all been from completely different corners of the metropolis, for a start. Ah, which reminds me, did you talk to the "hermit"?'

'Why, do you think he *knows* who it was, sir?' says Bartleby with a grin.

'Sergeant,' says Webb in gruff admonition.

'Sorry, sir. I did. No joy there. He's an old fellow, theatrical sort, made a point of telling me how he knew Macready. Was in his "cave" the whole time. The thing is, he wears spectacles when he's not on duty. He might have second sight but I wouldn't say his regular eyes are up to much.'

'Hmm,' replies Webb.

'Maybe it wasn't the same man that stabbed Miss Hockley as attacked the others,' continues Bartleby. 'Maybe it was more personal-like?'

24

'Yes, well, you should look into the girl's circumstances,' replies Webb. 'That would be wise. At least you are thinking it through. But did you see her dress?'

'Her dress, sir?'

'I meant to point it out when we saw her at the infirmary. It looked to me like the cut of a pair of scissors – not a puncture or a gash like a knife might make, but a series of three or four sharp lacerations along a line, then the tear. No, I rather feel it is the same man. You know, I am not even sure if he meant to stab her.'

Webb pauses and frowns. 'Telegraph the mad-houses in London and the counties. A madman seems the most likely explanation. If it is some escaped lunatic, I don't want anything missed.'

'Yes, sir.'

⸺

John Boon opens his afternoon's post. The first item is, however, not at all to his liking: it is a pamphlet of a biblical nature, containing several odious comparisons between the entertainments on offer at Cremorne Gardens, the 'New Sodom upon the Thames', and the Canaanites' worship of idols.

Boon rips the paper to shreds.

CHAPTER FOUR

'Rose! Must you constantly watch the street? I have told you before.'

'Sorry, Mama. I was just looking out for Father.'

Mrs. Perfitt looks indulgently at her daughter.

'Rose, I will speak to him as soon as he comes home. I am sure he will say yes.'

~

Charles Perfitt is a tall, well-proportioned man, forty-five years of age, with smartly trimmed whiskers of the mutton-chop variety. Like most of the gentlemen arriving at Chelsea Station of an evening, he wears an immaculate business suit and hurries off the train as quickly as possible, walking briskly down the platform to the exit. He makes a point, however, of nodding to the booking-clerk as he passes the ticket office. It is his custom, upon his return from the City, to pay this small homage to the old party in question. For the clerk has taken the receipts of the London Western Extension Railway at Chelsea for as many years as Mr. Perfitt can recall. The old man, of course, nods back. Mr. Perfitt, as satisfied with this transaction as with any of his cleverly calculated dealings with jobbers upon the Stock Exchange, then turns his steps towards the King's Road.

Mr. Perfitt's journey is an agreeable walk by any standard. The route passes the Italianate towers of St. Mark's Training College – which look rather pleasing in the evening light, hinting at some forgotten corner of Tuscany – and, upon the opposing side of the King's Road, lie the famous nurseries of Messrs. Veitch, whose rose gardens and treasured exotic blooms, concealed by a high wall, lend a sweet fragrance to the surrounding suburban streets. But Mr. Perfitt does not linger, even as he passes the gates to Cremorne Gardens. In fact, it is only a matter of five minutes or so before he arrives at his front door. Once inside, he makes his way to the first-floor drawing-room, as is his custom. He finds his wife pacing rather nervously around the hearth-rug.

'Charles! You are back at last!' she exclaims.

'I find it's rather expected of me, this time of day, Caroline.'

'I thought you might have gone to your club.'

Mr. Perfitt sits down in the nearest armchair. 'Now why should I do that?'

'Oh, I don't know!' replies Mrs. Perfitt, a little annoyed at his calm response. 'I have such news – you will never guess!'

'Tobacco running high? I know already. They say it's the scarcity of western leaf. I should have bought last month. Would have made quite a tidy sum.'

'Charles, for pity's sake, don't tease. Alice Watson called this afternoon . . .'

Charles Perfitt rolls his eyes.

'Alice Watson called this afternoon . . .' says Mrs. Perfitt, but then hesitates. 'No, wait, I must find Rose.'

Charles Perfitt takes a deep breath, as his wife bustles from the room, almost catching the hem of her dress in the door. She returns, in a matter of moments, with her daughter in tow.

'Out with it,' says Mr. Perfitt, observing his daughter's rather animated and cheerful expression. 'I can see it will cost me money.'

'Papa, don't be a beast!' exclaims his daughter.

'Alice Watson called today,' continues Mrs. Perfitt, 'and she has spare tickets for a ball at the Prince's Ground upon Saturday. It is such a stroke of luck!'

Mr. Perfitt raises his eyebrows. 'Are you quite sure? Thought it was strictly the *bon ton* at the Prince's?'

'Alice, as you well know, is a personal acquaintance of Lady Astbury, who herself is a close friend of the Princess Louise.'

'I do know rather, as she never ceases from telling me. I thought one had to be introduced at Court before the Prince's Club would so much as glance at you.'

Mrs. Perfitt looks askance.

'Not that you aren't good enough for such society, my dear,' adds her husband, drily.

'It is a charity night, Charles, for the Society for the Suppression of something or other. A grand ball. Members may bring guests.'

Rose Perfitt takes her opportunity. 'May we go, Papa, please?'

Her father says nothing for a moment.

'Very well. I do not see why not.'

Mrs. Perfitt smiles. 'I should think so too.'

Rose, meanwhile, bends down to her father, and kisses him lightly on the cheek. 'Thank you!'

'Now,' continues Mrs. Perfitt briskly, 'there is the matter of a new dress. I will send a note to Alice. We must find out what her Beatrice is wearing.'

Mr. Perfitt looks at his daughter significantly. 'There, I told you it would cost me money.'

'Papa!'

Mr. Perfitt looks reprovingly back at his daughter, but then turns his attention to the magazines kept by his chair, in a wooden rack by the fire-place. He pulls out one item and brandishes it in his hand.

'I don't recall a subscription to this, Caroline.'

Mrs. Perfitt looks down, distracted from her mental calculations on the cost of certain fabrics suitable for ball-gowns, and glances at the cheaply-bound sheets.

'Ah, you have Mrs. Featherstone to thank for that.'

Mr. Perfitt flicks through the pages of pamphlet. 'She called again?'

'My dear,' replies Mrs. Perfitt, 'you know she makes a point of it; she visits every house in the street at least once a week.'

'Well,' says Mr. Perfitt, hastily putting the rather inky paper down, 'I suppose we shall never run short of reading matter. I just wish Featherstone might get his way and the place might close. At least then we could all be done with it.'

'They can't close the Gardens, Papa!' protests Rose.

'My dear girl,' says Mr. Perfitt, 'you do not know what goes on there nowadays. Everyone in Chelsea would be grateful to see it go. Am I not right, Caroline?'

'Of course you are,' replies Mrs. Perfitt, taking her daughter's hand. 'Come on, my dear, we will go and look at your wardrobe. We have lots to do.'

CHAPTER FIVE

Whatever their views upon Cremorne Gardens, it must be admitted that many of the inhabitants of Edith Grove look to the heavens at the mention of a certain Mrs. Bertha Featherstone. For she constantly appears uninvited in their drawing-rooms, in the aid of one good cause or another. Moreover, her husband, the Reverend Featherstone, is not the ordained minister of the parish, but rather one of several staff members employed by the National Society at St. Mark's Training College, an institution for the instruction of Christian school-masters. Thus, Mrs. Featherstone does not even call upon her neighbours *ex officio*. It is, perhaps, something of a testimony to her character that she persists with such enthusiasm and diligence, and that she does rather well for the Society for the Suppression of Vice and several other august bodies.

As Mr. Perfitt calls her to mind, however, Mrs. Featherstone has already finished her round of calls for the afternoon and returned home to St. Mark's College. Indeed, her rather stout, corseted form is quite striking as she enters the grounds. She receives a particularly servile bow from the gate-keeper, and there is something of the ironclad battleship about her as she glides towards the suite of rooms that belong to

31

her husband. She finds him bent over his books, preparing his monthly report upon one of his pupils – not one of the College's trainee pedagogues, but rather one of the boys who attends the College's school-room, to act as an experimental subject. Mr. Featherstone, a grey-haired man in his late fifties with rather aquiline features, looks up at his wife as she enters the room.

'Do you know Hughes, Bertha? Capital little chap. His Euclid is excellent.'

Mrs. Featherstone states that she is sure she does not. She looks around the study. 'Augustus, has Jane not done this room?'

Mr. Featherstone puts down his pen and looks up. 'How am I to know such things?'

Mrs. Featherstone runs her finger along the surface of the nearby chiffonier. 'I'll swear she has not.'

'There is no need to swear anything, Bertha. Really.'

Mrs. Featherstone, however, not one to let a matter rest, proffers her dusty forefinger to her spouse.

Mr. Featherstone gives in. 'Then have words with her, if you must. But I sometimes think that you do pick at the servants, dear.'

Bertha Featherstone's face turns rather dark. Her husband, sensing he has gone a little too far, tries to add a note of contrition to his voice. 'Bertha, you might open the evening post.'

Mrs. Featherstone obliges. She takes up the pile of letters, and applies the silver letter-opener provided by her husband, with a vigour that disturbs his concentration and altogether defeats the object of her assistance. As she sorts through each one, she places the opened letters in two neat piles upon the chiffonier, one for more urgent items, one for the remainder. Or,

32

rather, she does so until she comes to a particular envelope, whose contents are quite different from the daily ecclesiastical correspondence with which she is familiar.

'Good Lord!' exclaims Bertha Featherstone. 'This is dreadful!'

Her husband, quite startled, gets up from his desk.

'What on earth is it?'

'Augustus,' she says, clutching his arm in a fashion with which he is quite unfamiliar, 'I'd never have believed it.'

'Whatever is it?'

Mrs. Featherstone does not release her grip.

'You must call the police, Augustus. This instant. It says he intends to kill you!'

⸺

It is late in the evening when, having been summoned by the local constabulary, Sergeant Bartleby sits down in the room that serves as the Featherstones' parlour at St. Mark's College. His slightly awkward posture in the armchair is suggestive of a certain degree of discomfort and it is not merely the chair's ageing upholstery. For there is something rather uncomfortable and stuffy about the room itself, not least the heavy velvet curtains, which drape the windows. Indeed, it is altogether a dull, sombre sort of room, plainly decorated, whose only obvious nod to ornamentation is a glass-domed bell-jar that sits upon the mantelpiece. The jar in question contains a stuffed owl, perched on a little branch, which, thanks to some considerable artifice in its re-creation, possesses a peculiarly lively expression. An uncharitable person might say considerably more lively than that of its owner.

'Sergeant is your rank?' asks Mrs. Featherstone, seated opposite the policeman.

'Yes, ma'am,' replies Bartleby, 'of the Detective Branch.'

'I rather expected an inspector.'

'It is quite late, ma'am,' replies Bartleby. 'I assure you I will consult with Inspector Webb tomorrow, once we have the facts.'

'I should hope you will,' replies Mrs. Featherstone. 'I gather you insisted on seeing someone from the Yard, rather than a local man?'

'Of course. This is a serious business, Sergeant. But here is my dear husband at last.'

Bartleby stands up as the Reverend Featherstone appears at the door, still dressed in the long black gown, which marks him out as one of the masters at St. Mark's.

'This is the police sergeant, Augustus,' says Mrs. Featherstone, laying a rather negative stress on Bartleby's rank.

Bartleby offers the clergyman his hand. 'Sergeant Bartleby, sir.'

'Forgive me, Sergeant. A meeting; I have certain responsibilities in the College, I am afraid. They cannot be abrogated. Please, sit.'

'It's no trouble, sir,' says Bartleby, eager to proceed. 'Now, I gather from Mrs. Featherstone that you received an unfortunate letter earlier this evening?'

'Not merely "unfortunate", Sergeant,' says Mrs. Featherstone. 'Do show him, Augustus.'

'My dear, please,' replies her husband, handing Bartleby a folded piece of note paper. 'This is the item my wife is concerned about. It came in the post.'

Bartleby opens the letter and reads it through:

Dear Feathers,

Damn all your infernal squawking – <u>you</u> are the honest nuisance in the Gardens. I know you and Mother Goose and I will have my say. I would beware of dark lanterns and sharp daggers, if I were in your shoes. I have talked to the United Brotherhood of Chelsea and they all say I should set your little castle in flames, and roast you, old bird. I will do it too, you just wait, and I will carve up the meat good and proper.

THE CUTTER

The sergeant is silent for a moment. 'The red ink is a nice touch,' he says.

'You mean it is not . . .'

'Not blood, ma'am, no, I shouldn't say so. Doesn't dry quite that colour, if you think about it.'

'But these threats, Sergeant,' says Mrs. Featherstone. 'It is a very serious matter. That is why I specifically asked the constable for Scotland Yard. I mean to say, we know this awful creature is in earnest – the wretched girl he assaulted only the other night . . .'

Bartleby nods, then looks up at Reverend Featherstone. 'Forgive me saying so, sir, but you don't seem so concerned as your wife.'

The clergyman smiles. 'I think it is an idle boast, Sergeant. Someone hopes to deter me from my mission. I can readily defend myself, if needs be. I have the Lord on my side.'

'I see. And, forgive me, what is your "mission", sir?'

'Why, to remove the stain of Cremorne Gardens from Chelsea. I expect you have come across my tracts?'

'Well,' says Bartleby, apologetically, 'Chelsea's not my part of the world.'

'Wait one moment, Sergeant,' says Mrs. Featherstone, quitting her seat. 'I will get one for you.'

Bartleby is too late to protest, as Mrs. Featherstone bustles from the room. 'Perhaps, sir,' he suggests, 'you might just give me the gist of your, ah, work?'

'You must have heard of Cremorne Gardens' ill-fame, Sergeant? It goes back a good number of years. Mr. Boon is the most recent lessee; I am sure you have heard of him.'

'Met him today, as it happens, sir.'

'Did you? Well, his so-called "management" has made matters much worse. Even if one puts aside the noise and inconvenience of the place – just try and walk along the King's Road of a night! There are fast young men and loose girls in every state of degradation and vice. Quite disgusting.'

'I have heard something of the kind, sir,' replies the Sergeant, tactfully.

'And it is quite true,' says Mrs. Featherstone emphatically, overhearing as she re-enters the room. 'Here, Sergeant,' she continues, offering him a pamphlet, 'you may keep it, we have others. You will find it quite informative.'

'"Dancing to Satan's Hornpipe in Chelsea,"' reads Bartleby out loud.

'You would not believe what goes on behind those gates, Sergeant,' says the clergyman's wife. 'And we call ourselves a Christian country.'

'Yes, well. Thank you, ma'am. Thank you very much. But you think there is nothing in this letter, sir?' says Bartleby, turning back to address the Reverend. 'You think it is all bluster?'

'It is the work of some crank. Utter nonsense – the

36

"United Brotherhood of Chelsea" indeed!' Reverend Featherstone pauses for thought. 'Unless, of course, he is trying to intimidate me. But I doubt that even he would stoop so low.'

'Who?' asks Bartleby.

'Boon, Sergeant! Who else? I have the measure of that man, I can tell you.'

'Forgive me, if those are your feelings on the matter, why did you ask Scotland Yard to get involved, sir?' asks Bartleby.

'To be frank, Sergeant, my dear wife—'

'Augustus!' exclaims Mrs. Featherstone. 'Really, it quite terrified me.'

Bartleby looks hard at Mrs. Featherstone. There is something about her imposing manner that suggests it would be very difficult indeed to do such a thing; nonetheless, he does not contradict her display of womanly feeling.

'Well, we shall look into it, ma'am, I promise you.'

'And what should we do, Sergeant?' asks Mrs. Featherstone.

'Ah,' replies Bartleby, considering the question. 'I should lock all your doors of a night, ma'am. Just in case.'

Mrs. Featherstone looks back at the sergeant, not at all satisfied with this response. It is a look that leaves him quite certain she would have definitely preferred an inspector, without any shadow of a doubt.

⸺

Sergeant Bartleby quits the Featherstones' room at a little past ten o'clock and retraces his steps through the college's corridors, into the central cloister. He walks briskly, the letter safe in his jacket pocket, his mind turning over how to report the matter to Decimus

Webb. He is sufficiently distracted that, as he turns a corner into the quadrangle, facing the main entrance, his feet slip on the polished stone, just as a maid-servant comes walking briskly in the opposite direction. He narrowly avoids falling into her, bracing himself awkwardly against the wall.

'Beg your pardon,' says Bartleby.

'No harm done,' replies the young woman, brusquely.

'No, but all the same,' replies the sergeant.

The maid is a ruddy-faced, muscular-looking woman, clad in a white pinafore, about twenty-five years of age. She stares at Bartleby with a certain degree of disdain, saying nothing. Bartleby is about to walk on, when he stops and turns back.

'Here, what's your name?'

'Jane Budge,' she replies, a little wary.

'Have you worked here a long time?' asks the sergeant.

'Five year. What's that to you?'

'Do you know Reverend Featherstone?'

'Course I do.'

'And do you know of any party that might bear some grudge against him?'

'You a peeler or something? I ain't done nothing.'

'I never said that you had. Do you though – know of anyone?'

'Shouldn't be surprised if there was. His Missus told us I was going to bleeding burn in hell-fire today, just 'cos I ain't dusted her precious shelves.'

Bartleby cannot help but smile. With a nod and brief thanks, he bids the maid good night.

It is too dark for him to notice the nervous expression that passes over Jane Budge's face as he departs; nor the peculiar haste with which, once he has gone, she walks in the opposite direction.

Chapter Six

In Edith Grove, Charles Perfitt stands up and lights the fish-tail burners above his drawing-room mantelpiece. The gas splutters to life, as the flames flicker on either side of the tall gilt mirror above the hearth, their light reflected in the glass.

'Shall I do the lamp?'

Mr. Perfitt nods towards the gasolier that hangs from the ceiling but his wife, seated at the small writing desk against the wall, does not turn her head.

'Or shall I just throw myself on the fire?'

Mrs. Perfitt looks up. 'I'm sorry, dear, what did you say?'

'Shall I light the lamp?'

'Yes, dear, you may as well.'

Mr. Perfitt strikes a match and turns on the gas-tap.

'Is your correspondence particularly enthralling?' he asks.

'Alice has sent a note. Beatrice is to wear that green surah she wore at Easter, so, thankfully, everything is all right.'

'Is it?' replies her husband.

'Charles, you don't see at all. It means Rose can

39

wear the *poult de soie* that Madame Lannier showed me last week; I knew I was wise to have her put it aside. I am so pleased.'

'Is that so? I swear, I should have never agreed to you attending this wretched ball in the first place. Rose is quite beside herself already. And you are little better.'

'Charles! It is the perfect occasion. Rose may be introduced to – well, Lord knows who!'

'That is precisely my concern,' says Mr. Perfitt, his expression suddenly more serious.

Mrs. Perfitt gets up and puts a gentle hand on her husband's arm. 'You must let her go into society, Charles. She is eighteen. It is expected. She will have no better chance. Besides, what would you do? Lock her in her room until she is an old maid?'

Mr. Perfitt shakes his head. 'I only want her happiness. It is just that I am not sure she is quite level-headed enough to cope with such excitement. I should not like her to fall in with the wrong sort.'

Mrs. Perfitt removes her hand.

'How could that happen at the Prince's Ground, of all places? Charles, please. She will never improve if we keep her cooped up like some caged bird.'

Mr. Perfitt smiles faintly. 'You may be right.'

'Of course, I am. Now, don't take on so, please. I must write back to Alice.'

Mr. Perfitt nods, and returns to his arm-chair, picking up the newspaper he put down earlier. He reads for a minute or two, then looks up at his wife.

'Where is Rose?'

'In her room. I think she was a little tired. We spent such a long time talking about her dress; and she will argue so. I expect she is asleep.'

40

Mr. Perfitt looks at his wife, already absorbed again in her correspondence, and shakes his head.

———

Rose Perfitt does not sleep. Rather, though the bedroom curtains are all drawn, she is seated at her desk, with all the accoutrements of letter-writing laid out in front of her, and an old brass Argand lamp to provide illumination. She takes up her pen, dipping the metal nib into the inkwell, and puts it to paper, writing in a neat hand:

My Dear Love,

Another month has gone by and you have not come. I have waited and waited but you never came. Please come, beloved, and clasp me to your heart. I know you will be true. I have not forgotten you, but I know you shall come.
A kiss, fond love, a kiss.
Your own ever dear

R.

Rose looks down at the paper, carefully dabs it with a sheet of blotting paper, then folds it and presses it to her lips. She holds it there for a good while, her eyes closed, as if repeating some silent ritual. Then, at last, she returns it to the desk, and slides it into an envelope. She does not, however, pen any address, but merely closes the flap of the envelope and opens a concealed drawer, adding it to a large bundle already there.

There is a knock at the door. She hastily closes the desk.

'Come in?'

The Perfitts' maid-servant enters.

'Would you like any supper, Miss?'

'No, Richards, thank you,' replies Rosc.

'It's just the Missus said you didn't eat much at dinner, Miss. I thought I'd ask.'

'Even so.'

'Yes, Miss. Thank you, Miss.'

The girl leaves, closing the bedroom door behind her. Rose Perfitt tidies away her stationery, running her hands over the wood of the desk.

On a whim, she leans over the surface, laying her head upon her hands, and closes her eyes.

———

She is a little girl lost in the maze at Cremorne; the endless green hedges that seem to turn and twist in an infinite puzzle. She is there as it grows dark, the heavens seemingly descending lower and lower, extinguishing the sun.

She grows tired; she sits upon the path until a boy comes along. He teases her; chaffs her about her frock. She does not like him and runs.

There, that is when it happens. It is inevitable. The sound of footfalls on the grass, catching up to her.

That is what makes her heart race.

Then her mother calls out to her.

———

Rose Perfitt wakes up. The lamp still burns beside her, but not as brightly. Her hair has come loose, and her neck is stiff. For a moment, she recalls her dream.

But only for a moment.

CHAPTER SEVEN

Not a half mile distant from the Perfitts' home, Mrs. Bertha Featherstone lies in her bed. It is unusual for the bells of St. Mark's chapel to wake her during the night and the mere fact of being conscious at such an ungodly hour rather disturbs her. She blinks, listening to the seemingly endless peals, estimating that it must be midnight.

Then she hears footsteps outside.

It is perhaps rather foolhardy of her to put on her dressing-gown, without alerting her husband in the adjoining room. Nonetheless, she does so, and proceeds into the narrow hallway outside her bedroom. In a matter of seconds, she reaches the door that leads into the cloisters and swings it forcefully open.

'Who's there? Show yourself!'

She peers round the darkened quadrangle. She can hear the sound of footsteps again, clicking on the stones.

'Don't skulk in the shadows – I know you are there.'

'Ma'am?'

Mrs. Featherstone turns, startled, to face the figure of Jane Budge. The maid-servant is wrapped in a tartan shawl, a crumpled white bonnet upon her head.

'I weren't skulking anywhere, ma'am,' says the maid emphatically.

Mrs. Featherstone looks a little relieved. 'What in heaven's name are you doing?'

'Going home, ma'am, as it happens,' she replies, her voice rather tart. 'We don't often see you at this hour.'

The clergyman's wife pulls her dressing-gown tightly around her body. 'No, indeed. I was asleep. I thought I heard something.'

'Likely it was me, then.'

'Yes, I see. Well, good night. Go carefully.'

'I always do, thank you, ma'am,' she replies. 'Good night to you.'

And, with a glance at Mrs. Featherstone, and a haughty look rather unsuited to her position in life, Jane Budge cuts across the courtyard, out onto the cobbled drive towards the gate-house.

The gate-keeper himself, whose nights are spent in a small wooden hut by the entrance, is nowhere to be seen. Only the sound of his snoring announces his presence to any would-be intruders. Miss Jane Budge, therefore, does not trouble to wake him, but lets herself out, and walks briskly eastwards along the King's Road.

———

Jane Budge's walk home takes her past the gates to Cremorne Gardens, as it does every night. She herself has little doubt that the pleasure gardens are not quite so bad as they are painted. True, she notices a couple of hansom and clarence cabs waiting by the gate. And it may be that some of those getting in or out of the vehicles are somewhat the worse for drink – but there is nothing so unusual in that. And if the women whom

44

certain gentlemen have upon their arms are not their wives or daughters – well, who is to know? It does not matter to her, in any case.

A mile down the road, she comes to the old World's End inn, then walks down to Lindsey Row, which runs along the river. The end of the row is where the Thames Embankment begins: a grand gas-lit carriageway stretching eastwards, on to Westminster and beyond. But Jane Budge's journey takes her south – to Battersea Bridge.

To anyone unfamiliar with the crossing, it might seem a bold move. Built upon rickety-looking wooden pilings, sloping at a steep angle, the bridge gives the impression of an altogether makeshift affair, thrown together in haste. Admittedly, it boasts a quartet of lamps, mounted on the iron railings that run along either side; but it is principally a timber construction; and old timber at that, nailed together in odd proportions and angles, occasionally giving out a mournful groan, complaining in vain at the shifting waters below. Still, it is safe enough; Jane Budge knows the bridge of old. She pays the toll-keeper and crosses the Thames, alone in the moonlight.

On the Surrey shore, the Battersea Road is devoid of activity. The handful of public houses along its length have, by and large, dispersed their customers into the night, and the labourers and factory workers who inhabit the area are mostly in their beds. Further from the river, it becomes quieter still: the houses diminish in number, and the gas-lights disappear; for Battersea is still a half-finished suburb, a place where clay soil is being churned up to make bricks, and where plots of ground, once fields, are marked up with lengths of rope, in anticipation of putative terraces and villas. It is, moreover, a rather hazardous place in darkness: trenches and pits

45

abound upon either side of the road, and there are odd turnings, barely visible in the nocturnal gloom. But Jane Budge seems perfectly familiar with the Battersea brick fields, only slowing down when she comes to a dirt-path known in the vicinity as Sheepgut Lane, a lonely road in the shadow of the railway lines that criss-cross nearby Lavender Hill. She trudges along, passing several old cottages – where there is a not a single light visible – until she comes to a slightly larger building, set back a little from the road. It resembles an old, rather dilapidated farm-house, with a solitary candle that burns in the parlour window. The light faintly illuminates a handwritten sign upon the front door: 'Budge's Dairy'. Jane Budge lets herself in.

'That you, Janey?' says a voice from the candle-lit parlour.

'Who were you expecting, you old whore?'

There is a laugh from the parlour, as Jane Budge unwraps her shawl. She opens the connecting door and walks in.

The front parlour of Budge's Dairy is a low-ceilinged room, thick with smoke, emanating from a small brick-built hearth that gives out more fumes than heat. As for the room's decoration, there is little to speak of: some plain-looking crockery sits upon an old oak table that has seen better days; a couple of wicker baskets lie heaped up in a corner. There are, however, two persons inside. One is a woman of about sixty years, seated upon a chair by the fire. She is a little plump, with grey hair pulled tightly back from her face, and wears a voluminous russet-coloured dress that balloons out from her legs, entirely concealing their very existence. Almost hidden in her arms is the second inhabitant: a baby of some three months, swad-dled in a grey blanket.

46

'What's the fire going for?' asks Jane Budge.

'The little 'un's got a chest,' replies Mrs. Budge.

'I ain't surprised with you smothering him like that.'

Mrs. Budge tuts. 'I looked after you, Janey girl, didn't I? I knows what I'm doing.'

Jane Budge walks over to the baby and looks at his face, touching his cheek with her finger. 'It ain't his chest, Ma. He's got a fever.'

'That's his natural complexion. Quite healthy.'

'If you like.'

Mrs. Budge purses her lips. 'Well, did you see your father on the road?'

Jane Budge shakes her head.

'How about Madam? Did she pay her dues today?'

'No, she wrote us a letter, though,' replies Jane.

'Did she now?'

'You won't like it. She wants to see the boy. Won't take no for an answer.'

Mrs. Budge lets out a long breath. 'Is that what she said? Well, I'll be blowed. After all this time.'

As Mrs. Budge speaks, the movement wakes the baby in her arms. The child lets out a pitiful cry, halfway between mewling and choking, its face reddening. Mrs. Budge looks down at the infant, then stands up.

'Bring that light, will you, Janey?' she says, nodding to the candle. Her daughter obliges.

'That's enough of you, little 'un,' she says, walking towards the back of the parlour. With her daughter holding up the candle, she pushes open a low wooden door with her foot. Jane Budge follows idly behind her.

The second room is a little cold and lacks a single window. Once, it most likely was a store-room of some kind. Mrs. Budge lays the infant down in a simple cot that lies upon the stone-flagged floor.

47

'She wants to see the child,' repeats Jane Budge.

'Then she'll have to see him,' replies her mother. 'Seeing is believing, ain't it? What about Mary Whit's boy?'

'You wouldn't!'

Mrs. Budge smiles, showing the rather irregular contours of her teeth. 'I'll send her a note. Here, come and have a proper sit. I've got a drop of something strong that your Pa got hold of.'

'If you like,' says Jane Budge. As she follows her mother, she raises up the candle, casting its meagre glow on half a dozen similar cots that lie arranged in twin rows upon the flag-stones.

'How many today, Ma?' says Jane Budge, peering at the infant face in each cot.

'Five little angels,' replies Mrs. Budge. 'None of 'em a bother. Two is ailing, though. Won't be long.'

'That's a shame.'

'Ah, it is, Janey,' replies Mrs. Budge, complacently. 'Terrible.'

CHAPTER EIGHT

'Good morning. Your number?' asks the warder.

'D4-3-10. Ticket-of-leave,' replies the young man.

'Sign here or make your mark, 4-3-10,' says the warder. The young man obliges.

The warder looks down at his papers. 'Nelson, is it?'

'Yes, sir.'

'You have your freedom, Nelson. Do not squander it.'

'No, sir. I don't intend to.'

'Very well,' continues the warder, handing the young man a small book from a pile of identical volumes upon his desk. 'The chaplain wishes to give you this, for your moral welfare. You can read, I take it?'

The young man nods.

'Good,' continues the warder. 'I commend it to you. It has the address of the Discharged Prisoners' Aid Society; you will find them at Charing Cross – make that your destination and you will not go far wrong.'

The young man casts a cursory glance over the gift.

'Be on your way, then. Next!'

It is a little past nine o'clock on a Monday morning when George Nelson quits the confines of Pentonville

Prison. There is no mass exodus of freed inmates from the gaol. Instead, they trickle through in ones and twos during the morning, at carefully timed intervals, to avoid any possible disturbance. Thus Nelson is quite alone as he passes the Warden's lodge and walks beneath the rather fanciful portcullis of the prison's gate-house. In fact, as he goes down the avenue that leads to freedom, beside the yellow brick of the outer wall, his footsteps echo on the stone pavement, a strangely solitary, lonely sound.

The guard who stands at the prison's perimeter looks at him sternly as he passes.

'Mind you don't come back, eh?' says the man in question.

George Nelson looks at the official, pauses for a moment, then spits on the ground.

'Hook it,' says the guard, a look of unconcealed contempt on his face.

Nelson does not reply but walks on, round the corner of the gaol, onto the Caledonian Road. He pauses, standing in the shadow of the prison walls. Perhaps his only reason to stop is the ill-fitting discharge suit, which, he discovers, obliges him to adopt a somewhat shuffling gait. Or it may simply be the sight of the traffic – the waggon that slowly passes by; the omnibus in the distance; the dozen people making their way along the pavement – the ebb and flow of daily life he has not seen for five years. Regardless, he stands there, seemingly frozen, for a good few minutes, before he recovers, and directs his steps to the opposite side of the road, where the Bull in the Pound public house is conveniently situated.

The landlord does not even blink at the spectacle of George Nelson as he enters the public bar. He is used to the rather shabby fustian outfits provided by

Her Majesty for those quitting Pentonville. In fact, though he keeps early hours for the nearby Metropolitan Cattle Market, the convenience of his hostelry as a watering-place for the ex-residents of the prison is not lost upon him, and he makes no effort to discourage such custom.

'Give us a pipe and some baccy, for God's sake,' says Nelson, placing his hands on the bar. 'And a pint.'

The landlord smiles at the familiar request.

'Been a long time, has it, old son?'

'Five years,' replies Nelson, as the landlord pulls on the beer-pump.

'Need lodgings? I know a good few places. Cheap 'uns.'

Nelson shakes his head. 'I know where I'm going.'

The landlord shrugs.

<hr>

George Nelson stays for an hour or so in the Bull in the Pound, seated by the door. As occasional customers enter, he peers out, back at the high wall of the gaol, as if to reassure himself of his location and that his freedom is not illusory. At last, with every ounce of tobacco burnt through in the clay pipe, and his pint pot quite empty, he reaches inside the unfamiliar jacket of his suit, and retrieves an envelope, stamped with Her Majesty's crest, the lion and unicorn. Unfolding the contents, he reads it through:

Order of Licence under the Penal Servitude Acts, 1853 to 1864

WHITEHALL
17th day of *May* 1875

HER MAJESTY is graciously pleased to grant to *George Frederick Nelson* who was convicted of *Rape* at the *Central Criminal Court* on the *14th* day of *June 1870*, and was then and there sentenced to be kept in Penal Servitude for the term of *six years* and is now confined in the *Penitentiary Prison, Pentonville*, Her Royal Licence to be at large from the day of his liberation under this order, during the remaining portion of his said term of Penal Servitude, unless the said *George Frederick Nelson* shall be convicted on indictment of some offence within the United Kingdom, in which case such licence will immediately be forfeited by law, or unless it shall please Her Majesty sooner to revoke or alter such Licence.

Nelson looks at the document long after he has finished reading it. He takes a long breath, then returns the ticket-of-leave to its envelope, replacing it in his jacket pocket.

Standing up, he nods to the landlord, who has long since lost interest in him, and makes his way out of the bar. Behind him, upon the small deal table at which he was seated, lie the crumpled remains of a pamphlet, entitled *The Long Road that leads to Heaven*.

CHAPTER NINE

Decimus Webb takes a sip from his mid-morning mug of coffee, as he stands and stares out of the narrow window of his office, looking at the cobbled yard below. It is a warm day, even for the time of year, and he notices that the mud between the stones in the courtyard has disappeared, baked into a dry layer of dust. Then he hears the familiar sound of someone ascending upon the stairs at a brisk pace.

'Good morning, Sergeant,' says Webb, even before Bartleby opens the door.

'Morning, sir,' replies Bartleby.

'You needn't look so cheerful,' mutters Webb. 'Unless you've just captured our wretched scissor-man single-handed.'

'No, sir. Beautiful day, though, isn't it?'

'I suppose so. Do you have anything further to report? I can make out the weather for myself.'

'Well, I've been and seen Miss Hockley in the infirmary; she seems to be doing well enough. They reckon the wound will heal quite nicely, given time. And then I went and had a word with her mistress.'

'And?'

'Decent sort. Runs a little confectioner's on the Old Kent Road. Nothing to say against her. She came to

53

her with a good character and she was happy to let her go out to Cremorne on Friday night.'

'Very liberal,' replies Webb, taking another sip of his drink.

'What's more, sir, she doesn't know of anyone who might have a grudge against the girl. Apparently she'd been keeping company with the young man she was with for a few weeks, but nothing untoward – no rows or nothing.'

'Yes, well, I do not think we will find anything there,' replies Webb. 'She was certain that her young man was ahead of her, not behind. I think *our* man is a simple opportunist. The way he cut at her, there is nothing to suggest great preparation, or even much determination.'

'And what do you make of that, sir?' asks the sergeant, gesturing to the Featherstones' letter, which sits atop a pile of papers on Webb's desk. 'Have you had a chance to look at it?'

'Yes, and I have read your report. I think the Featherstones are safe enough. To my mind, it smacks of a prank – red ink, for pity's sake!'

'Do you think Mr. Boon sent it?' asks Bartleby.

'That, Sergeant, is rather a can of worms, is it not? I certainly have no wish to be dragged into this ridiculous dispute over the Gardens.'

'Still, perhaps we should talk to Boon again, sir?' suggests Bartleby.

'No need,' replies Webb. 'As it happens, I had a letter from Mr. Boon this morning. He says that he plans to call on me shortly – for what reason I cannot quite make out. And I can tell you, for what it is worth, his handwriting appears quite different to that of your "Cutter".'

'Are you sure, sir?'

54

Webb, however, does not reply, as something catches his attention outside.

'Ah, here he is, I think. Yes – keeps his own carriage, too, by the look of it – no expense spared.'

'Mr. Boon?'

Webb nods. 'And with a young lady as his companion. You had better find us a couple more chairs, Sergeant.'

—

Mr. Boon enters Decimus Webb's office with a young woman upon his arm. She is smartly dressed in a dark emerald day-dress, and carries a folded parasol in her hand. After a brief introduction, both parties are seated in front of Webb's desk.

'Now, sir, what may I do for you?' says Webb.

'You have no news, then, Inspector?' asks Boon.

'Not since we last spoke, sir, no.'

'Very well, as I thought. Then I have a proposal for you. This is, as I say, Miss Richmond. I expect you recognise her.'

Webb looks at the young woman, whose rather average features bring no-one particularly to mind. 'I can't say as I do, sir.'

'Come, sir. Miss Richmond, one of our fair city's greatest artistes. You tell me you do not know her?'

Webb shakes his head rather wearily. 'Perhaps my sergeant can assist – Bartleby?'

Sergeant Bartleby frowns as he looks at the young woman. 'There is something, sir, but I can't quite place it.'

'Please, Inspector,' says Boon, 'I did not intend a guessing game. Miss Richmond is *The New Female Blondin* – The Most Astounding Aerialist and Mistress of the Gymnastic Art". Her performances have engendered adulation and astonishment in all who have seen her. Now, if you dare, tell me you have not heard of her!'

'Of course!' says Bartleby, with some enthusiasm. 'I saw you at Astley's last year, Miss. Pleasure to make your acquaintance.'

'Mr. Boon, Miss Richmond,' interrupts Webb, 'this is delightful, I am sure. But I seem to recall you mentioned a "proposal"?'

'Quite right! I have a plan, Inspector. We cannot wait on this maniac to strike at will. We must lure him out. Miss Richmond has a delightful head of hair, as you can see' – the young woman blushes rather fetchingly – 'and she assures me that she is happy to oblige, if it may help rid us of this danger to her sex. And, besides, she has her own contract to consider; we had planned three shows a night from June.'

Webb clasps his hands together. 'I struggle to get your meaning, sir.'

'A trap,' says Boon, in the manner of a conspirator. 'Miss Richmond waits in a quiet spot – and then we have him!'

Webb sighs. 'Am I to understand you propose to entice the wretch to assault this young woman?'

'And then we pounce!' says Boon, banging his hand on Webb's rather cluttered desk for emphasis. Several pieces of paper fall to the floor.

'Oh good Lord,' says Webb. 'You are not serious?'
'Of course.'

Webb smiles politely in the direction of Miss Richmond. 'I am sorry, Miss. I applaud your courage, but I could not allow such a thing. The danger to yourself would be far too great.'

'But, Inspector!' protests Boon. 'Surely with trained men at hand—'

'No, sir. Categorically no.'

'Very well,' says Boon, a hint of indignation in his voice, 'then you leave me no choice in the matter.'

'No choice?'

'I had hoped I might be spared the expense. But I can see there is no other way. I give you notice, Inspector, that I intend to place an advertisement upon every wall in Chelsea. A fifty-pound reward to whomever can accomplish this lunatic's capture.'

'I hardly think that is a good idea, sir,' says Webb.

'I have no choice, if you cannot find this fellow. I think the promise of a reward may work wonders.'

Webb shakes his head, but Boon interjects before he can speak.

'My mind, Inspector, is quite made up. Come, Miss Richmond. We will leave the inspector to his work. Good day to you both.'

And, with that, John Boon rises dramatically from his chair, straightens his jacket, and leads the rather submissive Miss Richmond from the room. Decimus Webb watches them go and then places his head in his hands, rubbing his temples.

'Hot-headed, these theatrical types, sir,' says Bartleby, going over to the window and looking at Boon's carriage pulling out of the courtyard. 'But a reward – can't be that bad, surely?'

Webb casts a despairing glance at the sergeant. 'Bartleby, really. Do you think, knowing the sorts who visit Cremorne, that they will be overly scrupulous about finding the right culprit? For fifty pounds we'll get a dozen "Cutters" a night; and none of them our man, I'll lay odds. One may have a squint; or he may have a low brow; or merely look askance at some female. That will be all it takes; anything will suit. It will work against us.'

Webb places his hands on his forehead.

'Just once I would like to meet a simple out-and-out villain.'

———

George Nelson looks at the room on offer. It is a small space in the attic floor of a somewhat below-par lodging-house, in a rather dingy side street. It is barely large enough for the bed, wash-stand and dressing table within.

'Meals included?'

The landlord shakes his head.

'Laundry?' says Nelson.

The landlord smiles, but shakes his head again.

'I'll take it.'

'How long for?' asks the landlord. 'Month? I can't say less than a month. I'd be doing myself a disservice if I said less than a month. In advance.'

'A month then,' says Nelson, shaking his hand.

'What's your line of work?'

Nelson pauses. 'Nothing in particular.'

'Lost your position, eh? What brings you here?'

The ticket-of-leave man walks over to the room's small window and peers out. 'Thought I'd look up some old friends.'

CHAPTER TEN

Rose Perfitt stands perfectly still upon a low stool in
the work-room of one Madame Lannier, 'Superior
Milliner and Dressmaker', as the latter circles about her,
minutely examining her form, like a scholar pondering
some marble Venus in the basement of the British
Museum. Rose's appearance is a matter of professional
pride to Madame, who has spent fifteen minutes adorning
her in a garnet-coloured ball-gown of corded silk, albeit
one as yet with no trimmings, the body and cuirasse
held together with a temporary arrangement of cleverly
placed pins. Madame Lannier, it must be said, is a
renowned perfectionist and must have things 'just so'.

Rose's mother, meanwhile, accompanying her
daughter to the fitting, merely sits upon a wing chair
by the door, observing the proceedings.

'You must keep the back straight, Mademoiselle, if
you please,' insists the dressmaker, a thin woman with
a surprisingly firm manner, who tugs gently at the
dress's putative cuirasse, then, seeming to change her
mind as to the cause of the difficulty, manipulates
Rose's shoulders, pushing them firmly into an accept-
able posture. Rose does her best to oblige.

'Now,' says Madame Lannier, turning to Mrs.
Perfitt, 'the skirts are tied back like so, yes? *Vous*

comprenez, Madame? That is *la ligne* for the season – you see the waist, yes? *Très prononcé* – here and here. Then, of course, we attach the train. My girls will add the lace trim tomorrow.'

Mrs. Perfitt beams. 'I think it will be delightful, Madame Lannier. What do you think, Rose dear?'

'I do like it, Mama, but I would rather—'

'*Attendez*!' interrupts Madame Lannier, observing a slight turn by her model. 'Do not move, my child, please, not yet.'

'Rose,' says Mrs. Perfitt, 'please do not make a fuss. It is quite perfect. Your father will be so proud.'

⬤

'*How* much?'

Mr. Perfitt's query resounds throughout the Perfitts' drawing-room.

'Charles, do not pretend for a moment that you even care about such trifles.'

'You know I do not hold with such extravagance, Caroline. It will quite turn Rose's head. She is in the clouds enough, as it is. You saw her at dinner – I could barely get a sensible word out of her.'

'My dear, we have discussed this,' replies his wife, reaching for his hand and taking it in hers. 'One cannot turn up to the Prince's Ground in some ready-made from Marshall and Snelgrove. This is your daughter's entrée into Society.'

Mr. Perfitt replies with a rather indistinct murmur of disapproval.

'You will come too. And I shall be her chaperon – why, don't you trust me to keep my eye on her?'

'I should hope I did.'

'Well then. You need not worry so. She will be quite safe.'

Mr. Perfitt looks to the floor, and says nothing. His wife squeezes his hand.

'I expect,' he says at length, 'it is one of those modern articles, all waist and whalebone.'

'Madame Lannier makes everything to the latest fashion, if that is what you mean,' replies his wife, smiling gratefully at the touch of good humour returning to his voice.

'Then I am sure it will be something no decent young woman would wear.'

'I shall be wearing something similar myself,' replies Mrs. Perfitt. 'If you do not think it is suitable . . .'

'I suppose if she must go, she ought to look her best.'

'Thank you, Charles,' says Mrs. Perfitt. 'Thank you. Oh Lord, that reminds me,' she continues, 'I shall need something to settle Madame Lannier's account. It is due the week after next.'

～

Rose Perfitt sits at her desk. Instead of opening her treasured cache of letters, a daily ritual she has already performed, she begins a new missive, addressed to her older sister:

17 May 1875

My Dearest Laetitia,

Just a little note, as I said I would write. Today we went to Lannier's, an awful bore, though Mdm. made herself very agreeable afterwards. She said I shall look like a princess at the ball – très gentile, n'est ce pas? But I think Mama hopes I shall be a Cinderella. Of course, my dress will

not be magicked up, except by Papa's ten guineas!
HE thinks it is all nonsense – poor Papa! I confess,
my dear Letty, I am getting <u>so</u> excited about the
dancing that I know I shall be quite out of my
mind with it on the night; and I cannot believe
that three whole days remain until Saturday. I
mean to enjoy it like anything. Mama says no-
one present will have less than seven thousand a
year – she thinks that I shall go fishing out one
of them like a prize angler. I cannot say why, my
dear Letty, if you can forgive me a little secret,
but I do not think such men will ever capture
your little one's heart; but I expect they shall all
mark my programme. For I long to <u>dance</u>!!
I trust your Mr. Worthing and the boys are keeping
well. The weather here is heavenly – I hope it
lasts. I shall write to you properly, I promise,
once the agony of waiting is over!

> *Your loving sister,*
> *Rose*

Rose smiles, satisfied with her prose, folds the letter
into an envelope and rings the servants' bell. Her maid
arrives promptly.

'Can you see this is posted tonight?'

'Yes, Miss.'

❦

An hour later, as Rose Perfitt is completing her evening
toilette, assiduously brushing her long hair, she is
interrupted by a knock at her door.

'Come in?'

The Perfitts' maid reappears. 'Beg pardon, Miss.'

'Yes?'

'I posted that letter, Miss.'

'Thank you,' replies Rose, perplexed. 'Richards – whatever is it?'

'There was a gentleman, Miss. He came up to us when I was at the pillar-box.'

'I do not follow. Was he pestering you?'

'Yes, Miss. Well, not exactly,' replies Richards, blushing. 'He gave me this envelope, Miss. He said I was to take it just to you, seeing how it was a secret.'

The maid holds out a rather dusty-looking envelope. Rose takes it swiftly from Richards' hand.

'You may go, Richards.'

'Thank you, Miss,' replies the maid, a conspiratorial twinkle in her eye.

Rose Perfitt waits until the maid has left the room before taking up her silver letter-opener. She slices open the envelope, peers inside and turns it inside out.

A single petal from a red rose falls onto her desk.

CHAPTER ELEVEN

'A warm night, ain't it?' says the toll-keeper upon Battersea Bridge, tugging at his shirt collar. 'I reckon there's a storm brewing.'

'Is that right?' replies Jane Budge, surrendering a copper coin to pay for her crossing.

'Aye, that's right,' says the toll-keeper, gesturing magnanimously towards the turn-stile. 'Us old 'uns can feel it in our bones.'

'You're like my old Ma, 'cepting with her it's rain, snow, and who'll win the bloody Derby.'

'You laugh, my girl. You laugh when you're soaked through and no 'brella.'

'I'll be all right,' she says, over her shoulder, walking on across the bridge.

In truth, Jane Budge wonders if the old man's prediction may prove correct. The nocturnal sky seems black as pitch, punctuated by neither the moon nor the stars. She sets herself a brisk pace, past the gas-lights upon the bridge, quickening her step down to the Battersea Road. There, for want of any better mental exercise, she estimates her progress by ticking off each public house as she goes past, useful milestones along the rather dingy thoroughfare. It is only when she passes the Red Cow, considering herself quite alone on the road, that she hears the distinct sound of foot-steps on the stone paving behind her.

She turns around, but there is no-one to be seen. Pausing for a moment, the only figure she can discern in the gloom is several hundred yards away, in the side road next to the last public house, a man bracing his body against a wall with one arm, relieving himself of an excess of beer. He looks far too unsteady to be any danger. She shakes her head and walks on, looking back at him two or three times, to be sure he is not following. But the man merely remains against the wall, as if determined to prop it up all night.

Jane Budge's nerves become calmer by the time she reaches the brick fields. Perhaps she reasons that her familiarity with the half-made roads is a charm against danger – for any drunk would be as likely to trip and break their neck somewhere along the way, as catch up with her. In any case, she strides along the darkened lanes with some assurance.

But, again, she hears the sound of someone walking. Not the firm clatter of boots on stone, but soft muddy footfalls on the new unpaved street, not far behind her. She rather fancies that she can hear a man breathing.

'Who's there?' she says, stopping in her tracks, looking about her. But she can only see the black outlines of the brick kilns in the nearby fields, which appear rather like malign carbuncles upon the rugged landscape, and there is no reply except the echo of her own voice.

She takes a deep breath and quickens her steps.

It comes as a relief to find the turning down Sheepgut Lane. The two familiar rows of dilapidated cottages doubtless seem comforting, even if indistinct in the pitch darkness. She can, at least, make out the candle in her mother's window.

There it happens again. A man breathing heavily; the sound of someone moving about.

This time she runs, though she does not quite have the confidence to turn around. But as she approaches Budge's Dairy, within inches of the gate, a man's hand grabs her wrist, yanking her body about.

'Who you running from, Janey?' says George Nelson.

'Bleedin' hell!' exclaims Jane Budge, her face a picture of astonishment.

'I knew I'd find you here. Still clutching at your mother's apron strings.'

Jane Budge shakes her arm, but does not remove her captor's grip. 'I thought you were still inside.'

George Nelson looks at her contemptuously. 'Did you now? Well they gave me a ticket, you see, for good behaviour. So I'm a free man. Can do as I like.'

'As you like?' she replies breathlessly. 'The peelers won't stand for you coming here.'

Nelson tilts his head quizzically, still maintaining his grasp of her arm. 'To say hello to my old sweetheart? It'd be a hard man who could object to that, eh? Where are you working now, Janey? I looked for you at the old place, but you weren't there. I thought you were their little treasure.'

'Will you let go of me? You're hurting me.'

'That's a shame. Don't squirm so. Where are you working?'

Jange Budge bites her lip. 'Down at the Training College. What's it to you?'

'Just wondering who'd have a cheap whore like you, that's all.'

Jane Budge swings her free hand in a swift arc

67

towards Nelson's face. He, however, is far too quick for her, grabbing her so that he has both her arms firmly in his grasp.

'What do you want from us, George?' she says angrily.

'What do I want? I spent nigh on five years in Pentonville on account of you, Janey. I suppose I didn't have much else to think on: what I'd say to you when I got out; what I'd do—'

'You ain't man enough to do nothing,' says Jane Budge defiantly.

George Nelson scowls. 'Five years, Janey. Hard bed, hard board, hard labour. Leaves a man liable to do anything. Every other day on the 'mill, turning that blasted wheel, till I was fit for nothing. And not allowed to say a word, except "yes, sir", "no, sir", "thank'ee, sir". Imagine that, eh?'

He tightens his grip on her wrists. Jane Budge grimaces in pain.

'It changes a man,' he says. 'It changes him all right.'

As he speaks, there is the sound of a door creaking open. George Nelson turns his gaze to the exterior of Budge's Dairy. The substantial figure of Mrs. Budge stands upon her doorstep. In one hand she holds an oil-lamp, casting an orange glow, which illuminates the darkness; in the other is a small pistol, the burnished metal of its barrel glinting in the light.

'Reckon you look much the same to me, George Nelson. Now, let go of my Jane before you get hurt.'

'You wouldn't dare,' says Nelson.

'Do for a villain like you? Trespassing on a person's property in the middle of the night, when you've hardly set foot out of the jug? If I killed you stone dead they'd give me a medal and draw up a subscription.'

Nelson's hesitation, his eyes fixed on the gun, is

sufficient for Jane Budge to wring her hands free of him. She hastens to her mother's side.

'Off you go, then,' says Mrs. Budge, with considerable authority.

Mrs. Budge gestures with the gun. George Nelson does not reply. With a silent and sullen parting glance at Jane Budge, he turns back down the path.

Mrs. Budge watches him leave. When she is quite certain he is not coming back, she shepherds her daughter inside.

'Lor!' she exclaims, once the front door is bolted. 'Who'd have thought it?'

Jane Budge shakes her head. 'What will we do? You heard him. He won't just let it go, not now he's out.'

'I didn't think he'd have the nerve to come round here, pestering you,' says Mrs. Budge, standing in front of the fire, a rather worried look upon her face.

'Where did you get that?' says Jane, looking at the gun.

'Your Pa won it – must be ten year back; made a wager with a commercial traveller. Thought I'd best keep it safe.'

'It ain't loaded, is it?'

Mrs. Budge shakes her head, placing the pistol on the wooden mantel. She does it rather too casually, however, and the gun falls from the shelf as she lets go of it, landing on the stone floor – with a terrific noise and a sudden explosion of smoke.

Both women instinctively freeze. When the smoke has dissipated, a small china tea-cup that rested decoratively above the fire-place is smashed into half a dozen pieces.

'Bless me!' exclaims Mrs. Budge. 'It was an' all.'

From the rear of the room comes the sound of a crying child.

CHAPTER TWELVE

'So, another clue falls into our laps, courtesy of your clergyman,' says Decimus Webb in a tone that would extinguish the enthusiasm of the most eager detective sergeant. 'But we do not know what it is?'

Bartleby, however, refuses to be quenched. 'It's just that the wife was quite insistent you turned out and talked to her husband, sir. Inspector or nothing. I think she thought we weren't taking her seriously last time.'

'I hold you responsible for that misapprehension, Sergeant.'

The cab carrying the two policemen pulls up outside the Fulham Road entrance to St. Mark's Training College.

'If you met the lady, sir,' says Bartleby, 'you might understand.'

'I will admit,' replies Webb, paying the driver, 'that any female that sends you away with a flea in your ear has my utmost respect.'

Bartleby adopts the resigned smile he reserves for such exchanges and seeks directions from the gate-keeper. The two policeman are directed to a peculiar stone octagon that nestles inside the college walls. Two storeys high, it is in a similar Italianate style to the college's principal buildings, even down to a miniature eight-sided campanile that forms the summit of its tiled roof.

'Apparently it's the Practising School, sir,' says Bartleby. 'The Reverend should be there this time of day.'

If anything, it seems to Webb that the building has the look of some obscure chapel, rather than any school with which he is familiar. The interior does nothing to dispel the impression: a cruciform space within the octagon, with boys on various benches and forms in each arm of the cross, both on the ground floor and in a gallery above. The scholars themselves receive attention from individual monitors, pupil-teachers learning the art of pedagogy, but all of the boys face the centre. And there, seated on a tall chair, is the Reverend Featherstone, his eyes roving around the room. The clergyman's field of vision is not quite three hundred and sixty degrees, for at the heart of the room is a multi-sided chimney, extending up to the roof, with four substantial fire-places at its base. And yet, there is undoubtedly something of the prison panopticon in the unusual design and, although not given to sentiment, Decimus Webb feels a stab of pity for the pupils in St. Mark's model school.

'Ah, Sergeant,' says the Reverend Featherstone. 'My wife said you might call.'

'This is Inspector Webb, sir,' replies Bartleby. Webb, however, seems a little distracted, leaning over the shoulder of one of the nearby pupils.

'Sir?' says Bartleby.

'Ah, Sergeant. Yes, forgive me,' says Webb, turning and offering his hand to the clergyman. 'Pleased to meet you, Reverend. Now, perhaps you could tell us what is the matter? I gather you have received another little missive.'

'Not quite, Inspector. Perhaps if you might come with me.'

The policemen follow Reverend Featherstone who,

signalling to his juniors to continue, quits the school-room and leads them outside. He walks in the direction of the main buildings.

'Have you worked here long, sir?' asks Webb.

'Three years or so, Inspector.'

'And do you find it rewarding work?'

The Reverend Featherstone smiles indulgently, as if humouring his interlocutor. 'It is my calling, Inspector. So, yes, of course I do.'

'I would not be responsible for a mob of children if you paid me, sir. I expect the younger boys are the worst, eh?'

'Inspector, I fear your work must have engendered an unfortunate cynicism. One must simply show them a firm hand. Then one earns their respect.'

'Ah, well, of course,' replies Webb.

Featherstone leads the two policemen into the main quadrangle but not to his suite of rooms. Instead, they turn down a rather dark corridor, to a small box-room, tucked away from public view, where the college's servants keep their cleaning utensils.

'My wife would not have it in our rooms, Inspector. The smell, you see? I thought it best to leave it here but the servants have complained. The sooner you remove it, the better.'

'Complained of what, sir?'

Featherstone frowns, and retrieves a rolled-up newspaper from a nearby shelf. Gingerly, he unwraps it with his fingertips, revealing the rather ripe carcase of a scraggy-looking plucked chicken – minus its head.

'Pungent, I'll grant you,' says Webb.

'Here, Inspector,' says the clergyman, proffering a piece of paper.

Webb takes it and reads the contents.

Watch out, old bird!

'This is everything?' says Webb incredulously. He casts a rather irritated glance at Bartleby.

'Is it not enough, Inspector?' asks Featherstone. 'I mean to say, I have no great concern for my safety, but you must take this sort of thing seriously. If some party, whether it is Mr. Boon or not, is hounding me in this way – however ridiculous it may be – well, surely it is a criminal matter.'

'I should not make wild accusations, sir,' suggests Webb.

'But surely you must look into it.'

Webb nods. 'Well, of course, sir. I can assure you I will give this matter the attention it deserves. You have my word.'

Reverend Featherstone looks relieved. 'Mrs. Featherstone will be so glad, Inspector.'

Webb nods. 'Thank you, sir. It is an . . . interesting development. We can find our way out – no need to accompany us – your students will be missing you. Sergeant . . .'

'Sir?'

'Be a good man and bring the evidence, will you?'

Bartleby casts his eye over the dead bird and grimaces, holding his breath.

~

'I have never, Sergeant, wasted my time in such a ridiculous wild goose chase.'

Sergeant Bartleby begins to speak, but is cut short.

'Don't even contemplate that remark, Sergeant.'

'No, sir. One moment, sir?' he says, spying a familiar figure crossing the college quadrangle and running back, before the inspector can reply.

'Miss? Miss Budge, isn't it?' asks the sergeant.

Jane Budge looks up, startled. 'Can't you leave me be?'

'I am sorry. I did not introduce myself when we met – my name is Bartleby, Sergeant Bartleby.'

'Sergeant? And I thought you was a chief inspector,' replies Jane Budge sarcastically. She looks at the newspaper in the sergeant's hand, her nose curling up. 'Lor, if that's your fish supper, I'd take it back.'

'It's a dead bird. It was left here last night, outside Reverend Featherstone's rooms.'

'Was it?'

'Did you see anyone prowling here last night?'

'I'd have smelt 'em first if I did.'

'No-one?'

Jane Budge shakes her head. 'Won't you take no for an answer?'

'Sergeant!' shouts Webb.

'Well, if you see anything out of the ordinary, Miss, you let me know. At Scotland Yard.'

Jane Budge shrugs. 'If you like. Your old man's calling, you know.'

'I know,' replies the sergeant with a grin. As he turns away, however, he notices Jane Budge's hands – the skin around both her wrists mottled with bruises.

'How did you get those?' he asks.

Jane Budge pulls her sleeves further down her arm. 'Well?'

'Mind your own business, Sergeant, eh?'

The sound of Decimus Webb's voice interrupts him again, and Sergeant Bartleby reluctantly returns to the inspector, leaving Jane Budge to her own devices.

'I warn you, Sergeant,' says Webb. 'You are not brightening my mood with your disappearing tricks.'

'She's one of the servants, sir. Does for the Featherstones. I thought she might have seen something.'

'I don't care if you were asking her to a matinée at the Alhambra,' says Webb as they reach the southern gates of the college, which lead out to the King's Road. 'Come and let's find another cab. Good God! And throw that wretched thing away, won't you?'

'But I thought you said it was evidence?'

'Evidence of a juvenile prank is all it is, Sergeant. Do you know what I saw scratched on one of those forms in the schoolroom?'

'Sir?'

'A small representation of a bird, with a cap and gown. Quite artistic for a youngster. And the word "Feathers". It is Featherstone's nickname amongst his pupils, though he appears not to know it. These notes are the productions of some wretched schoolboy with an over-active imaginative faculty.'

'Are you sure, sir?'

'Not only am I sure, Sergeant, I suspect we can look forward to more of the same from all quarters. Look over there.'

Webb points to the wall of Veitch's Nursery, upon the opposite side of the King's Road. A row of colourful red and green posters, each identical to the other, have been papered over the bricks.

REWARD of £50
For Information which leads to the
CAPTURE of the
Dreadful Fiend known as 'THE CUTTER'
APPLY Mr. J. Boon, Cremorne Gardens

'You know, Sergeant,' says Webb, 'I do not think this could get any worse.'

Bartleby does not disagree, tossing the rolled-up news-paper into the gutter and wiping his hands on his trousers.

CHAPTER THIRTEEN

'Mama, I said I might see Beatrice at Barassa's at half-past three.'

'Oh really, Rose, must you? The cab is an awful expense. When did you make this arrangement?'

'Bea wrote to me this morning.'

'Beatrice Watson should know better. What would your father say if he thought you were running off to some dingy confectioner's every other day?'

'Mama!' protests Rose Perfitt. 'It is not dingy. You know it isn't. Nor every other day.'

'And the cab, Rose?' replies Mrs. Perfitt. 'Your Papa is not made of money.'

'Then I shall walk.'

'You shall do no such thing!' exclaims Mrs. Perfitt. 'Very well, I suppose you cannot disappoint Beatrice. Have Richards find a cab. And be back by five – or your father will have something to say about it, I am sure.'

'Thank you, Mama!' exclaims Rose, running up to kiss her mother. Mrs. Perfitt smiles, but does not let her daughter leave the room without offering some further advice.

'Remember, Rose, we expect certain standards of behaviour now you are a grown woman. If we are to be introduced at the Prince's on Saturday no-one will care to hear about the ices at Barassa's. You must put aside these girlish things, dear.'

'Yes, Mama,' replies Rose Perfitt dutifully.

'And do take your sun-shade.'

In a matter of minutes Rose Perfitt is seated in a four-wheeled cab, wearing her best linen day-dress, a maroon check, and carrying her favourite Japanese parasol. With her fare paid in advance, the cab ought to speedily progress eastwards towards Barassa's Fancy Confectioner's, a popular resort for young ladies taking tea in the purlieus of Chelsea and Brompton. Instead, contrary to Miss Perfitt's supposed itinerary, it stops just round the corner from Edith Grove, on the King's Road.

It is Rose Perfitt herself who pulls the check-string that calls the driver to a halt. Moreover, she opens the door of the cab, stepping onto the pavement before he can even inquire what is the matter.

'You may go,' she says. 'I shall walk from here. It is such a beautiful day, after all. Please, keep the fare.'

'Walk, Miss?' says the cab-man, utterly perplexed, not having travelled more than four hundred yards.

'Yes, thank you,' replies Rose with a distinct nod, as if to signal a polite end to the conversation.

The cab-man raises his eyebrows – in a manner calculated to suggest he possesses certain doubts as to the mental faculties of his passenger. However, with a fare already in his pocket, he resolves to let the matter rest, and so instructs his horses to 'walk on', albeit allowing himself a brief glance over his shoulder. Rose, for her part, waits until the cab is in the far distance, then turns round, walking hastily across to the opposite side of the King's Road – to the very entrance of Cremorne Gardens.

'On your own, Miss?' asks the clerk on the gate. 'One shilling.'

The clerk's initial question is not a pointed one. For the daytime reputation of the Gardens is not so bad as the night. Indeed, it is not unknown for nurse-maids and governesses, from more liberal households, to bring their infant charges, as a special treat, to listen to the concerts of Cremorne's own brass band, or to the see the matinée performances of Senor Rosci's Astounding Dogs and Educated Monkeys in the Theatre Royal. If a certain proportion of Chelsea's inhabitants consider even these innocuous daytime amusements to be tainted, it is only a small propor-tion. It is certainly not a consideration in the mind of Rose Perfitt – she eagerly buys her ticket and makes her way through the gates.

Once inside, Rose walks with confident steps along the Gardens' central tree-lined avenue. As she walks, however, she constantly scrutinises the horizon for something or someone – although, by her expression, she does not seem to find it. Nonetheless, she carries on: past the American Bowling Saloon and the Hermit's Cave, until she comes to the Gardens' famed glass fountain. It displays a kneeling Grecian nymph, upon a crystal dias supported by a trio of long-necked storks, perpetually pouring out an endless stream of water from a bounteous jug. The fountain is in a secluded spot – nestling in a rose garden, beneath the shadow of the twin Moorish towers of the Fireworks Platform. Rose finds herself quite alone.

Rather than sit down upon one of the nearby benches, she begins to pace around the fountain's round basin.

— ◆ —

Rose Perfitt re-emerges onto the King's Road as the church bells of the parish ring five o'clock. Her face is rather gloomy, a hint of tears upon her cheeks, and an air of solemn disappointment about her. She hardly pays attention as she crosses the road, and she is surprised to hear her name called out as she turns onto Edith Grove. She looks round to see the Reverend Augustus Featherstone approaching.

'Miss Perfitt?'

Rose blushes. 'Yes, sir?'

'Are you quite all right, Miss Perfitt? Forgive me, you look a little distressed.'

'No,' protests Rose, forcing a smile, 'I am fine, I assure you.'

'Are you alone?'

'Yes, sir. I mean, I have just come back from tea with a friend. I asked the cab to drop me just along the way, so I might take some exercise.'

'Is that wise, Miss Perfitt?'

'Whatever do you mean, sir?'

'Well, the Gardens. You know the sort they attract, my dear girl. I would not wish to hear of a young lady such as yourself subjected to the insults of the idlers who frequent that place.'

'I am sure I have not seen any idlers, sir,' replies Rose. 'And if there were, I am sure I should be quite safe in broad daylight.'

The Reverend shakes his head, as if to admonish Rose for her naivety. 'Sad to say, Miss Perfitt, there is a class of ill-conditioned blackguards who do not hesitate to presume upon the good nature of innocent creatures such as yourself. Now, shall I accompany you home?'

'There is no need, sir. It is not far now.'

'No? As you wish, my dear,' says the Reverend

Featherstone, his thin aquiline features wrinkled in an expression of deep concern. He reaches out and clasps Rose's hand in a rather bony grip. 'Good day, then. But do take care, I beg you.'

Rose bids him goodbye, and hurries down Edith Grove. The clergyman lingers upon the corner, watching her disappear up the steps to her home.

He turns his gaze from the Perfitts' residence to the gates of Cremorne Gardens, and then once more back to Edith Grove, a look of consternation upon his face.

CHAPTER FOURTEEN

There is a light summer drizzle falling on the muddy ground of Sheepgut Lane, as one Alfred Budge departs for work. He is a short man of fifty years or so, stocky in build, with craggy features and a slouching cloth cap that barely conceals a thick mop of rather dirty-looking brown hair. With his rugged face and fustian coat, he very much resembles the archetype of a London 'rough', only differing from that happy ideal in his gait. It is a lame, lop-sided progress, caused by a crushed foot, trapped beneath a beer barrel some years ago, which remains stubbornly twisted at an odd angle to his body.

His cap does little to protect his head from the rain. In consequence, Mr. Budge mutters sundry curses to himself as he walks, his eyes fixed upon the ground, wary of pot-holes and other obstacles. Presumably, were he to meet one of his neighbours on the way, despite his displeasure at the weather, he would make some desultory nod or greeting. But he is quite alone, for the casual labourers and down-at-heel navvies who inhabit the lane's tumble-down cottages have long since gone to look for work. Mr. Budge, on the other hand, potman of The Old King's Head, keeps the civilised time of the victualling trade. In fact, he considers the present hour, at just gone ten o'clock in the morning, 'a precious early start'.

But Mr. Budge has little option in the matter. For his departure has been superintended by his wife of some thirty years, who stands indoors at the window of Budge's Dairy. As is often the case, she has an infant child in her arms. But she holds the baby in a rather disinterested fashion, seemingly oblivious to its cries, and the distinct tearfulness about its eyes, her attention focused on the figure disappearing down the road. Only when she is quite certain that her husband has receded out of sight, does she glance at the child and, even then, it is only to put it down in the cot that sits by the fire-place.

'Hush,' she says.

The baby does not oblige her. Mrs. Budge turns to the other individual in the room: a four-year-old boy who sits quietly upon a chair by the hearth. He is dressed in what is considered 'Sunday best' in Sheepgut Lane, a little suit of cheap cloth that boasts at least a couple of buttons and a shirt that might loosely be described as white.

'And how are you keeping, Davey?' she asks the boy.

The little boy nods in a rather timid way.

'Come now, dear, don't be shy,' says Mrs. Budge, coaxingly. 'Remember what your Ma told you?'

The little boy nods again.

'Good. Now, let me tell you something. I know a shop, not far from here, Davey, that sells the sweetest hardbake that any little boy is ever likely to taste. But they only sell to them that is good boys. What do you think of that?'

The mention of the sugared delicacy in question brings a rather more cheerful, expectant expression to the boy's face. Mrs. Budge smiles.

'That's it, Davey,' she continues. 'You be a good boy, like your Ma told you, and keep thinking on that, and we'll have a fine old time. Now, we're going on a little outing.'

⟡

An hour passes and Margaret Budge stands upon the pavement of the approach to Vauxhall Bridge, with an umbrella under one arm, and Davey Whit at her side. She takes the umbrella and points out the spectacle of the Houses of Parliament upon the far shore, and a steamboat heading up river, but the little boy in her charge seems disinterested. He is more struck by the sight of a soot-black pigeon that walks confidently along the gutter, occasionally pecking at the dirt, oblivious to the proximity of passing carriages. It is only when the bird flies away, as a clarence cab draws to a halt along side them, that the little boy looks up.

In truth, he looks startled. A judicious whisper of the word 'hardbake', however, serves to calm his nerves. As for the carriage, it remains motionless, with no sign of movement from within. Mrs. Budge, therefore, walks the boy to the kerb. At last, the window of the clarence is lowered by a black-gloved hand, revealing a female face inside, hidden by a dark veil, of the sort normally reserved for the mourning of close relatives.

'Ma'am,' says Mrs. Budge, with a rather awkward curtsey, made problematic by the balancing of her umbrella and Davey Whit's hand tightly clasping her own. 'I trust you are well, ma'am.'

'Thank you. I am well enough. Is this the child?'

Mrs. Budge places Davey in front of her, one shoulder firmly in her grip, as if fearing he might bolt at any moment.

85

'This is the boy, ma'am. Answers to Davey – David, ma'am.'

The woman in the carriage pushes the door ajar. 'Come here, David.'

Mrs. Budge ushers Davey forward. As he seems a little reluctant, she does not release her grip on his shoulder until he is on the carriage step.

'Just the boy,' says the woman inside, rather sternly. Mrs. Budge nods and steps back.

'Come, boy, you needn't be afraid of me,' says the woman. 'Step in so I may see you properly.'

The little boy looks back anxiously at Mrs. Budge, who urges him onward. Once he is inside, his interlocutor says nothing, but merely stares at him.

'He's a fine lad,' says Mrs. Budge from the roadside.

The veiled woman says nothing. At one point, she seems to raise a hand, as if to touch his face, but the boy flinches, and she withdraws it. At length, at what must be an interval of two or three minutes, she bids the boy to step down.

'Is everything all right, ma'am?' asks Mrs. Budge.

There is a silence from within the cab.

'He has changed a good deal,' she says at last.

'Oh, they do, ma'am. It's a year or two since you saw him; he were just a little whelp before.'

There is no reply.

'Ma'am?' says Mrs. Budge at last.

'I would have him emigrate,' says the woman in the cab, bluntly.

'Ma'am?'

'Emigrate. That is why I came here. To the colonies. I am sure a good place can be found for him by one of the societies. He has been in your care long enough.'

'We've looked after him well, ma'am,' says Mrs.

Budge, shaking her head, and putting a finger to her eyes. 'I don't know, I really don't. This is a hard blow.'

The woman in the carriage turns her head, her eyes hidden behind the black gauze of the veil.

'You will respect my wishes.'

'Of course, ma'am. But there is all sorts of difficulties . . . I mean, to separate him from those what have loved and cherished him all these years.'

'I will pay a premium, of course.'

'A premium?' replies Mrs. Budge, her tone of studied regret somewhat diminished. 'That puts a different face on it, begging your pardon, ma'am. It would be hard on a body, but, put that way, I can see as how it might be for the best.'

'Twelve sovereigns. By the usual arrangement.'

'And when would that be, ma'am?' asks Mrs. Budge.

'Tonight. You shall have it tonight.'

'Thank you, ma'am. That's a comfort.'

The woman closes the carriage window and slams the door, without uttering another word. The driver, in turn, makes the gentle tug upon the reins that drives the horses to trot on. As the vehicle departs, Mrs. Budge looks down at her youthful companion, ruffling his hair, much to his obvious discomfort.

'Regular Young Roscius, you are, Davey,' she says. 'Your Ma should put you on the stage.'

'I want my hardbake,' says Davey, quite emphatically.

~

True to her word, Mrs. Budge satisfies Davey Whit's appetite upon their return to Battersea. The little boy, in turn, is then collected from Budge's Dairy by his mother, who gratefully accepts two shillings for the services of her offspring. Once this transaction is completed, Mrs. Budge bids mother and child goodbye, and watches them depart along Sheepgut Lane. At length, when they have disappeared into the distance, Mrs. Budge turns away from the window, and walks into the back parlour. Her infant charges still lie there, side by side, and she crouches down beside a particular crib. Peeling back the grey linen, she touches the skin of the child, which feels decidedly damp. It cries out, but only a little, as if it cannot quite muster the power to complain any further.

'Not long till the good Lord gathers you up, eh? Most likely it's for the best, dear.'

Mrs. Budge smiles sympathetically, gets to her feet and returns to the front parlour. She goes over to the table, where a paper and pen lie ready. She dips the pen in the ink, and composes a brief note for the morning paper, with an ease and fluency bred of long experience.

NURSE CHILD WANTED, OR TO ADOPT –
The Advertiser, a Widow with a little family of her own, and a moderate allowance from her late husband's friends, would be glad to accept the charge of a young child. Age no object. If sickly would receive a parent's care. Terms, Fifteen Shillings a month; or would adopt entirely if under two months for the small sum of Twelve pounds.

Mrs. Budge reads her handiwork with pride, then gets up to search for an envelope.

CHAPTER FIFTEEN

Mr. John Boon waits behind the ticket booth at the gates to Cremorne Gardens. Decimus Webb stands a few yards distant, silently observing the night's steady stream of revellers tender their shillings and stroll merrily into the Gardens' landscaped walks. Boon, having finished a conversation with the clerk in the booth, walks back over to the policeman.

'Would you believe it, Inspector? Receipts are up!' he remarks cheerfully.

'Your notice has done the trick, then, sir.'

'Inspector!' protests Boon. 'That was never my intention. I merely wish to see the devil caught, as quickly as possible.'

'Of course, sir,' says Webb. 'And if the public has a natural curiosity to see it happen, then what are we to do about it?'

'Quite,' says Boon, uncertain whether Webb is mocking him. 'And you have no news I take it?'

'Three reports this afternoon, sir. All of them seem thoroughly specious. I've left Bartleby to make certain of it.'

'I am sure we shall catch the man, Inspector. Either that or he will not dare make another attempt, when the whole of Chelsea is looking for him.'

'Well, you will win out in either case, sir.'

'Inspector, I do not think that I care—'

Boon's words are cut short as he hears some kind of disturbance on the far side of the gates.

'What the deuce is that?' he exclaims, pushing his way past the booth, where a group of would-be visitors have halted. The cause is the approach of a large group of black-robed figures along the King's Road, all of whom are singing at the top of their voices.

The King of love my shepherd is,
whose goodness faileth never.
I nothing lack if I am his,
and he is mine forever . . .

Webb steps up beside Boon, as the group draw to a halt by the gates. He recognises the leader as the Reverend Featherstone, and a couple of the younger men, dressed in their cassocks, as the junior masters he saw in the Training College's schoolroom.

Perverse and foolish, oft I strayed,
but yet in love he sought me . . .

Featherstone does not interrupt the verse, but nods politely to Webb who, despite himself, cannot quite conceal a smile at Mr. Boon's almost apoplectic rage.

'Inspector!' exclaims Boon. 'You must put an end to this . . . this intrusion!'

'What intrusion, sir?' asks Webb. 'I believe they are on the public highway.'

'It is persecution, Inspector! Does the Law countenance such behaviour?'

'I'm rather fond of a good tune, myself, sir,' says Webb.

———

'Rose?' says Mrs. Perfitt, opening the bedroom door. 'My dear, must you keep disappearing to your room?'

Rose Perfitt turns from her seat by the window. 'I am sorry, Mama, I just felt a little seedy.'

'You do look tired. Are you coming down with something? Oh, I do hope not – not now. Why, I should think you might be a little more excited.'

Rose smiles. 'I do want to go to the ball, Mama, I promise. I shall be better tomorrow.'

'Well, Madame Lannier will bring the dress in the morning. I expect that will raise your spirits?'

Rose nods.

'Good. Now your dear father is still at his club, so Lord knows what hour he may come home. And I said I would call on Elspeth this evening – she has had one of her turns again.'

'I hope it is nothing serious?'

'You know your aunt, Rose – a slight head and she is convinced she has a brain fever. I expect it is nothing. Still, I shall not be back before ten. Tell your father if he comes home before you retire, will you?'

'Yes, Mama.'

'You will be quite all right on your own?'

'Mama!'

'Very well, dear. Have Richards bring you some supper. You must keep up your strength.'

Rose casts a chastening look at her mother, who smiles and withdraws from the room. She remains seated until she hears the sound of a cab arriving outside, and the front door of the house opening and close. Getting up, she watches her mother climb into the four-wheeler.

As the cab departs, Rose turns and looks around for her summer shawl.

⟋⟍

It is approaching nightfall as the Reverend Featherstone's amateur chorus come to a pause, in order to light the lanterns they have brought with them. John Boon has already disappeared, annoyed and exasperated, back into the gas-lit gardens. Decimus Webb, upon the other hand, remains by the gates. He takes advantage of the pause in the *al fresco* concert to speak to the clergyman.

'Good evening, Reverend.'

'Ah, it is you, Inspector, I thought it was,' replies Featherstone. 'I feared you might arrest us.'

Webb shakes his head. 'You aren't causing that much of an obstruction, sir. Nor a great public nuisance.'

'Mr. Boon might disagree with you.'

Webb shrugs. 'There doesn't seem to be many takers for your pamphlets, sir,' continues the Inspector, nodding at the handful of bills that one of the Reverend's juniors holds out to those approaching the gates.

'We only hope for "one sinner that repenteth", Inspector. Anything more is a great blessing.'

Webb nods. 'I trust your good wife has found nothing else upon her doorstep today, at least?'

'Thankfully not, Inspector.'

'Well, that is something. I see you have all your young men assisting you?'

'Everyone at St. Mark's is of a like mind, Inspector. We must see Cremorne closed. It is the Lord's will.'

Webb nods, but does not comment.

⟋⟍

In truth, if the Reverend Featherstone's protest has any obvious effect, it is principally to empty St. Mark's College of its staff and pupil-teachers, leaving the college buildings rather devoid of activity. The few persons that remain behind are mostly wives and servants, and several take the opportunity to visit the college chapel, and spend an hour or two in prayerful contemplation, Bertha Featherstone amongst them.

After the chapel bells are rung for ten o'clock, however, Mrs. Featherstone resolves to return to her rooms. She quits her place at the rear of the chapel's nave and gently opens the heavy wooden door that leads out into the college grounds. The short walk to her apartments in the main building is a peaceful one, and there is nothing in the warm summer night to disturb her serene progress, save the creaking iron weathercock that roosts atop the chapel's summit.

But even Mrs. Featherstone visibly jumps when she hears a strange, muffled scream, as she enters the college quadrangle. Even though the sound is somehow muted, it is unmistakably frantic, a raucous and primitive cry.

For a moment, she cannot quite believe her ears. Echoing stone walls can play tricks, after all; it is, she reasons, an animal, some wretched cat or fox. But then it comes again. She can do nothing but pursue the sound, completing almost a full lap of the cloisters until she realises the noise comes from the servants' quarters, not far from her own rooms. In fact, from the servants' scullery.

In her heart, she knows something of what awaits her, before her eyes see the evidence. For, mixed with the screams, there are repeated desperate thuds against some hard surface, and a sound like the crackling of autumn leaves upon a bonfire. It takes only the sight of smoke creeping beneath the scullery door to confirm her worst suspicions.

Instinctively, Mrs. Featherstone rushes forward, heedless of any danger to herself, and, as the smoke rises around her, struggles to free the heavy bolt that holds the scullery door firmly shut. The metal is already warm with the blaze, and it takes all her strength to move it. Moreover, she does not anticipate the sudden rush of acrid air and belching fire as the door flies open, singeing her dress; it compels her to run back along the corridor to safety.

It is probably for the best that she does not come too close. For it means she does not see the full horror of Jane Budge's face as she tumbles from the blazing inferno, her body writhing in agony, her hands scratching senselessly at the floor, as the flames dance gaily on her back.

PART TWO

CHAPTER SIXTEEN

Decimus Webb stands alone in the well-kept grounds of St. Mark's in the first light of dawn. The towers of the college buildings seem strangely insubstantial, almost one-dimensional, silhouetted in the early-morning half-light, like shadows from a lantern-show. In the background he can hear the morning chorus of the neighbourhood's sparrows, underscored by the distant bass rumble of a freight train on the London Western Extension Railway, its line adjacent to the college's grounds. The policeman's face looks a little troubled; it may be that he simply regrets there is no breeze to remove the noxious smell of burnt matter that lingers in the air.

'Sir?'

The figure of Sergeant Bartleby approaches, coming from the college.

'Sergeant.'

'I wondered where you'd got to, sir.'

'I was just taking a moment to gather my thoughts. What progress?'

'We'll move the body this morning, sir, to the Chelsea Infirmary. Autopsy this afternoon. Coroner's tomorrow.'

'Well, I should be surprised if we are mistaken as

to the cause of death,' replies Webb. 'Still, it is best to be certain that we have not missed anything. And the rest?'

'I've made arrangements to interview everyone on the premises; there's about sixty resident pupil-teachers, and half a dozen staff and three wives – though most of them seem to have been absent.'

'I can vouch for that. They were outside Cremorne Gardens, at the Reverend Featherstone's impromptu prayer-meeting.'

'Ah, yes, sir, you did say.'

'Did you look at the body, Sergeant?'

Bartleby visibly winces. 'Yes, sir.'

'A peculiar murder, all things considered,' says Webb, disdaining to notice his sergeant's queasy reaction. 'I suppose we should be grateful the whole place did not burn down, and not merely the scullery.'

'The brigade came out pretty sharp,' replies Bartleby.

'I know, Sergeant, I was here myself.'

'You're sure it was no accident, sir?'

'I should be impressed if Miss Budge managed to set herself alight, and bolt herself inside the room, locking it from the outside.'

'Well then, what next, sir?'

'I think we may now interview Mrs. Featherstone,' says Webb. 'She seemed a little too distressed to be questioned last night.'

'Still a bit early in the day, though?'

'Is it? Well, let us find her husband and see what he says about it. I am loath to delay any longer.'

Bartleby assents and the two policemen walk in silence across the lawn, back towards the college. As they approach the cloisters, Bartleby turns to Webb.

'You weren't to know this would happen, sir. To tell the truth, I didn't take that letter too seriously myself.'

Webb pauses, causing Bartleby to draw to a halt beside him.

'When I require your opinion, Sergeant, I shall ask for it.'

———

Mrs. Featherstone sits in her parlour, a strong cup of tea by her side and the two policemen seated opposite, together with her husband. If there is any change to her normal rather implacable appearance, it is only that her dress is a little more creased than might be expected, and her eyes a little tired and bloodshot.

'Thank you for seeing us, ma'am,' says Webb. 'Your husband said you might be agreeable to a brief interview.'

'One must do one's duty in such terrible circumstances, Inspector,' replies Mrs. Featherstone. 'In truth, I have not slept since the incident.'

'My wife is a woman of spirit, Inspector,' adds the Reverend. 'You may rely on her.'

'Of course,' agrees Webb. 'So, tell me, ma'am, if you can, precisely what happened?'

Mrs. Featherstone takes a deep breath. 'I came back from the chapel, Inspector, not long after the stroke of ten. I often go there to pray in the evening. I heard a scream. I thought it was some distressed animal. I could not locate it at first.'

'But you realised it came from the scullery?'

'At length, yes. After a minute or two. Then I smelt something burning. Naturally, I went directly to see what was wrong.'

'And it was you who opened the door?'

'With some difficulty. I did not think I would find . . . well, I did not think.'

'There, Bertha, please, do not distress yourself,'

interjects the Reverend, placing a hand on his wife's arm.

'Do go on,' says Webb.

Mrs. Featherstone takes another breath. 'I shouted for help. Some of the servants came to my aid. Jane . . . I believe they managed to extinguish the flames with a blanket, but she was beyond help. God rest her poor soul.'

'Tell me, ma'am,' persists Webb, 'was it usual for Jane Budge to be on the premises at such an hour? She did not lodge here, I understand?'

'No, Inspector, she did not. But she had chores that might take up most of the evening.'

'I see. And what of the scullery itself? Who would normally use it?'

'Jane and the other servants, I suppose. There are five or six girls who work for the college.'

'So Jane Budge was not your own maid?'

'No, she was employed by the college,' interjects Reverend Featherstone. 'But principally she was engaged to clean our rooms, and those of the pupil-teachers on the adjoining landings here, for whom I am responsible.'

'Ah. Well, thank you, sir. Now, I do not suppose, to your knowledge, or yours, ma'am, that she had any enemies?'

'Enemies, Inspector?' asks the clergyman, as if rather perplexed.

Webb frowns. 'Forgive my bluntness, sir, but it is undoubtedly a case of murder. It is no accident.'

'Yes, yes, Inspector, I realise that much,' replies Reverend Featherstone, with impatience. 'But we know who is responsible, do we not? I admit I did not take him seriously at first, but all the same.'

'Sir?'

If the Reverend Featherstone is about to elucidate, he is given no opportunity. 'This man who calls himself "The Cutter", Inspector!' exclaims Bertha Featherstone, jumping in. 'Heavens! Have you not even read the letter we gave your man here?'

'I have, ma'am,' says Webb cautiously, 'and I would not race to such conclusions, not yet.'

Mrs. Featherstone gives Webb a look of utter incredulity. 'Race? What "conclusions" will you draw, Inspector, when this lunatic murders us in our beds? What then?'

'Bertha, please,' says the Reverend, attempting to placate her. 'You are over-tired. I am sure the inspector meant no harm.'

'We are obliged to keep an open mind at this stage, ma'am,' says Webb. 'And whether we attribute this to our friend "The Cutter" or not, I fear it does not help us identify the person or persons responsible.'

Mrs. Featherstone says nothing, though the stern fixity of her gaze is eloquent in itself.

'I think, Inspector,' suggests the Reverend Featherstone, 'that might do for now?'

'Of course, sir,' replies Webb. 'I shan't be a moment; one last point. If I may, Mrs. Featherstone, what was your opinion of Jane Budge?'

Mrs. Featherstone relaxes her stern expression of contempt only to the degree that it allows her to speak.

'As a servant, Inspector, I would say she was not of the best class. Her work often left something to be desired.'

'And what of her character, ma'am?'

'I know of nothing against her, Inspector. Why?'

'It is only that we are having a little difficulty establishing where she lived. The address she gave, upon starting work here, turns out to be a common lodging-house in Battersea. We sent a man down there to make inquiries last night. They claim not to have seen her for more than two years, and that she never lived there for any length of time.'

'Indeed? Well, that is curious. Still, I believe her last position was with a very respectable family, with whom I have the honour of being acquainted.'

'I see. Who might that be, ma'am?'

'The Perfitts, Inspector. They reside quite near here – in Edith Grove.'

CHAPTER SEVENTEEN

The town houses of Edith Grove are typical examples of a certain breed of London terrace. For, with a nod to the civilisation of Ancient Greece, they are of the classical style, much favoured in the western portion of the great metropolis, that places an Ionic portico above every doorstep, and a stucco pediment above every window. In size, they are a little smaller and more stunted than the fashionable homes of Belgravia or even Mayfair; but they are respectable houses, nonetheless, whose polished front steps are regularly washed down and whose black iron railings, tipped with gold points, are regularly repainted.

'You're sure someone was trying to do away with Jane Budge, sir?' asks Sergeant Bartleby, as the two men walk along the road. 'I mean to say, not just our man trying to burn the place down, and the girl got in the way?'

'Anything is possible, Sergeant, but ask yourself this about your scissor-man. First, why does a man with some morbid urge to remove the hair of young women suddenly decide to murder a respectable clergyman? Second, why do so by fire? Is the man suddenly a pyromaniac too? It is hardly the most efficient or likely way to effect his object, is it? Third, it is a peculiar time and place – why not in the Featherstones' apartments whilst they slept? Why the scullery?'

'But the letter, sir? It said he'd "roast" him. That can't be a coincidence.'

'Why start a fire when Featherstone was out?'

Bartleby shakes his head.

'If we are searching for a genuine lunatic, Sergeant, who acts utterly at whim,' continues Webb, 'then I confess that any further cogitation upon the subject is wasted. But we are required to investigate this matter and, therefore, we may as well assume some logic exists, some cause and effect?'

Bartleby nods. He knows Webb well enough to recognise a purely hypothetical appeal to his own judgment.

'Now,' continues Webb, 'here we are at last. Ring the bell, will you?'

Bartleby rings the bell. It is swiftly answered by a young maid-servant. Webb, in turn, inquires if either the master or the mistress of the house is at home. After a brief period of consultation, during which, doubtless, the inspector's calling card causes a degree of consternation, the two policeman are relieved of their hats and shown up to the Perfitts' first-floor drawing-room. They find Mrs. Caroline Perfitt ready to welcome them.

'Inspector Webb?' she asks, in the polite but slightly haughty tone that is her custom.

'Yes, ma'am.'

Bartleby coughs.

'And this is Sergeant Bartleby, ma'am. You must forgive our intrusion at such an early hour.'

'Of course. But did you wish to see my husband, Inspector? He has already left to catch his train. I trust there is nothing wrong?'

104

'I hope not, ma'am,' says Webb, as affably as he is able. 'Merely you might be able to help us with some information. Either your good self or your husband might suffice; but we can call another time, if it is more convenient.'

'No, please, if I can be of any assistance, of course, ' replies Mrs. Perfitt. 'Please – Inspector, Sergeant – do take a seat.'

'Thank you, ma'am,' replies Webb, as Mrs. Perfitt herself sits down. 'It relates to a former servant of yours, so we understand – one Jane Budge.'

'Jane? Poor creature. I trust she is not in any trouble?'

'"Poor creature", ma'am?' asks Bartleby.

'Forgive me, Sergeant. An awkward turn of phrase. Inspector, what is it?'

'May I be blunt, Mrs. Perfitt?' asks Webb. 'I do not wish to shock you.'

'Of course, Inspector,' she replies, with considerable calm. 'Really, you must tell me. I am quite in suspense.'

'She is dead, ma'am.'

'Dead?'

'Murdered, I am afraid. She died last night. We are trying to learn something of her history.'

'Good Lord,' says Mrs. Perfitt. 'Last night? Who would do such a thing?'

'We do not know yet, ma'am. Forgive me, I must persist. You were once her employer?'

Mrs. Perfitt nods. 'For two years or so. She left us . . . well, it would be almost five years ago.'

'Any particular reason for her departure, ma'am?'

'The family quit London for a few months' holiday, Inspector. She did not wish to travel with us to the country.'

105

'I see. Can you tell me anything about Miss Budge? Did you provide her with a good character? I assume so, as she found a place quite readily at St. Mark's?'

'I did, Inspector. She was an excellent maid-of-all-work. But,' says Mrs. Perfitt, pausing, as if vacillating whether to speak any further, 'well, I suppose it must out. You will soon hear about it, I am sure.'

'What, ma'am?'

'You ask about her character, Inspector. There was one particular circumstance, though I would not wish it to reflect badly upon her. It is rather delicate.'

'Speak plainly, ma'am, I beg you.'

'Very well,' replies Mrs. Perfitt, although she seems a little affronted by the policeman's lack of politesse. 'My husband, at one point, did suspect her of improper conduct.'

'Theft?' suggests Bartleby.

Mrs. Perfitt shakes her head. 'No, Sergeant, nothing of that sort. It was, rather, he thought that she was engaging in relations of a questionable character with a particular young man.'

'Ah,' says Webb. 'I see. But your husband was proved wrong?'

'I almost wish he was right, Inspector. You see, he discovered the man in question . . . his name was Nelson, I recall . . .' says Mrs. Perfitt, faltering, her cheeks colouring a little. 'You must forgive me . . . he discovered him forcing himself upon her.'

Webb frowns. 'I am sorry you are obliged to recall such matters, ma'am.'

'Quite. Charles – that is my husband – insisted the fellow was brought to trial. And, I am glad to say, he was convicted and sent to gaol. We did not feel it would be right to make any reference to it in Jane's character, but the whole business was rather awkward.'

'And how long was this before she left your employment, ma'am?' asks Webb.

'Perhaps a month or so,' says Mrs. Perfitt. 'Poor girl.'

'And is there anything else about her that you recall? Did she have any family? How did she come to you?'

'I believe it was through one of the local agencies, Inspector. My husband may have the correspondence. As for her family, I am not so intimate with the personal affairs of my maids.'

'Of course, ma'am,' replies Webb. 'Well, in that case, I think it might be best if I returned for a quick word with your husband, perhaps this evening?'

'I can provide you with the address of his firm, Inspector,' suggests Mrs. Perfitt. 'Barker and Co., in the City.'

Webb smiles politely. 'Thank you, but tonight would be more convenient, ma'am, if you don't mind. What time shall we say?'

'You might come at seven o'clock,' suggests Mrs. Perfitt, 'before dinner.'

'Excellent,' says Webb, moving to stand up. 'Then that is all, I think. Again, I am sorry for intruding, ma'am.'

'Not at all,' replies Mrs. Perfitt. 'Inspector, you did not say how poor Jane died?'

'I hoped to spare you the details, ma'am. They are rather unpleasant.'

'I am sure I will hear them at some point, Inspector.'

'Very well. She was caught in a fire, ma'am.'

'A fire? Really? It was not an accident then? You are certain?'

'No, ma'am,' says Webb. 'Quite deliberate.'

'Why did you want to leave seeing his nibs until tonight?' asks Bartleby, as the two men walk back down Edith Grove.

'It is merely because I think we would do better to spend a little time over this "awkward" business of Miss Budge and – Mr. Nelson, was it not? – before we talk to Mr. Perfitt. It may provide us with a few more questions about the girl, even if it does not provide any answers. You can talk to the local division about it, for a start. Find out where Nelson's serving his time. We might even pay him a visit.'

Bartleby nods, notebook already in hand. 'And what about Mrs. Perfitt, sir?'

'What about her, Sergeant?'

Bartleby pauses for thought. 'She said she wasn't intimate with her maids, but her husband seems to have kept a close eye on Jane Budge – close enough for him to discover this fellow having his way with her.'

'And then they got rid of her; because no-one cares for soiled goods, do they, Sergeant? A good character supplied to compensate, naturally.'

'You don't think it was Jane Budge's aversion to country air, then?'

Webb allows himself a derisive snort. 'I should think not.'

There is another pause before Webb turns to the sergeant. 'Did she strike you as an "excellent" sort of servant, Sergeant?'

'Hard to tell, sir. More the skivvying sort, rather than your lady's maid, I'd say.'

'But Mrs. Perfitt described her as "excellent". That was not Mrs. Featherstone's opinion, by any means. Curious, eh?'

'Perhaps Mrs. Featherstone has different standards, sir.'

'I doubt they are higher than those of Mrs. Perfitt,' replies Webb. 'I'd say she has fairly high standards herself.'

'It could be that she didn't want to speak ill of the dead,' remarks Bartleby.

'I suppose that must be it.'

———

'Who was that, Mama?' asks Rose Perfitt, entering the drawing-room. Her mother stands by the window, watching the street.

'No-one, Rose,' replies her mother. 'No-one at all.'

CHAPTER EIGHTEEN

Reports of murder are not uncommon in the great metropolis. Some may even be all but overlooked: a brawl in an East End beer-shop may result in a fatal wound, but merits only two lines in the day's *Police News*. The wife-murder; the poisoning; the mutilated corpse – anything with a hint of sensation – is another matter entirely. Rumour of such dreadful events is carried not only by the papers, but by word of mouth, passing from one man or woman to another, travelling at speed like some dreadful contagion. And the murder of Jane Budge is no exception. Whether it is the association with the peculiar reputation of the 'Cremorne Cutter', or the effect of the words 'Woman Burnt Alive' rendered in bold type, her demise swiftly becomes the subject of common gossip. Thus, in due course, less than twenty-four hours after Jane Budge has breathed her last, the news reaches one Mrs. Margaret Budge in Battersea.

It arrives in the form of a neighbour, a woman hesitantly bearing a copy of the *Battersea Evening Record* who finds Mrs. Budge at home, alone but for an infant in her arms. The woman is, in truth, no great friend of the Budge family and merely stops long enough to offer some words of comfort – and, perhaps, to observe the effect of her evil tidings. But if the woman expects tears, she is disappointed. Mrs. Budge appears perversely calm; and so the woman excuses herself and leaves, audibly muttering the word 'unnatural'.

Mrs. Budge watches her visitor depart, then casually places the baby she is holding, a small undernourished creature, to one side. There is almost always one such child in Mrs. Budge's tender care. Indeed the presence of a mewling infant is something Margaret Budge rather takes for granted; an almost comforting constant in her life. On cue, the child cries out a little at being abandoned, immediately missing the warmth of her adoptive mother's bosom.

Mrs. Budge herself puts her hands to her head and lets out a sigh, a low throaty sob. Her round face trembles and tears trickle down her cheeks. The child responds in kind, its cry more insistent and aggravated.

'Hush now,' says Mrs. Budge, at length.

But the child does not oblige.

'Hush,' says Mrs. Budge, placing a finger on the child's lips. 'Hush.'

Still it screams.

Mrs. Budge rises wearily from her chair, to the small cupboard that serves as her medicine cabinet.

'You need something to calm your spirits, little 'un,' she says out loud, a distracted expression upon her face. 'A nice dose of quietness, eh? I expect we both do. And what will I tell her father? Not that he'll care, the old sot.'

The child screams all the more. Mrs. Budge sighs a second time, her face still wet with tears, and pours out a spoonful of Godfrey's Cordial, her hand rather unsteady, spilling a good deal upon the floor. She puts the bottle down, laying the spoon beside it, talking to the infant, her tone shifting to a harsh whisper.

'I hope that bastard Nelson swings for it.'

The object of Margaret Budge's curses is, in fact, not many miles distant. He sits alone in the tap-room of the World's End tavern, a quiet, smoky resort of Chelsea's labouring classes, concealed from the outside world by frosted glass and separate from the more refined snug by a nicely carved wooden partition. It is suited to men who enjoy a quiet drink at the end of a day's work; its seats are plain and wooden, without padding or ornament; its tables made of cheap varnished deal. A handful of locals sit chatting animatedly near the bar but George Nelson remains on his own, seated at a small table, a pint pot in his hand. He does not look up when two newcomers enter from the King's Road – or, at least, not until they stand directly over him.

'George Nelson?'

'Who's asking?'

'No need to take that tone,' says Decimus Webb.

'Peelers, ain't you?'

Webb smiles, apparently gratified to be recognised. George Nelson puts down his drink.

'My name is Inspector Webb. This is my sergeant. May we join you?'

Nelson looks up, as if about to say something rather forcefully against the idea. But he seems to hold himself back. 'Join me? You buying then?'

Webb shakes his head and sits down beside Nelson.

'Shame,' says Nelson.

'I think you know why we're here,' suggests Bartleby.

Nelson shrugs. 'I ain't done a thing. I've got my

113

ticket; I already reported to the station. I don't want any trouble.'

Webb raises his eyebrows. 'I'd have thought a man in your position would steer clear of Chelsea in the first place; make a fresh start.'

'I've pals here. What do you want with us?'

Webb looks directly into the ticket-of-leave man's eye. 'I think you know, Mr. Nelson. But I'll happily spell it out for you. A strange coincidence, you see – I've been making inquiries today into the murder of a young woman named Budge; she was killed last night. I find out this morning that five years ago she was assaulted by a certain George Nelson – a nasty piece of work by all accounts. I make further inquiries. It turns out that our Mr. Nelson has just finished his penal servitude; that he's out on leave.'

'Bad business that fire,' replies Nelson, taking a gulp of his drink. 'I just read about it, as it happens. In the paper.'

'Is that so?'

'What, you don't think I can read?'

'You don't seem very sorry about it,' says Bartleby.

Nelson looks up at Bartleby. 'Maybe I ain't.'

'Where were you last night, Mr. Nelson?'

'Here.'

'All night?' asks Webb. 'Between, say, nine and eleven o'clock?'

'I was here. Ask the landlord there; he knows me. Ask anyone you fancy.'

Webb looks at Bartleby and nods. The sergeant heads off in the direction of the bar.

'When did you last see Miss Budge, then?' asks Webb.

Nelson frowns. 'Five year back, I should say.'

Webb pauses. 'I don't see many of your pals about,

Mr. Nelson. Why did you really come back, eh? Did you want to punish that wretched girl for what she did to you? For putting you away?'

'I said already, I was here the whole night,' repeats Nelson, in monotone.

Webb pauses. 'A costly habit, drink. Have you found employment?'

'The Gardens.'

'Cremorne?' asks Webb.

'I used to work there. They're happy to have me.'

'What is your position?'

'General labourer. Scene-shifter.'

'They must have thought highly of you, to take you back, knowing the sort of man you are. A risk for them. All those young women, actresses, ballet girls . . .'

Nelson places his drink firmly down upon the table, turning to look Webb directly in the eye. 'Look here, Inspector – I know your game. But I never did nothing to that damn girl.'

Webb does not reply. Nelson takes a deep breath.

'Ah, here's your poodle now,' says the ticket-of-leave man as Bartleby returns.

'Well?' says Webb.

'He was here, sir,' says Bartleby. 'The landlord and two others will vouch for it.'

Nelson takes another sip of his drink. The hint of a smile curls at the edge of his lip. 'That's cooked your goose, ain't it, Inspector?'

Webb ignores the remark. If he is about to ask Nelson any further question, he thinks better of it. 'We may wish to speak to you again, Mr. Nelson. Do not leave your current lodgings without notifying us.'

Nelson nods, an expression of mock gravity upon his face. 'I know the rules of the ticket, Inspector. I know 'em all right.'

'I am glad to hear it,' says Webb, getting up from his seat.

'One thing, Inspector,' says Nelson.

'What?' says Webb.

'Who do you think killed her then? They say it's this "Cutter" fellow, don't they?'

Webb wordlessly gets to his feet.

'Let me know if you catch up with him,' says Nelson, grinning. 'I'd very much like to stand that gentleman a drink.'

'Warm sort of chap, wasn't he?' says Bartleby, as the two policemen walk along the King's Road.

'I've yet to meet a convict with great love for the police, Sergeant,' says Webb. 'Still, these men who vouched for him – did they seem reliable?'

'Far as I could tell, sir. They didn't seem to have been put up to it. I've got their names. And I'll ask the lads at T Division what they know about the landlord.'

Webb nods. 'He had a grudge against the girl, we know that much.'

'You think he had someone else do it?'

'Possibly; though he does not strike me as the type. A queer way to go about it, too. One might imagine a garrotting would suit his purpose; a knife in a dark alley as the girl made her way home. This fire smacks of something different; hardly the act of a determined assassin.'

'Spur of the moment?'

Webb smiles. 'Correct, Sergeant. Improvisation. Or, perhaps, desperation.'

'Where now, sir?'

Webb pulls out his watch from the pocket in his waistcoat.

'Back to Edith Grove.'

CHAPTER NINETEEN

Webb and Bartleby find Charles Perfitt already returned home, expecting their arrival, waiting together with his wife. Introductions are swiftly made, and soon the policemen are seated once more in the Perfitts' drawing-room.

'I fear you have wasted your journey, Inspector,' says Mrs. Perfitt. 'I have talked to Mr. Perfitt—'

'Caroline, please,' interrupts Charles Perfitt, rather firmly. 'I am quite able to speak for myself.'

Mrs. Perfitt blushes and falls silent.

'I am sure that you are correct, ma'am,' replies Webb, tactfully. 'And I don't wish to detain you or your husband longer than is necessary. I gather then, sir, that you do not have any further particulars regarding the personal circumstances of Jane Budge?'

'I looked through my papers, Inspector. She came to us through an agency, as we were new to the area. She was only a young girl at the time. We took her on trial, and she proved suitable. I can provide their address, if you like, though I am not sure they are still in business.'

'Thank you, sir. Bartleby here will make a note of it. Did you have any contact with Jane Budge after she left your employment? I suppose you or your wife must have passed her in the street upon occasion, the college being so near by?'

'Not to any great extent, Inspector,' replies Mr. Perfitt. 'I may have seen her, in passing, on occasion.'

'So you do not know, for instance, if she had any particular acquaintances or friends? Or if there was someone who might wish her harm?'

'I have no idea, Inspector,' replies Mr. Perfitt. 'Why ever should I? Besides, from what I hear, some lunatic is responsible – that same fellow who's been molesting these girls in the Gardens?'

'We cannot be certain of that, sir,' says Webb. 'I merely wondered if you took any particular interest in Miss Budge's welfare, after she left you. Mrs. Perfitt explained you decided to give her a good character, even after the unfortunate business with Mr. Nelson.'

'I would prefer not to discuss that painful affair, Inspector, if it is all the same to you. I know that my wife has already mentioned it – and I would rather she had not – but, really, I cannot imagine that we need to rake it up again.'

Webb frowns. 'I fear we policemen must grub in the dirt upon occasion. One never knows what one may find. I would not wish to distress Mrs. Perfitt, however . . .'

Webb's implication is not wasted on Charles Perfitt. 'Yes, Caroline, perhaps you might be spared this, at least.'

'Really, Charles,' replies Mrs. Perfitt. 'There is no need.'

'Caroline,' returns her husband firmly, 'I rather think the inspector is right.'

'Very well,' replies Mrs. Perfitt. And with a polite, if somewhat forced, smile, she gets up and quits the drawing-room.

'You must forgive my wife, Inspector. She can be rather headstrong.'

Webb dismisses the apology with a wave of his hand. 'I am sorry to be the cause of any awkwardness, sir. But I fear we do need to discuss George Nelson. He is, at least, the only person we have yet discovered with any grudge against Jane Budge. An unpleasant character too, though he appears to have an alibi.'

Charles Perfitt smiles ruefully. 'Yes, well I expect Pentonville Prison will stand for that.'

'No,' says Webb. 'I am afraid it is not quite so cast-iron as Pentonville. You see, he was released on ticket-of-leave two days ago.'

Charles Perfitt's face becomes suddenly pale.

'You seem surprised, sir?'

⏤

As Caroline Perfitt quits the drawing-room, she finds her daughter loitering near by, upon the stairs.

'Rose! Heavens, were you eavesdropping?'

'No, Mama!' replies Rose indignantly. 'I just heard we had guests, that is all. It is the same men that came this morning, isn't it? I saw them in the road.'

'Did you now? Rose, I swear, I sometimes think you spend half your life gazing out of that bedroom window. I have told you a thousand times – it is so common.'

'I'm sorry, Mama,' replies Rose, a little shame-faced. 'But it is the same men, isn't it?'

'Rose – please, it need not concern you.'

⏤

Charles Perfitt sips from a glass of brandy.

'You know how servants will have hangers-on, Inspector,' he says at last. 'I mean, one tries to discourage it, but it is to be expected.'

'I've heard it said, sir.'

'But I began to see this fellow Nelson – a labouring man by the look of him – loitering in the street, late at night – almost every night, in fact. Then my wife noticed him in Jane's company when the girl returned from running an errand. There seemed a disagreeable intimacy between them. I told Jane it had been noted and she must desist from seeing him. She protested her innocence of any mischief.'

'You did not believe her?'

'I had some doubts. In any case, it was not more than two or three days after I made my opinions clear, that I saw the fellow loitering once more, just as I was going to my bed. Worse – he went down into our area; I was sure it was for some pre-arranged nocturnal assignation.'

'So you went to have words with him?' asks Webb.

'With them both. But it was not as I had imagined. Well, it was a fearful attack, Inspector. Rape, that is the only word. The girl was struggling against him, struggling for her life – the way he held her down – she was fortunate not to be seriously injured. Naturally, I intervened. Floored the brute, I am proud to say.'

'And you gave Nelson in charge?'

'I made sure there was a prosecution, Inspector. Any decent man would have done the same for the poor girl – for the common good.'

'Quite, quite,' says Webb.

'Do you believe it was Nelson that killed her?' asks Mr. Perfitt anxiously, taking another sip of brandy.

'He claims to have an alibi, sir. And he would have to have made his way into the college somehow. But it's clear he had no great fondness for the girl, let me put it that way.'

'You have spoken to him?'

'Not fifteen minutes ago, sir. He's lodging by the

World's End; we found him there, drinking in the public house.'

Charles Perfitt's face freezes into a stony, shocked stare.

'The World's End?' he says after a brief pause. 'I rather wish that's where he were, Inspector. I would happily put ten thousand miles between us.'

'I do not blame you, sir,' replies Webb. 'But I think he should know better than to give you any trouble. We've marked his card, as it were.'

'But if he bears a grudge against me, Inspector? I have to think of Rose and Caroline.'

'Rose?'

'My daughter, Inspector. I would not put her in any danger,' says Mr. Perfitt.

'I'll have a word with the local constables, sir,' says Bartleby. 'Make sure they keep a special eye on the premises. And I think we'll be doing likewise for Mr. Nelson's movements?'

Bartleby's query is directed to Webb, who nods his approval.

'Tell me, sir,' says Webb, 'why did Jane Budge leave your employment?'

'Ah, well, we decamped to the country, Inspector. If I may be honest, my wife took the whole business with George Nelson rather badly. My part in the trial was rather a strain on her nerves; our doctor, marvellous fellow, recommended a thorough rest; I took her for the water-cure.'

'And Miss Budge was unwilling to accompany you to . . .'

'Leamington Spa. Dr. Malcolm has his own establishment there. I confess, the baths did Caroline a great deal of good.'

'A pleasant holiday, you might say.'

'Yes,' replies Mr. Perfitt. 'I suppose you might.'

'Well, I am sure we have wasted enough of your time, sir,' says Webb, raising himself from his chair. 'Now if you can just find that address for my sergeant, we will be on our way.'

———

Caroline Perfitt waits until the two policemen have left the house before she rejoins her husband. She finds him sitting before the drawing-room hearth with an half-empty glass of brandy held loosely in his hand. He looks around as she enters.

'Caroline,' he says, extending his arm towards her, 'sit down.'

'Charles, whatever is the matter?'

'George Nelson has been freed. They have released him on leave.'

Mrs. Perfitt puts her hand to her mouth.

'Good Lord,' she says in a whisper.

'Perhaps,' continues Mr. Perfitt, 'we might take a holiday for a month or so; the firm would not object, I am sure. We might even go abroad?'

'Charles, no! Rose is coming out this season; we have the ball at the Prince's Ground – and then . . . no, I cannot possibly allow it.'

'It might be for the best,' says Mr. Perfitt. 'For Rose's sake if nothing else. I do not want any unpleasantness.'

'Charles, I assure you, if you have any fears . . .'

'I just thought this whole business was behind us.'

Mrs. Perfitt rallies. 'And it is. There is no need to be so rash – promise me you will sleep upon it, at least.'

Mr. Perfitt looks solemnly at his wife.

'I doubt I shall get much sleep at all.'

CHAPTER TWENTY

Decimus Webb bites into a slightly stale piece of buttered bread provided by Metcalf's Temperance Coffee House, chewing it rather ruminatively. The bread itself comes upon a plate in four thick slices, almost sufficient to constitute a loaf. Served to complement the Coffee House's stock-in-trade, it provides a 'fourpenny breakfast' for weary travellers – a modest outlay for a distinctly modest form of early-morning refreshment. It is, however, eminently suited to the drowsy clerks and impecunious cab-men who constitute a majority of the clientele. Decimus Webb himself might certainly afford somewhere a little better. But he makes the Temperance Coffee House a stop upon his way to work in nearby Scotland Yard whenever he notices that a certain table is free by the window – a table that provides a panorama of Trafalgar Square. And if it is free, and he has anything upon his mind, he makes a point of sitting there. For he can watch through the plate glass and observe the progress of the hundreds of souls who pass by, until the chimes of St. Martin-in-the-Fields eventually persuade him it is time to visit his office.

Unfortunately, as he looks out of the window, the approach of Sergeant Bartleby from Whitehall often serves to jolt Decimus Webb from whatever reflections, pleasant or unpleasant, might play upon his mind. Today is no exception. The sergeant waves cordially as he catches the inspector's eye through the glass.

'Morning, sir,' says Bartleby, as he enters the coffee house. 'Thought I might catch you here. The Clarence not open yet?'

'Spare me, Sergeant, it is too early in the morning. I take it you have some news?'

'Looks like it. A fellow made himself known to V Division last night – seems he's Jane Budge's father.'

'V Division? Wandsworth?'

'Battersea Rise. He's a potman in some local public house. I said you'd want a word with him.'

Webb takes a sip of coffee. 'I suppose it would be wise, before we see the Coroner.'

'The Coroner will have to say it's murder, though?' suggests Bartleby. 'Persons unknown?'

'I should imagine that will be his verdict. Unless you intend to solve the whole business before breakfast, Sergeant. Now find us a cab while I finish my coffee.'

'You not having that bread, then, sir?'

Webb pauses for a moment, then shakes his head. The sergeant, in turn, takes a slice of bread and bites into it.

'Well,' says Webb impatiently, 'what are you waiting for, man?'

Bartleby swallows, with a little difficulty.

'Cab's already waiting, sir,' replies the sergeant.

❧

The policemen's cab takes them from Westminster down to Battersea, until they come at last to Mr. Budge's given address – The Old King's Head, situated upon Folly Lane, not four hundred yards from Battersea Bridge. It proves to be a small rather dingy-looking public house with the external appearance of a run-down labourer's cottage, marked out only by the wooden sign that projects from its upper storey. This bears the head of the house's titular monarch – although the bewigged face is so dirty and smutted that no particular royal resemblance is visible – and provides a useful clue for the cab-man, who reins in his horse.

Webb looks around as Bartleby pays the cab-man to wait. There is no doubt that the pub possesses a rather seedy aspect, surrounded on every side by large commercial premises, manufactories with small soot-blackened windows. At one point, doubtless, it sat in a scenic spot, a stone's throw from the mighty Thames. But now, with a foundry on one side and bridle-maker's upon the other, it seems very distant from the river, which flows unseen, concealed behind the brick wall of King and Cosgrove's Turpentine Works, upon the opposing side of the road.

'Mr. Budge told them we could generally find him here,' says Bartleby.

'That bodes well,' says Webb.

The door to the public house lies open, though it is a good two hours or more before drinking may commence. The interior proves to be little better than the outside, a darkened parlour into which sunlight seems reluctant to intrude. There is no landlord behind the modest counter that takes up one corner of the room and there is no-one else in the bar – save for a man in his fifties, clad in a grimy rust-coloured jacket, slumped over one of the tables.

Bartleby walks over to the man, and bends down by his side.

'Dead drunk. We should have the landlord for breaking his licence.'

Webb joins the sergeant, and tilts back the man's head, observing his rather ruddy complexion and heavily-lidded eyes, which do not fall open.

'I know my lushingtons, Sergeant, and I suspect this gentleman is of the confirmed variety. I would not blame the landlord. He probably had his fill last night and stayed put.'

Webb releases the man's head, letting it fall heavily back down onto his arms, folded across the table. The shock, however, seems to stir him to a semblance of consciousness, and a pair of bloodshot eyes reveal themselves.

'Who's that?'

'Inspector Webb of the Metropolitan Police,' says Webb firmly. 'Am I addressing Mr. Alfred Budge?'

Mr. Budge somehow contrives to both sit upright and then immediately slump backwards in one continuous motion. 'That you are, 'Spector. I am that unlucky fellow,' he replies, after a considerable pause, his voice quite slurred.

Webb rolls his eyes. 'Sergeant, find the landlord – he must be out the back if his door is open – and get this . . . Mr. Budge a cup of something suitable.'

'Rum'd do it, old man,' says Alfred Budge. 'Drop of rum'd do it.'

———

'A fellow speculates on his family, don't he, 'Spector?' inquires Alfred Budge, some twenty minutes later, and a little more sober.

'Is that so?'

'Don't matter whether it's a boy or a gal, he speculates his own life-blood on the return, don't he? He

126

invests what he has, what he knows, in that little individual what is the fruits of his loins.'

Budge's speech is still rather slurred, albeit with a certain world-weary consistency. Webb cannot help but frown as 'fruits' and 'loins' take on a peculiar elasticity of pronunciation.

'And this,' he continues, 'is what he gets for his trouble.'

Mr. Budge pauses and sighs, closing his eyes.

'There will be a Coroner's inquest, today, if you wish to attend,' suggests Bartleby.

Mr. Budge merely shakes his head.

'There is the question of a burial,' says Webb. 'Or will it be upon the parish?'

Mr. Budge opens his eyes. 'No, not a parish job, 'Spector. You send her here when you're done.'

'You live here then?'

'Potman, you see?' says Budge, waving his hand indiscriminately at the room.

'That cannot pay much, in a small place like this?'

'He's paid in kind, I reckon,' whispers Bartleby.

'I gets by, 'Spector,' says Budge, seemingly oblivious to the sergeant's comment. 'You send Janey here. We'll see her done right. Proper send-off.'

'Is there a Mrs. Budge?' asks Webb.

'There was a sweet creature of that name, 'Spector. But I don't care to recall her. Beyond price she was – the old girl.'

Budge seems to sag as he speaks, his eyes faltering. Webb shakes his head, casting a glance to Bartleby that suggests he is ready to leave. As the two policemen rise, however, the drunken man recovers himself a little.

'Nelson. That's your man, 'Spector. Pound to a penny, it were Nelson.'

Webb stops as he reaches for the door. 'George Nelson? What about him? Have you spoken to him, Mr. Budge?'

'No, I don't bloody speak to him. I don't needs speak to him. He's the one – I'll swear it blind. If it weren't for my old 'firmity,' says Budge, slapping his leg, 'I'd settle him. I'd settle him, all right. My poor sweet little girl.'

'Mr. Budge, please,' says Webb, 'think for a moment. Anything in connection with George Nelson might be important to us. Did your daughter say anything about Nelson before she died? Or was there anyone else, perhaps, who might bear her a grudge?'

Budge drunkenly waves his hand at the inspector's questioning, as if attempting to swat a fly. 'Here, who are you anyway? What's your game, pestering a honest man?' he mutters, his eyes drooping once more.

'Thank you, sir,' replies Webb, courteously as he can manage. 'I am sorry for your loss.'

Alfred Budge remains at his table until the policemen have gone; to all appearances barely conscious. It is only when he is joined by his wife, who walks cautiously into the tap-room, that he shows some signs of wakefulness, assisted by a firm poke in ribs.

'Wotcha do that for?' exclaims Mr. Budge.

'Did you tell 'em what I said? About Nelson?'

'I told 'em, for pity's sake,' says Mr. Budge, in a rather self-pitying tone.

'Where they keeping our little girl?'

'Chelsea dead-house. We can have her tomorrow. Poor thing.'

Mrs. Budge scowls. 'You old fool. Much good you were to her when she was alive.'

128

'Don't say that, Maggie – don't be harsh,' replies Mr. Budge. 'I did what you said, I swear I did. I don't see why, mind you.'

Mrs. Budge pokes her husband more vigorously, producing an audible yelp.

'Because, I has to be discreet, Alfred Budge. I have a handful of little reasons at home to be discreet, don't I? Or do you think the bloody peelers would turn a blind eye, if they came sticking their beaks in?'

'I swear, I told them,' protests Mr. Budge, as if still arguing the point.

'You'd better have,' replies Mrs. Budge emphatically.

CHAPTER TWENTY-ONE

20th May 1875

My Dearest Laetitia,

Forgive your foolish little sister – whom you must think an ungrateful, spiteful creature – for not replying sooner. I confess, Letty, the ball is never out of my thoughts – to think that there is only tomorrow! – and I have been awful slow with my letters.

The gown is now finished, you will be glad to hear; I have shown it to Bea and she is quite <u>green</u> and says she now think hers is frightful! Mama still frets about it! Papa, meanwhile, says nothing – he considers Mama and myself quite empty-headed.

Now, Letty – I must ask you something – as a dear sister who is in my confidence, as I hope I am in yours. A queer thing happened yesterday. Two strange men visited us twice and Mama positively would not tell me who they were. This morning – at breakfast – Mama and Papa <u>both</u> seemed so very quiet and low in spirits, I almost thought they were ill. It is as if they know some awful secret, which they will not tell – please,

Letty, I hope that neither you nor the boys are in a bad way? <u>Please</u>, you would not keep such a thing from your own Rose? I am quite grown up enough to know the worst.

Please answer and put my heart at ease.

Your loving sister,
Rose

Charles Perfitt picks his silk hat from its stand, and opens his front door. He looks outside with the wary glance of a seasoned commuter, and finds that the sky has darkened since he enjoyed his breakfast, and that specks of rain have begun to fall. He steps back, therefore, to grab the elegant ivory-handled umbrella that is always left by the door. His wife appears upon the stairs.

'Charles?' she says, hurrying down to the hall. 'You did not say you were going?'

'Did I not, my dear? I am sorry. You know I always leave at this hour.'

'Mind you do not get soaked through.'

'No, my dear, that is not my intention,' he replies with a rather forced smile, brandishing the umbrella in his hand.

'Charles?'

'Really, Caroline, what is it? I will be late.'

'Have you thought about what we discussed last night? You were so quiet at breakfast, and I did not want to mention it in Rose's presence.'

Charles Perfitt nods. 'I have.'

'Well?'

'I think you are right. We should stand our ground; a coward would run away, and I am not a coward.'

'I never said you were, Charles. But you mean it – we may go to the ball? You realise it is tomorrow night?'

'The ball! As if I could forget,' says Charles Perfitt. 'Yes, why let that wretched man ruin everything? Now, I shall see you tonight.'

'Tonight,' replies Mrs. Perfitt, smiling with relief, closing the door as her husband departs.

Mr. Perfitt walks swiftly out onto the road, raising his umbrella. His wife does not observe his progress down Edith Grove, which is perhaps fortunate. For at the Grove's junction with the King's Road, facing Cremorne Gardens, he turns left instead of right, walking away from Chelsea Station, in the direction of the World's End public house.

Mr. Perfitt's journey is a brief one, no more than ten minutes' walk, if that. He finds the World's End itself to be shut at such an early hour, as he expected, and therefore makes several inquiries of passing strangers – inquiries as to the availability of cheap lodgings in the vicinity. Dressed in his fine black City suit, with rain spattering off his umbrella, he elicits more than a few puzzled looks from the maid-servants and delivery boys whom he importunes. Nonetheless, he eventually finds himself in a narrow side street behind the public house called Albion Terrace, where several of its old tenements are let by the room. And, by persevering further, it is not long before he is welcomed into a particular establishment. The landlord of the place is quite happy to present Mr. Perfitt's compliments to one George Nelson and returns to announce that Mr. Perfitt is cordially invited to 'go up'.

The staircase in question turns out to be a rather

ancient assemblage of bare boards, with its banisters preferring to arrange themselves in twos and threes at odd intervals, suggestive of comrades long since lost – perhaps to the unchecked descent of a heavy piano, or substantial chest of drawers. Nelson's attic room is upon the third floor, the door slightly ajar. With no word from inside, Mr. Perfitt knocks and walks in.

He finds George Nelson standing bare-foot in front of him, tucking his shirt into his trousers.

'Ah, now then, look who's come to see me,' says Nelson, 'so early in the morning.'

'I did not intend to wake you,' says Mr. Perfitt, warily, his voice sounding far from confident.

'I ain't too particular. It's just a fellow likes his sleep, after he's been in the jug,' says Nelson, picking up a grubby-looking mirror from the nearby dressing table and straightening his hair with his fingers. 'Even this here object,' continues Nelson, returning the mirror to its place, and nodding at his rather Spartan bed, 'feels like you're on the softest feathers there ever was.'

'I expect you would care to know why I have come here,' says Mr. Perfitt in his best business-like fashion.

'I can guess.'

'I will be blunt, Mr. Nelson. I will pay you money. Good money. One hundred pounds to leave us alone; to quit Chelsea.'

George Nelson smiles. 'Mr. Nelson is it? Now why would a fellow do something so contrary to his wants and inclinations?'

'Two hundred then.'

Nelson positively grins. 'Is that what I'm worth? I remember it were only fifty last time, weren't it?'

'Two hundred and fifty. My final offer,' says Mr. Perfitt.

134

'Not three?' says Nelson, cheerfully. 'And here's me reckoning my stock was up.'

'Three then, damn you, but not a penny more,' exclaims Mr. Perfitt.

George Nelson shakes his head, a mocking smile upon his lips. Then, without any warning, he lunges towards Charles Perfitt, pushing him backwards against the half-open door, so that it slams shut with the full weight of his body falling against it. With one hand, Nelson presses hard against Perfitt's chest; with the other he grabs him violently by the throat, his rough fingers crushing his victim's starched collar. Mr. Perfitt in turn, can do little but struggle in vain, barely able to breathe.

'Damn me, would you? Damn me? If I'm going to hell, I reckon I'll be seeing you on the way down, eh? I bet you bloody laughed, didn't you – you and that bitch of yours – when they sent me down. I bet you split your bloody sides?'

Mr. Perfitt tries to speak, his words coming out in a whisper. 'One word from me—'

'And what? It'll look pretty queer the likes of you sniffing round here, I reckon.'

Mr. Perfitt can barely utter a reply. Looking at Perfitt's flushed features, Nelson leaves the question hanging in the air, stepping back and releasing his grip.

'No-one will take the word of a convict,' splutters Mr. Perfitt, recovering his equilibrium.

Nelson shakes his head and picks up the razor that lies besides his mirror, moving with slow deliberation. 'I tell you straight, you bastard, if you try that game again, I can bide my time. And when I come out, I'll do for you, and that wife of yours. And I'll take my bloody time about it.'

'Then just tell me what you want,' exclaims Mr. Perfitt, frustration in his voice.

'I don't want nothing,' replies Nelson. 'Well, excepting the love of a good woman. Now, you know what that's like, don't you?'

'Listen to me – I swear, if you so much as come near my wife or daughter—'

Nelson laughs in derision. 'I wouldn't so much as piss on your Missus if she was on fire.'

Mr. Perfitt blanches a little, but ignores the taunt. 'And Rose – give me your word that will not come near her. Give me your word and I will say nothing of this encounter. We may call our account settled.'

Nelson pauses for a moment, as if in thought. 'If you like.'

'I have your word?'

Nelson nods.

'Very well,' says Mr. Perfitt. 'That is settled.'

Nelson says nothing. His guest, therefore, opens the door and quits the room, descending the stairs in a hurry. It is only his pride that prevents him from running; and it is only when he is sure that he is out of Nelson's sight that he wipes the sweat from his brow.

George Nelson sits on his bed, a smile of evident satisfaction in his face. He reaches into the pocket of his coat, laid by his side, and pulls out an envelope. Reaching over to his dresser, he roots inside one particular drawer with his hand. At length, he retrieves a handful of dried red petals, which he slides carefully into the open envelope.

'I don't need to go near her, old man,' he mutters to himself. 'She'll come to me, will your little Rosie. She always had a fancy for me. And then we'll see who's laughing.'

CHAPTER TWENTY-TWO

The police station of T Division at Chelsea, which sits upon the King's Road, is located not half a mile east of Cremorne Gardens, a little past the World's End public house. It is not so large or bustling as many of its contemporaries in the great metropolis, a plain brick building, distinguished only by the customary blue lamp above its front door. Indeed, were it not for that distinctive light it might be easy for a stranger to pass it by, quite unaware of its function.

Inside, however, there are clues for the discerning eye: walls are plastered with police notices, half a dozen bearing photographic likenesses of certain 'wanted' gentlemen; there is a wooden dock, with a regulation height-gauge beside it, to measure the precise dimensions of those brought up on a charge; and in the small offices that lead off the hall, one or two of the desks boast not only pen, paper and ink, but a pair of handcuffs or a wooden truncheon laid carefully to one side.

It is in one such office – an hour or so after the Coroner's jury has returned a verdict of 'wilful murder' upon Jane Budge – that Decimus Webb sits, his forehead creased in concentration, with a small black notebook in front of him.

'Any luck, sir?' asks Bartleby, appearing at the door. 'How are you getting on?'

'Inspector Cheadle – the fellow in charge here – was at Nelson's trial. He has kindly provided me with his notes – but his handwriting is almost as bad as yours.'

'I am sure it can't be that bad, sir.'

'Hmm. It seems Nelson pleaded innocent, said the girl consented.'

'They always say that, don't they?' replies the sergeant.

'In this case, however, the testimony of Mr. Perfitt said otherwise. Miss Budge was quite fortunate in that respect, at least.'

'Sir?'

'It appears she let Nelson into the Perfitts' kitchen voluntarily; they were also seen keeping company on several occasions. Now, in such circumstances, how would you rate her chances of seeing Mr. Nelson convicted, without a witness?'

'Not good.'

'I think you are too optimistic, even in that. But there is something wrong here, if one reads this account of the trial and we assume that Inspector Cheadle is a reliable reporter. You recall Mrs. Perfitt's comments – that she did not want to cast aspersions on Jane Budge's character, given what happened?'

Bartleby nods.

'But Budge did not deny in court that she was on familiar terms with Nelson; in fact, it appears that she had let him inside the house on at least two other occasions – well, Mr. Perfitt almost said as much, did he not?'

'He did, sir. But I don't quite take your point.'

'She deceived her employers, Bartleby. Whatever

her relations with Nelson – whether carnal or otherwise – they were hardly proper; certainly not what respectable people like the Perfitts expect from their servants. So why did they keep her on? Why give a good character to this girl who repeatedly admitted this villain into their home?'

'Pity, sir?' says Bartleby.

'You may think me a cynic, Sergeant, but Mrs. Perfitt did not strike me over much as the pitying kind.'

'Well, I wouldn't like to say, sir,' replies Bartleby. 'Not when you hear who Constable Dawes saw visit George Nelson this morning. He just sent word with the local man on the beat.'

Webb looks up. 'Dawes?'

'Our plain-clothes, sir. Had him stationed at the World's End, if you recall.'

'Ah, yes. Well, who was it?'

'Mr. Perfitt. Made a point of finding where George Nelson lived, asked directions, and then went and paid a call.'

'You are sure it was Perfitt?'

'Our man followed him. Then the local constable identified him.'

Webb closes the notebook in front of him. 'I trust Dawes was not seen.'

'I don't think he was spotted. He's a good man.'

Webb taps his fingers upon the desk. 'Mr. Perfitt, eh? Rather curious for a man who wanted absolutely nothing to do with Nelson.'

Webb pauses for a moment.

'Tell me, Sergeant, do you recall how the Perfitts described their trip to Leamington Spa, after Nelson's trial?'

Bartleby smiles. 'Made a note of it, sir. Mrs. Perfitt said it was a holiday; her husband said it was a rest-cure. I thought she was probably being discreet, sir – not wanting to admit to trouble with her nerves.'

'Possibly,' says Webb, musing for a moment. 'He gave us the name of their doctor, did he not?'

'Reginald Malcolm,' replies Bartleby, without even referring to his notes. 'Looked him up yesterday – office in Harley Street.'

'Very good, Sergeant,' replies Webb. It is a rare moment of praise untinged by sarcasm; Bartleby cannot quite contain a triumphant smile.

'When you have stopped grinning like a lunatic, perhaps you might care to arrange an interview for me with Dr. Malcolm – at his convenience, of course. There is something amiss with this whole business, I am sure of it. Something does not quite ring true. I just cannot put my finger on it.'

'Yes, sir.'

Bartleby pauses upon the threshold.

'Well, Sergeant, what is it?'

'No more thoughts on The Cutter, sir?'

Webb sighs. 'I have not forgotten him, Sergeant. There were no reports last night?'

'No, sir. Perhaps he's gone to ground. I just wondered if this business with Nelson is . . .'

'Well, out with it?'

'Distracting us, sir. I mean, even if The Cutter's nothing to do with this Jane Budge case – we still have to nab him.'

'Your opinion is noted, Sergeant,' replies Webb. 'And if you have any suggestions, I am happy to hear them.'

Bartleby pauses.

'I thought not,' says Webb. 'Now let me return to my reading.'

Decimus Webb quits Chelsea police station at a little after seven o'clock in the evening. Rather than walking directly towards his home in Clerkenwell, he turns his steps westwards, back along the King's Road towards Cremorne. He passes the World's End tavern with barely a sideways glance and only comes to a halt when he reaches the great gates to Cremorne Gardens. For, standing upon the pavement, addressing anyone who comes to the Gardens' ticket booth, is the Reverend Featherstone, with a Bible in one hand, and a bundle of pamphlets in another.

'Back again, sir?' asks Webb.

'Ah, Inspector. Yes, I am afraid the Lord's work must still be done. One must persevere. And my wife is a little less delicate today; I will not say she has quite recovered from her experience, but she is much better.'

'I am glad to hear it,' replies Webb.

'I do not suppose you have any news for us? You have not caught The Cutter, I take it?'

Webb looks away, as if reminded of something he would rather forget. 'Not yet, sir. I was just taking a stroll, mustering my thoughts. Is Mr. Boon not with you?'

Featherstone smiles. 'He was here a little earlier, but does not have much patience. That is how we shall defeat him, Inspector. With God's love and patience.'

'Defeat, sir? You make it sound like a battle.'

'It is, Inspector. For the souls of the poor wretches who are lured here to Cremorne. You have not come to remove me, I trust? I had assumed, after our last discussion, that there could be not objection to my coming here.'

'Not if you are polite and peaceable, sir. It's not Scotland Yard's business to interfere in such matters.'

'I am gratified to hear it.'

As the clergyman speaks, a pair of coaches draw up, discharging a rather noisy party of smartly dressed young men and women onto the pavement. The Reverend Featherstone offers his pamphlet to the gentlemen as they pass by, but is thoroughly ignored – to the obvious amusement of their female companions.

'You don't seem to have much luck, sir, if I may say so,' observes Webb.

'We shall see, Inspector. It is a hard path I have chosen, but I am sure it is the right one. This place is a cancer in the very heart of our fair suburb. I have seen young persons – many of them of respectable families, mind you – corrupted, time and again. And now we have this business of The Cutter – I consider it the fruit of this social evil, which we have allowed to flourish, quite unchecked. Bitter fruit, Inspector. I only pray that a few of them may learn from it.'

Webb sighs. 'I rather gather from Mr. Boon that it's doing wonders for his business – apparently the public rather likes the mystery.'

'Lord preserve us!' exclaims the Reverend Featherstone.

'Some people don't know what's good for them, sir,' remarks Webb.

'No,' replies the clergyman, his face rather downcast, 'you are quite right. Some people do not.'

❧

Alone in her room, Rose Perfitt opens a sealed envelope with tremulous fingers. Dipping her hand inside, she finds its contains nothing but scattered red petals and a brief handwritten note, which she reads eagerly.

She smiles as she begins to get ready for bed, placing one of the petals to her lips.

CHAPTER TWENTY-THREE

Rose Perfitt sleeps uneasily as the church bells of Chelsea chime midnight, soft cotton sheets twined and trapped around her body. In her hand she clasps a folded piece of paper to her breast, unconsciously pressing it tight against the fabric of her nightdress, even as she tosses and turns in her slumber.

Outside, meanwhile, there is almost perfect silence in Edith Grove, only a faint rustling breeze, the soothing murmur of a warm summer's night. It does not rouse her. Instead she merely turns over once more, the pupils of her eyes moving rapidly beneath closed lids.

It is much the same every night. A carriage ride through unfamiliar streets; left and right, then left again. For in the dark recesses of Rose's dreaming, the streets of Chelsea take on a peculiar geography that she can never quite comprehend. Roads she has never known become roads in which she has lived; one is mixed up with the other.

And then they give way; they melt or vanish, as if the bricks and stone paving were merely snow or ice that dissolve in the sun; for all the terraces and winding paths of her imagination can only lead Rose Perfitt to one place – the ornate iron gates of Cremorne Gardens.

They are not quite identical to the reality, of course. They are a little bigger; somewhat more forbidding and grand than their worldly counterparts. And the man in the ticket booth has a sterner face, one that is somehow both awful and familiar at the same time. In fact, he is a little like her father; and this always disconcerts her.

But he lets her through; he lets her through every night.

Where next?

First, with the instantaneous progress of a dreamer, she comes to the Gipsy's Grotto or the Hermit's Cave or the Wizard's Lair – for they are all one and the same, the promise of reading from the dark page of futurity – where she pulls aside the muslin curtain and sits down upon a wooden stool.

The grotto walls are encrusted with oyster shells, plastered in pearly magnificence upon every surface. A single candle lights the face of the Hermit, who squats in the flickering shadow. An old man, he has the eyes of a gipsy, deep brown orbs that resemble dark caves themselves, infinite recesses in which one might become thoroughly lost. And Rose is sure she must know him too; for he surely knows her every secret.

'Cross my palm with a shilling, my dear.'

He hands her a piece of paper – the name of her first love.

⌒

In Edith Grove the wind grows a little stronger and the lace curtains in Rose's room flutter like the skirts

144

of a dancer pivoting on her toes. The gust of cool night air seems to breathe life into them, and Rose's own breath grows faster, as she clutches the piece of paper ever tighter to her chest.

—

'In consequence of its Immense Success, and by Particular Desire, the splendid Decorative entertainment "A Feast of Roses", illustrative of T. Moore's beautiful poem "Lalla Rookh" will now be repeated.'

Rose watches the stage of the old Marionette Theatre. She does not notice the man by her side at first. Rather, she dutifully observes the performance: as the Indian dancers begin to twine their arms into unlikely serpentine poses; as petals are strewn at their feet in extravagant explosions of colour; as the beat of the tabor grows ever quicker. The heroine appears stage right; the hero, turbaned and bejewelled, stage left.

But the man distracts her. A handsome young working man in his best Sunday suit, he lightly strokes her hand with his. He touches her gently, with peculiar confidence, as if he has every right to do so; as if her hand is a worthy object of his admiration. He touches her like she herself would run her hand along a piece of fine porcelain; he touches her and she forgets herself entirely.

'Come with me, love,' he whispers, his fingers interlocking with hers. 'And we'll make a night of it.'

And, if truth be told, she goes with him.

—

The breeze has died down. The room now is too warm; too suffocating. But the glass of mineral water that sits upon the dresser is untouched; the window still only ajar, when it might better be flung wide open. For Rose sleeps on, bound up in the crumpled linen, wrapped around her restless body like a winding-sheet. And her lips seems to move in sympathetic motion to unspoken words.

～

Hand in hand now, the two lovers move across the Crystal Platform, as if they are the only two dancing. He picks her up and lifts her, like she has no more weight than a feather. She can feel his arm upon hers, his hand holding the small of her back. He has no proficiency in the dance, this man who holds her in his arms, but it does not much seem to matter. For it is not quite a waltz, nor a polka; it is a dance both strange and familiar, that she swears to herself she will recall when she wakes.

Another glass of champagne, then the orchestra plays louder; it is fighting to be heard above the crowd around the bar, smart young men of the fast set, superior clerks, aspiring barristers, young doctors and lawyers, downing wines and spirits of the choicest quality. Another glass. Then another.

Faster goes the song, so fast that the steps become reckless, and they fall tumbling onto the wooden boards.

Then all is quiet; the dancing has stopped; the stars have gone out and the sky is as black as pitch.

And she falls, like a stone, dropped into a deep, deep well.

～

Rose Perfitt wakes, conscious only of being too hot, the silk of her nightdress sticking to her skin.

She sits up, takes her glass of water and looks

146

across her room in the darkness. Her eyes chance upon the outline of her ball-gown, draped flat across the ottoman by the door. For a moment, she fancies it resembles a woman's body laid out as if upon some funeral bier. But only for a moment.

Puzzled, she tries to recall her dreams, until she falls asleep once more.

CHAPTER TWENTY-FOUR

The suburban terraces of the capital each have their own rhythms, daily comings and goings that, in general, are quite unremarkable. Edith Grove is no exception. There is the dusky hour when a certain employee of the Gas, Light and Coke Company takes his ladder and attends to the street-lamps; then, in their glimmering light, the long night, the sole preserve of a solitary police constable, patrolling his beat. At dawn, a dozen or so cooks, full of age and domestic wisdom, scuttle down area steps. Breakfast is made and families roused from sleep. Front steps are freshly whitened – then scuffed by the boots of City gentlemen, marching for the morning train. It is something quite settled; a routine that suits the residents of Chelsea.

By day, even the calls paid by ladies upon their friends and acquaintances, the occasional visits of doctors or tradesmen, the importuning of pedlars and beggars, all have their place in the quiet, well-oiled mechanism of life in Edith Grove. New faces are generally noted; curtains twitch at the presence of an unexpected carriage and it is not uncommon for even the most respectable ladies, who have little else to do, to spend a good deal of their time casually observing the empty street.

The Perfitt household, despite the best efforts of its mistress, is most certainly not immune to such curiosity. Thus, when a substantial barouche, newly painted in green and gold, draws up in front of the house, with a coachman in matching livery, there is a small disturbance in the Perfitts' breakfast routine.

'Mama!' exclaims Rose. 'You must come and look.'

Mrs. Perfitt for once indulges her daughter and, though affecting disinterest, is equally impressed by the mysterious conveyance.

'Why has he stopped?' asks Rose.

'There is no-one inside,' says Mrs. Perfitt. 'Rose, call Richards – have her tell the man that he must have the wrong address.'

Rose nods, but is checked by her father, who raises his eyes from his copy of *The Times*.

'No need for that, my dear. I hired him. From a job-master in Brompton.'

'You, Charles?' replies Mrs. Perfitt, astonished.

'Is it not the ball tonight?'

'You know full well it is, ' replies Mrs. Perfitt.

'Well, I thought we might have a decent equipage.'

'I thought you said a cab would do.'

'My little surprise,' replies Mr. Perfitt, with a certain paternal complacency, as he observes his daughter's face.

'Oh, Papa!' exclaims Rose, rushing to his side and kissing her father's cheek, quite crushing his newspaper in the process. 'You are so clever!'

'We have him all day. I thought we might go for a little drive about the park, if the weather holds.'

'Charles,' says Mrs. Perfitt, 'we have too much to do. Rose's hair; the dress needs some final touches. And I have myself to think of.'

'You can spare an hour or so, Caroline, surely?

Either that or the wretched fellow will just sit there all day. Still, something for the neighbours to cast their eye over, I suppose.'

He says this with a smile, as if to imply that his wife and daughter might not be altogether adverse to such an outcome. Mrs. Perfitt blushes and though she vigorously demurs, her objections are not altogether convincing.

———

In the end, despite its recreative potential, the carriage stays firmly in place for much of the day. For Mrs. Perfitt does not feel that she can do it justice in anything but her evening dress; nor, she avers, can she risk the fatal effects of an unexpected shower upon her daughter's constitution – though the sky is as blue and cloudless as anyone might wish, and the barouche equipped with a retractable hood.

As for Rose, she is kept busy enough at home; there is, after all, the small matter of her dress, to be modelled both for her mother and Madame Lannier, who has engaged to pay a final call, to see her *pièce de résistance*. The result is that the silk and trim are nipped and tucked once more, here and there, for a good hour. Then there is her hair, to be dressed by her mother's own hand, each ringlet teased and trained with intense concentration; her skin anointed with the finest *eau de toilette*. Indeed, nothing is left to chance by Mrs. Perfitt. Moreover, her efforts are not wasted – for the result is, much to Mrs. Perfitt's great pride, something akin to perfection.

It is this sense of maternal satisfaction that buoys Mrs. Perfitt's spirits through all the preparations of the day, until the family quit the house at eight o'clock, and ascend into the waiting carriage. With mother

151

and daughter both thoroughly fashionable, it takes a moment for them to accommodate the long trains of their skirts. Mr. Perfitt, meanwhile, seats himself opposite, with his back to the driver, dressed in the plain black suit, white tie and waistcoat required of gentlemen upon such occasions.

'You both look like a pair of mermaids,' says Mr. Perfitt, as the two women finally settle, the backs of their dresses, tied with tulle ribbons, artfully arranged to one side.

'It is the fashion, Papa,' exclaims Rose. 'Don't tease.'

'I expect your father means we are fascinating creatures, Rose,' says Mrs. Perfitt, with a rather cutting glance at her husband.

'Goes without saying. You both look most becoming, I assure you.'

Mrs. Perfitt's look softens. Her husband, meanwhile, gives the word and the hired barouche goes at a leisurely pace along the length of the Fulham Road. It is nightfall by the time they reach Hans Place – an oval of rather grand houses in Brompton – around which a procession of carriages is already queuing for the narrow drive that leads to the Prince's Club. In the gas-light, Mrs. Perfitt peers at the vehicles ahead. Many of them have heraldic crests emblazoned upon their doors and, at the end of the drive, there is a grand landau with twin powdered footmen at the rear. Mr. Perfitt cannot help but observe his wife's gaze and whispers in her ear.

'Sorry, Caroline. I could only run to the coachman. And he doesn't come cheap.'

'Charles, really!' exclaims Mrs. Perfitt.

At last the barouche enters the courtyard of the Prince's Club and allows the Perfitts to alight. The club itself is of the sporting kind: a home to cricket matches and rackets tournaments. Its members are a famously select body, picked from the best families in Brompton and Belgravia. On occasion, however, it allows its buildings and grounds to be appropriated to the purposes of a charity ball, and its exclusivity is temporarily diminished. Such lapses are, of course, quite laudable. Whether the guests to such occasions, having paid for their tickets, then think much about charity is another matter.

Certainly Rose Perfitt appears more impressed by her surroundings than any such abstract notion, and gives little thought to the Society for the Suppression of Mendicity, in whose honour the ball is staged. For the hall in which they eventually gather has been laid out in breathtaking style. Indeed, the building itself, known as the Pavilion, a rather grand converted mansion, is quite impressive at the best of times, when no great effort has been made. Inside, however, rows of palms now conceal the wainscoting and regular furniture has been replaced by rout seats. Doors have been unhinged and mysteriously transformed into hangings of gossamer-thin muslin; a crystal fountain gushes in front of the main stairs, sparkling in the light of a dozen candelabras, which themselves supplement the colourful Chinese lanterns that hang from the ceiling. In short, it is a spectacle to gladden the heart of the most hard-hearted suppressor of mendicants.

It is unlucky, then, that the first person to greet the Perfitts, as Mrs. Perfitt strains to see her bosom friend Alice Watson, does not seem at all enthusiastic. It is Mrs. Bertha Featherstone, who emerges effortlessly from the crowd, dressed in black, as is her custom. Her only concession to gaiety are a small pair of jet earrings, that only serve to add to the drabness of her costume.

'Ma'am,' she exclaims, accosting Caroline Perfitt, 'how good to see you and your delightful family here.'

Mrs. Perfitt stops short, torn between appropriate politeness and a desire for superior company. 'Mrs. Featherstone. You are here for the ball?'

The question has an unfortunate hint of incredulity about it, but fortunately one that appears lost on its addressee.

'The Reverend is a governor of the Society, ma'am. We are rather obliged. I confess, I was not quite certain if I could bring myself to come, after our recent misfortune. But the Reverend insisted I rouse myself.'

'I am so glad,' says Mrs. Perfitt, though seemingly a little distracted. 'Oh, Rose – there is Beatrice Watson just gone by and she has no idea we are here. Do go and find out where her dear mother is – I must see her dress.'

Rose needs no prompting to speak to her friend. Before anyone else may speak, Mrs. Perfitt begins again. 'Charles – on reflection, I had best go with her. But what was it you said you must ask Mrs. Featherstone? I am sure there was something.'

Charles Perfitt struggles with a reply, as his wife and daughter disappear into the throng.

'I just wondered, ma'am,' he manages at last, turning to the clergyman's wife, 'how is your husband keeping?'

———

The Reverend Featherstone, in fact, stands alone upon the balcony that runs around the hall of the Pavilion, observing the gathering crowd, listening to the gentle babble of excited chatter amongst the ladies, leavened by the occasional guffaw that bursts forth from a rotund, military-looking man by the stairs. If his eyes fix anywhere, however, it is upon a certain mother and daughter, as they find their way round the hall; his eyes fix upon them, and do not let them go.

CHAPTER TWENTY-FIVE

The hour for dancing is ten o'clock. It is clearly marked upon the programmes distributed to ladies upon their arrival in the Pavilion. Unfortunately, this knowledge does little to quell Rose Perfitt's eagerness to begin. Thus, waiting in the ball-room, she repeatedly quizzes her father for the correct time and pays little heed to conversation between her mother and Alice Watson. The one thing upon her mind is the dance and, indeed, the only thing that fully commands her attention are introductions to prospective partners. And there are several such gentlemen that fall into the Watsons' circle – friends of the Watson family; a business acquaintance of her own father; a second cousin of her mother. In each case, Rose diligently takes up her pencil, attached to her programme by a red ribbon, and writes their name against the dance of her choosing. One, it transpires, is a naval officer; she reserves the lancers for him, perhaps in some unconscious idea of a military connection; for the younger men she sets aside the galops; for the older gentlemen – those of twenty-five years or more – she selects the more sedate waltzes. It is not long before a dozen arrangements are made and Rose's card is filled until midnight. The particular men are of little consequence to Rose herself, for she would gladly partner an automaton if it gave her the opportunity to dance upon the polished boards of a grand ball-room. Mrs. Perfitt, however, is rather a different matter. She sits with her daughter, sipping iced champagne, and looks over Rose's card with a discerning eye, one that replaces each dance with an estimate of the annual income, respectability and future prospects of the man whose name sits beside it. It grieves her that none quite meets her expectations.

At last, the band takes to the raised platform at the end of the ball-room, seating themselves beneath the purple satin canopy draped from the ceiling. They are military men in uniform, reputedly the string band of the Royal Artillery, and try Rose's patience by commencing upon 'God Save the Queen'. But once the anthem is complete, the master of ceremonies demands that sets be formed for the first quadrille of the evening. Whilst Rose Perfitt happily accepts the arm of her companion for the dance, her mother remains seated.

'You would not care to dance with your husband?' asks Charles Perfitt.

'Later, if I may, Charles. I prefer to watch,' replies Mrs. Perfitt, observing her daughter as she curtsies to her partner. 'I must say, I was not at all sure about her hair, but it has turned out just as I should like it.'

'She looks a picture,' replies Mr. Perfitt. 'Quite the belle of the ball.'

'Tell me again, Charles, who is that young man?'

'A junior broker. Nephew of old Chantry, I think.'

Mrs. Perfitt shakes her head. 'No, he will not do at all,' she says, in a hushed voice.

'Seems to know the steps.'

'You know precisely what I mean,' replies Mrs. Perfitt.

'I won't have Featherstone announce the banns next week, then, eh?' replies Mr. Perfitt.

'Do not joke, Charles, please,' replies Mrs. Perfitt, with no humour in her voice whatsoever, smoothing the grey silk of her dress.

'I am doing my best, Caroline, under the circumstances. I am sorry, but I cannot help thinking of other matters.'

Mrs. Perfitt frowns.

'I'm sorry, my dear,' she says, squeezing her husband's hand.

~

The band of the Royal Artillery calls a temporary halt to proceedings at the stroke of midnight. After two hours in a state of almost continual motion, Rose Perfitt appears content to separate from a certain City gentleman – of whose precise name she is rather uncertain, without reference to her card – and to return to her family.

'You look a little fatigued, Rose,' says Mrs. Perfitt, straightening a stray lock of her daughter's coiffure.

'I am quite all right, Mama,' replies Rose, although truthfully there is at least a pink blush to her cheeks.

'A bite to eat, I think,' suggests Mr. Perfitt, 'build our strength if we are to meet all Rose's engagements for the evening. How many is it, my dear?'

'Six more, Papa,' replies Rose, perusing her programme with the air of a connoisseur, the names of six more partners already in black and white.

'Come then, this way,' exclaims Mr. Perfitt, directing his wife and daughter in the direction of the supper-room.

A ball supper, as with most things that arise from necessity, is never the most relaxing affair. The supper-room laid on at the Prince's Club proves no exception. It is large enough to accommodate no more than fifty but, at the cessation of the dancing, it finds itself obliged to cope with almost five hundred. And, although the buffet is elegant and the company terribly polite, there is the inevitable heated overcrowding as gentlemen compete to retrieve the best of the game pie, whilst ladies tactfully strive to find suitable seats. For some, the omnipresent aroma of lobster salad becomes too overpowering, and they give up the notion of sustenance altogether; for others, the Perfitts included, seating simply cannot be found, and so they retire to a lamp-lit conservatory at the side of the building.

There they discover that a few small groups have also found refuge under its glass roof. Seated on wicker chairs, the Perfitts are swiftly joined by Mrs. Alice Watson and her daughter Beatrice. The night is still warm enough, thankfully, to enjoy the chilled champagne and what titbits of food can be salvaged. Thus, whilst the elders discuss the merits of the Royal Artillery Band, and Rose and her friend discuss the merits of their respective partners, a good hour or so is beguiled until the dancing is about to recommence.

The relevant announcement is made by a liveried footman, who appears at the door to the conservatory, looking rather weary. But before the Perfitts can return to the ball-room, they are interrupted by the tentative approach of a young man of rather handsome appearance and neat dress. Mrs. Watson effects an introduction and Rose's card soon bears one last name, destined for the penultimate waltz of the evening.

When the gentlemen in question departs, Mrs. Alice Watson leans over to Caroline Perfitt and whispers in her ear.

'My dear, what a stroke of luck! Poor Bea is so jealous! Do you know who that young man is?'

Mrs. Perfitt replies in the negative.

'The second son of Viscount Sedgecombe. Twelve thousand a year and his own estate in Hertfordshire.'

'Really?' replies Caroline Perfitt, as coolly as she can manage. 'Rose – my dear – do come here for a moment. Let me see your hair.'

⁓

Much to Rose Perfitt's delight, the ball at the Prince's Club goes on into the early morning, with the gallant members of the Royal Artillery Band performing sterling service for a good two hours more. Once they are done, the event draws to a close and the assembly at last begins to disperse, back to the snaking train of carriages that once more fills Hans Place. The process is a slow one, and little conclaves of ball-goers gather in the open courtyard outside the club, gossiping, exchanging polite conversation until the welcome approach of their vehicle, whether it be a landau, barouche, brougham or a mere clarence cab. In some cases, the champagne has loosened tongues. There are occasional bursts of raucous laughter from certain parties, which the more staid supporters of the Society for the Suppression of Mendicity look upon with a degree of disdain – a look normally reserved, perhaps, for beggars suspected of the worst impostures.

But there is nothing in the noise of the crowd loud enough to conceal a distinct sound from gardens at the rear of the Pavilion: the piercing cry of a woman's scream, that carries through the night air.

CHAPTER TWENTY-SIX

Decimus Webb stands at the rear of the Prince's Club, in the loggia beneath the iron-railed balcony that runs the length of the Pavilion's upper floor. He retrieves his tobacco-box and pipe, and strikes a match, watching the flakes grow red in the bowl, savouring the rich smell of Latakia before he puts it to his lips. Inside, the sound of furniture being moved resonates throughout the building: scraping and thumping, rumblings of activity from every room, as the traces of the previous night's revels are gradually removed. Outside, there are similar efforts: a pair of groundsmen assess damage to their cricket pitch, and shake their heads in disappointment; near the conservatory, the club secretary looks rather mournfully at chips in the paintwork of the rackets court. But these are all commonplace, the predictable results of hosting an evening of public entertainment. Less explicable, or at least less commonplace, is the presence of three uniformed policemen, moving carefully through the shrubbery that extends around the side of the house.

Webb, pipe in hand, walks a little way from the building, towards the men in question, where he finds Sergeant Bartleby superintending the procedure.

163

'Anything, Sergeant? Footprints?' asks Webb.

'The ground's quite hard, sir, with all this hot weather. Nothing to speak of. We found a couple of scraps of the girl's dress. Looks more like pieces she tore herself, running away from The Cutter. That's about our lot. Been over it twice.'

'Very well,' says Webb with an air of resignation, 'call the men off. Doubtless they have better things to do with their time.'

Bartleby obeys, and orders the three policemen to quit. Webb, meanwhile, extinguishes his pipe and looks back at the house.

'The girl still refuses to speak to us? What is her name again?' asks Webb.

'A Miss Mansell, sir. Society family, Belgrave Square. The parents insist she is too over-wrought – not up to it.'

Webb frowns. 'What do you make of it, Sergeant? It is the same as the other attacks?'

'I'd say so,' replies Bartleby, 'with the exception of the location, of course. The girl was answering a call of nature; sounds like she'd had a bit too much champagne – although I doubt you'll hear that from her family. I think the fellow was lurking here, waiting for someone to come his way.'

Webb nods. 'Possibly. The house and terrace were too well lit, that much is obvious. And the injury, it is not serious?'

Bartleby colours slightly. 'The man slashed at her dress and cut her rear, I believe, sir. That's what the doctor told me. As long as there's no infection, she should recover.'

'But she did not see her attacker?'

'No, sir. Not as far as I could make out, from what they said,' replies Bartleby, tailing off in mid sentence, as one of the uniformed policemen, having extricated himself from the shrubbery, comes running over.

'Sorry, sir,' says the constable, 'I just spotted this – snagged on that bush by the wall.'

Webb looks at the young policeman's offering, a ragged strip of black cloth. He takes it from him, rubbing it between thumb and finger.

'Silk, Bartleby. Good quality silk; not dirty or damp, so it cannot have been there long. A gentleman's suit, I should imagine.'

'You reckon it's our man, sir?'

'That I cannot say, Sergeant. But it offers one possibility, does it not? It must have occurred to you already. What if the reason that The Cutter chose to branch out from Cremorne Gardens to the Prince's Ground last night – and appeared at so late an hour – is that he was a guest at this ball too?'

'So you'll want a list of names, sir?' says Bartleby.

Webb looks back at his sergeant and nods. 'Names and addresses, if you please. And then I should like you to—'

'Interview all of them,' interrupts Bartleby, with a weary sigh.

Decimus Webb turns over the shred of material in his hand. 'Yes, all of them. If there is anyone at the Yard, get them to assist you. Here, you may as well have this – one never knows.'

Bartleby takes the piece of silk, looks it over, and places it inside his jacket pocket.

'I'd have preferred your traditional slipper.'

'Yes, Sergeant,' replies Webb without a flicker of amusement, 'very droll.'

'You won't be with us, sir?'

Webb takes out his pocket-watch. 'First I have a meeting with the Assistant Commissioner – a report upon our "progress". Then, this afternoon, I shall be seeing a certain Dr. Malcolm in Harley Street.'

'Do you think that's really worthwhile, sir?' asks Bartleby.

'Which?' replies Webb. 'If you mean the Assistant Commissioner, I would not care to comment. If you mean the doctor, that is another matter. I found something else in Cheadle's notes. It appears Dr. Malcolm gave evidence in court. He treated Jane Budge after she was assaulted.'

'Not too surprising,' suggests Bartleby. 'He was the Perfitts' doctor.'

'A good reason, then, why I should like speak to him.'

———

Dr. Reginald Malcolm turns out to be a short, robust-looking man, with a ruddy complexion and impressive side-whiskers, who maintains a consulting room in his home in Upper Harley Street, Marylebone. He greets Decimus Webb with a confident, professional smile, long practised upon his patients.

'Now, Inspector,' says Dr. Malcolm, as the two men shake hands and take a seat, 'I gather you wish to discuss something with me – though I did find your sergeant's note a little oblique. I assume it is not a medical inquiry?'

Webb smiles. 'I fear I am in the best of health, sir. It is in regard to a murder investigation.'

Dr. Malcolm nods. 'Is it the girl who was killed at St. Mark's, Inspector? Jane Budge?'

'Ah, I see you are familiar with the unfortunate circumstances, sir,' replies Webb.

'I read something in *The Times*. Terrible business.'

'Quite. I have been trying to learn something of the

girl's personal history. You treated her, did you not, some years ago? You were her employers' physician?'

'The Perfitts, yes. I still have that honour. I assume you know the facts of the matter, Inspector? The girl was violated by a brute of a man named Nelson. Mr. Perfitt asked me to do what I could for her.'

'You gave evidence at the trial, did you not?'

'Merely as to the nature of her injuries,' replies the doctor. 'Forgive me, Inspector – you think this is of some relevance to her death?'

'It might. George Nelson was given a ticket-of-leave shortly before Jane Budge's murder, sir. We know he still harboured a grudge against her; but I need to be sure of certain facts.'

'Ah, I see,' replies the doctor. 'Well, I can only give you my medical opinion, Inspector. I did not know the girl in any other capacity.'

'I understand, sir. The nature of her injuries then – what did they tell you?'

'That George Nelson was a savage. He struck her about the head and upper body repeatedly, if I recall. There was considerable bruising and the head was quite swollen. I had some fear for her sight in one eye. I am sorry, I cannot recall which without reference to my notes – it was some years ago.'

Webb bites his lip. 'Forgive the indelicate question, doctor, but I assume there was injury elsewhere? Her legs, perhaps?'

'Not that I recall. But she was not intact, if that is your question; I made a thorough examination of her person. I suppose the wretch beat her into submission.'

'And I gather you also treated Mrs. Perfitt for her nerves? I imagine the incident quite unsettled her.'

Dr. Malcolm waves his hand dismissively. 'Inspector,

I am quite happy to help with your questions about Jane Budge, but you can hardly expect me to comment upon my current patients.'

Webb smiles. 'I meant no offence, sir. But, if you will bear with me, am I right in thinking you have an establishment in Leamington Spa?'

'Indeed.'

'And I understand you practice the water-cure?'

'Yes I do,' replies Dr. Malcolm, suddenly a little annoyed. 'Inspector, please, do not insult my intelligence. I can tell you nothing about my treatment of Mrs. Perfitt. Such things are a confidential matter. I cannot imagine what prompts your interest – but I suggest you speak to the good lady directly.'

'Again, my apologies,' says Webb, getting up and offering his hand. 'Well, if that is the full extent of your recollection, sir, I won't waste your valuable time any further.'

Dr. Malcolm silently shakes the policeman's hand with a little less enthusiasm than upon his arrival. As he shows him to the door, however, Malcolm speaks up.

'You are the man charged with catching The Cutter, are you not?'

'Regrettably, I am,' replies Webb.

'The newspapers are not overly complimentary regarding your efforts.'

'We try not to pay too much heed to the press, sir.'

'Really?' continues Malcolm. 'You realise that this fellow must kill one of these females, in the end?'

'Sir?'

'I happen to have made several studies of lunacy and the action of the will, Inspector. These repeated attacks are a symptom of an ever-increasing derangement of the man's nervous economy.'

'I don't quite follow you, sir.'

'It is quite straightforward. The man has yielded to some primitive impulse to wound these women; it doubtless gives him some unnatural form of satisfaction. Unless you catch him, Inspector, that base instinct, which drives him on – which atrophies the will further with each assault – will only increase.'

Webb scowls. 'Well, I intend to catch him, sir, don't you worry.'

It is gone eight o'clock at night before Webb and Bartleby meet at Scotland Yard. The latter presents several folded sheets of paper, upon which a series of names and addresses is written out, together with a cash sum against each one.

'The Mendicity people gave me a copy of their subscription list for the ball, sir. Nearest thing we've got, when it comes to knowing who was there. Together with the ones we spoke to on the night, we're well on our way to seeing most of them. I've got three men working on it. Nothing to report as yet.'

Webb nods and scans the list. 'Quite an occasion. The Perfitts, I see.'

'Yes, sir. Guests of a Mrs. Watson, apparently. I've spoken to her. Friend of Mrs. Perfitt's.'

'And Reverend and Mrs. Featherstone. I would not have thought it their idea of an evening's entertainment.'

'I've not seen them yet, sir. Apparently he's a governor of the Society.'

Webb falls silent for a moment.

'Any luck with the doctor, sir?' asks Bartleby.

'No. But he got rather full of himself when I asked

him about Mrs. Perfitt's illness. More so than absolutely necessary, I should say. In fact, I have a task for you.'

'Sir?'

'Find out who goes to this spa of Dr. Malcolm's; see if you can get anything from the local constabulary. I should like to know a little more about it.'

'You think there was something queer going on there, sir?'

'Never mind what I think, Sergeant. Just send a telegram tonight. And be discreet.'

Bartleby nods. As he quits Webb's office, he stops on the threshold.

'How did it go with the Assistant Commissioner, sir?'

Webb looks up from his desk. 'He was quite satisfied, once I explained the principal obstruction to my inquiries.'

'Sir?'

'A particular sergeant who insists on asking idiot questions.'

Bartleby smiles rather nervously, not entirely sure whether his superior is joking.

CHAPTER TWENTY-SEVEN

22nd May 1875

My Dearest Laetitia,

Letty! I am so glad to hear there is nothing the matter with you or your darling little ones. Mama and Papa seem in much better spirits, so you most forgive your little sister's foolish imaginings.

What news? Of course, the ball! Letty, dear, I should like to tell you everything but I do not care to boast – suffice to say that I was quite in demand amongst the most handsome young gentlemen and that we danced until the very last. It might have been the perfect evening – but for the actions of some unmanly brute.

Have you heard of this monster, Letty? He is mentioned in today's Times *– Papa was reading it – they are calling him 'The Cutter' and he perpetrates horrible attacks on young women, stabbing at their clothes. I cannot imagine what sort of creature he is – but he attacked a girl at the Prince's Ground, just as Papa had gone to find our carriage – Mama and myself were quite defenceless! Bea said she thought it terribly* *exciting – she can be a silly goose – but the police did not catch him. It made me think of Spring-Heeled Jack – do you remember how you used to tell me those awful stories? How you used to scare me!*

Letty, dear, I am writing such nonsense, as I always do. But I have kept the good news until last – a certain Mr. Sedgecombe left us his card today – he is an acquaintance of Mrs. Watson – we danced a waltz – and he begs us to accompany him to the Prince's next week. There is to be a bicycle race between two members of the club and he requests the pleasure of our company as his guests. Mama is thrilled – he is the son of a Viscount!

Is he handsome, you ask? A little.

But then I do not think a girl should have two loves; you know my heart was stolen long ago. I used to think I was foolish to treasure such a notion; but no more. Now, can you keep that a secret, Letty? I will see him tonight.

Do not say a word to Mama and I will tell you everything in good time.

Your loving sister,
Rose
PS Do you recall Budge, who was our maid? Bea tells me she has been killed, poor thing, in a fire! Apparently it is common knowledge and the police suspect a murder! Some are saying it is this 'Cutter'. And Mama and Papa have not said a word! I wonder if this is what upset them. I wish they would not keep such things from me – I do not care to be wrapped up in clover and cotton wool.

Letty – write soon!

172

Rose Perfitt finishes writing to her sister at eleven o'clock, her room dimly lit by a single lamp. As she seals the letter in its envelope, she hears a muffled knock at her bedroom door. She walks swiftly over to open it and ushers in the maid, who carries a bundle of clothes under her arm.

'Is that everything?' asks Rose.

'Yes, Miss. Are you sure you want these, Miss? I don't want to lose my place.'

'I will not say a word, I swear. Now,' continues Rose, taking off a small silver ring from her finger, and holding it out, 'there – just as I promised.'

The girl looks uncertain.

'Go on,' urges Rose Perfitt. 'Remember – it will be our secret. Make sure Mama does not see it, mind.'

The maid stands still for a moment, then takes the ring and places the bundle upon the bed.

Rose swiftly ushers her from the room and then, bolting her door, begins to undress.

⌒

Rose Perfitt leaves Edith Grove, by means of the kitchen door, at half-past eleven. She has watched the policeman who makes a regular patrol along the street, and knows that she has a good ten minutes before he reappears. Even so, she creeps up the area steps with a cautious, hesitant tread. She wears a rather commonplace dress of brown serge, and a dull red shawl, wrapped about her shoulders and head. Both are borrowed from her maid.

She walks down to the King's Road and crosses it. At the entrance to Cremorne, there is a small queue, illuminated by the great octahedral gas-light that hangs suspended from the gates. Rose patiently waits her turn, trying not to heed the curious glances of several young gentlemen. She belatedly realises that her plain dress looks out of place, in the hour when pretty *demi-mondaines* in silk and satin take cabs down to Chelsea from the West End. The sight of a modest servant amongst the nocturnal denizens of the Gardens is itself a slight oddity. But it is too late to change and she has no wish to be recognised, so she pays her shilling and walks inside.

At first, she lingers by the gate, watching as young men in evening dress and young women in gaily-coloured costumes walk along the gas-lit gravel path, down the central tree-lined avenue that runs almost the length of the grounds. For the men, she notices, the fashion is light lavender gloves and patent leather boots. For the women it is an excess of Brussels lace around the neck. In both cases, she decides the gas imparts a glow of enchantment to their faces. And if a few of them stumble, hinting at intoxication, and a few more shout and call damnation upon this or that, it still seems to Rose Perfitt that it is a strangely magical scene.

Summoning her courage, Rose walks briskly down the avenue herself, taking care not to come too close to the more raucous pleasure-seekers. It is almost midnight, but she still passes several sandwich-board men, sullenly trudging along the path, who silently proclaim the merits of Senor Rosci's Astounding Dogs and Educated Monkeys, whilst another employee of the Gardens, dressed in a startling suit of red, white and blue, politely interrupts passers-by with vociferous directions to the American Bowling Saloon, and the mysterious promise of a gratuitous mint julep. Rose's poor dress, however, is ample protection against such importuning. In consequence, she proceeds quite unmolested to a certain quiet glade, where a glass fountain sparkles in the nocturnal lights, water cascading from the jug of a bronze cherubic youth perched upon its summit.

Rose pulls back the shawl from her face. There are two couples seated upon the benches that face the fountain, engrossed in their own company. Upon the other side of the clearing, a steady progression of men and women walk past, hastening in the direction of the Crystal Platform, intent on enjoying the last dance of the night. As Rose looks round, a pair of young men pause en route, and glance in her direction; a few words pass between them.

Rose turns away, but, as she does so, bumps into someone directly behind her. Before she can turn round, a man's hand suddenly comes up and covers her eyes; she gasps in surprise.

'Guess who it is, my little Rose.'

Rose Perfitt pulls away from the man's arm, spinning around. But there is no fear in her face as she confronts him, even though her eyes are suddenly moist with tears.

'George!' she exclaims. 'It is you!'

George Nelson smiles, reaching out to dab her cheek. 'You remember me then, Rose?'

'Oh! Don't say that!' she replies, looking him in the eyes, taking his hand and clasping it between her own. 'I knew you'd come back one day.'

'Did you?'

'I just knew,' she says fervently.

'Still, I don't expect they told you where I was, eh? Or what happened?'

'Jane just told me Papa had sent you away. She wouldn't say any more.'

Nelson allows himself a hollow laugh. 'Aye, he did that. But that's all done with now. I'm here now, working at the Gardens again; and I won't be going anywhere, not if I can help it. And I wanted to see you, Rose.'

Rose smiles a radiant smile. Before she can reply, however, there is a shout of 'Nelson!' from beyond the trees.

'Blast it!' exclaims Nelson. 'That's my lord and master; I'm not done for the night. Here, come on.'

Rose does not demur. Thus, she is pulled into the trees that surround the fountain glade, until the two of them are almost entirely concealed from passers-by. In Rose Perfitt's mind, the Gardens, the bushes and trees seem to disappear, so that the two of them are quite alone.

'Do you still love me, then?' says Nelson, reaching up and stroking her hair. 'That's what you told me, when I last saw you.'

'Of course,' says Rose, blushing as he touches her.

'Would you do anything for me, Rosie?'

'I might,' says Rose, adopting a mock conspiratorial tone. 'What should I do then?'

I'll show you,' says Nelson.

And then they kiss.

———

Rose Perfitt leaves Cremorne Gardens at half-past midnight. She walks hurriedly through the gates, her shawl once more artfully wrapped about her to conceal her face. She keeps her head down, avoiding the salutations of the gate-keeper, and the prying eyes of the departing votaries of the pleasure gardens. Consequently, she does not notice, at first, the presence of a certain clergyman and his wife, who mix with the crowd, accosting them with printed handbills.

But as Mrs. Bertha Featherstone thrusts a sheet of paper towards her, she cannot help but exchange a brief glance with the woman who virtually blocks her way.

Not a word is spoken. If she is recognised, then there is no denunciation, no cry of shame. Mrs. Featherstone, in turn, is distracted by another abandoned soul, in need of guidance, walking between them.

Rose Perfitt's heart races as she hurries home.

CHAPTER TWENTY-EIGHT

'Sir?'

Decimus Webb looks up from his desk, as Sergeant Bartleby appears at the door.

'There's a fellow from the *Illustrated Metropolitan News* outside in the yard,' continues Bartleby. 'He says he's been waiting since half eight.'

'Well, I told him I did not wish to comment at half-past eight, Sergeant. I do not know why he waits. What time is it now?'

'Gone eleven, sir.'

'Then go back and tell him he has wasted his morning.'

'He asked if you'd read the paper he gave you, sir.'

Webb scowls. 'Yes, Sergeant. I have. Here, see for yourself.'

Bartleby takes the copy of the *Illustrated Metropolitan News* that lies open on Webb's desk.

THE CUTTER

Many representations have hitherto been made to the Metropolitan Police as to assaults upon unprotected females in the vicinity of Chelsea by the miscreant known as 'The Cutter', whose outrages have been of an increasingly gross and violent nature. His ability to escape the notice of the constabulary has earned him, in some quarters, the reputation of a suburban ghost, a fiend able to strike at will and with complete impunity. We regret to inform our readers that we now possess further authentic particulars concerning this unmanly brute, following a new outrage committed in Brompton.

We understand that Miss Emma Wilmington, a young lady of 18 years of age, the daughter of a gentleman of considerable property, living at Woodbind Cottage, Brompton, stated to police that at about nine o'clock on the preceding night she saw a man loitering by her gate, in front of the house. On going to the door with a light, she inquired what was the matter, and why did he stand there. The person instantly replied that he was sick and 'For God's sake, do bring me a glass of water'. She returned indoors and brought him a glass. He wore a large blue cloak, such that she at first had mistook him for a policeman. The instant she gave the man the glass, he dashed it to the ground and threw off his outer garment. His visage presented a most hideous and frightful appearance. Without uttering a word, he flung himself upon the unfortunate Miss Wilmington, grabbing hold of her dress, and commenced tearing at her gown with his claws, which were of some metallic substance. She screamed out as loud as she could and it was only through considerable exertion that she escaped from him and ran towards the house. Her assailant, though he followed at first, was disturbed by the sound of an approaching policeman's whistle and fled. No trace of the villain was discovered.

Miss Wilmington further stated, we understand, that she had suffered an awful shock and was in much pain, from many wounds and scratches that had been inflicted upon her person.

We wonder that such a vile and cowardly assault can occur in our great metropolis, and only hope no pains will be spared to bring the miscreant perpetrator to justice.

'Doesn't sound like our man, sir,' says Bartleby. 'More like some penny dreadful.'

'Quite,' replies Webb. 'I checked with every division. There were no such reports last night, or the night before. But the gentlemen of the press have a story now, do they not? At least when the fellow confined himself to Cremorne, there was only a certain class of females in danger. Now, with the business at the Prince's Ground, it means every respectable maiden in London believes herself at risk.'

'And the press boys will pander to it.'

'You may count on it. Now tell that rogue downstairs not to trouble me again.'

'I'll tell him to hook it.'

'And you have no news, I take it? What about Dr. Malcolm's establishment?'

'Oh yes, sir – sorry. The local inspector says it's all very respectable, to the best of his knowledge – ladies with nervous complaints, that sort of thing. Mineral waters. Hot baths.'

'I had hoped for something more enlightening.'

Bartleby shrugs. 'Sorry, sir.'

Webb looks dejected. He takes the copy of the newspaper back from the sergeant, and tears it in half.

⌒

Caroline Perfitt starts as the door-bell rings in the hall. Although outwardly composed, seated in her drawing-room, she listens carefully for every tell-tale sound below, from her maid opening the door, to the sound of a hat dropped onto the wooden stand, to the distinct beat of a man's footsteps upon the parquet floor. In truth, she is somewhat nervous.

'Dr. Malcolm, ma'am,' announces the maid.

'Thank you, Richards, that will be all,' replies Mrs. Perfitt, dismissing her servant. 'Ah, Dr. Malcolm, how good of you to come at such short notice.'

'It is no trouble, ma'am,' replies the doctor, with the merest hint of a bow.

'Please, do take a seat. It is Rose, I am afraid.'

'I gathered as much, ma'am,' replies Malcolm, making himself comfortable in an armchair facing his client, the black bag of his trade placed carefully to one side. 'I am sorry to hear it.'

'Will you take some tea?'

'No, thank you, ma'am. I am here for Miss Rose and have another call to make in Kensington. Can you describe her symptoms?'

'Of course. It is quite odd – she was so pale when she came down to breakfast this morning. She told me she did not sleep and could not eat her food. That is not like her at all. And her constitution has been so much improved of late. I just cannot account for it.'

The doctor looks thoughtful for a moment. 'That is all, ma'am? It is not merely, forgive me, a question of the monthly function?'

Mrs. Perfitt colours a little. 'No, I do not believe so.'

'Then, I wonder, has she over-exerted herself in any way?'

'We attended a charity ball the night before last,' replies Mrs. Perfitt.

Dr. Malcolm smiles, as if struck by a sudden revelation. 'Then I am sure it is simple tiredness, ma'am. If one taxes the nervous economy, one must pay a price, especially in young ladies of tender years. I am sure there is nothing more to it.'

'I know you must think me a worrisome fool, Doctor,' replies Mrs. Perfitt.

'Not at all, ma'am. It is only natural. I would be happy to give her a thorough examination, if it is convenient.'

'Certainly. Both my husband and I would be very grateful.'

It is half an hour before Dr. Malcolm returns to the drawing-room. Mrs. Perfitt's face betrays little emotion, but her tense posture suggests a degree of anxiety.

'I am pleased to say, good lady,' begins Dr. Malcolm, 'that I can find little wrong with your daughter. A certain degree of nervous debility, perhaps, but only to be expected if you will have her dancing until dawn.'

'Nothing more?'

'No, ma'am. I recommend a day's bed-rest and lots of water.'

An unmistakable look of relief passes over Mrs. Perfitt's countenance. 'Thank you, Doctor. I am very grateful. We have an important engagement shortly, you see. I should hate for her to be indisposed.'

'Think nothing of it, ma'am. I trust your husband is keeping well?'

'Indeed, thank you.'

'I am glad to hear it,' replies Malcolm. 'Although I confess, it is a pleasant coincidence that you called upon me today. I would have come and seen you in any case.'

'Sir?'

'A gentleman from Scotland Yard came to see me the other day. I gather he has already spoken to you? A man by the name of Webb.'

'Yes, indeed. A detective. He is inquiring into the death of poor Jane Budge,' replies Mrs. Perfitt, though with little sympathy in her voice. 'Whatever did he want?'

'You may recall, ma'am, I gave evidence at the trial? In any case, I could not assist him to any great degree. But he had a particular interest in your stay at Leamington Spa. Quite insistent upon it. I wondered if you knew.'

Mrs. Perfitt falls silent for a moment. 'Good Lord,' she says at last, her voice a whisper.

'Naturally, I kept my own counsel, ma'am. I would not reveal any confidence placed in me by a patient. I merely thought you should be made aware.'

'Of course,' replies Mrs. Perfitt, recovering her manners. 'Thank you.'

Dr. Malcolm bows once more, opening the drawing-room door.

'Thank you, ma'am.'

CHAPTER TWENTY-NINE

Rose Perfitt stays in her room for the day whilst her mother and maid attempt to cater for her every need. Both the *Ladies' Domestic Journal* and the *Leisure Hour* are found for her amusement; meanwhile, a bottle of Pitkeathly Table Water is placed at her side, a tonic 'guaranteed to work as remedial agent upon plethoric states of the system, and all chronic affections of the organs of circulation'. Beef broth is considered appropriate nourishment, and supplied in abundance; windows are thrown open for ventilation and there is even talk of finding a man to clean the chimney, lest its blockage be a contributory cause of Rose's distress. In short, no effort is spared by Mrs. Perfitt to hasten her daughter's recovery; for, if nothing else, she has in mind the fast approaching date of a certain invitation to the Prince's Ground, by a certain Viscount-in-waiting.

As for Rose herself, she sleeps in fits and starts and eats small mouthfuls of broth. But, even after she has rested, and can sleep no more, she seems peculiarly nervous. Indeed, when her mother is absent she walks fretfully about her room, occasionally sitting down at her writing desk, or at the window, only to get up again almost immediately. It is only by the late afternoon that she finally summons enough vitality to dress and go downstairs. She finds her mother alone in the drawing-room, looking through her correspondence.

'I am glad to see you up and about, my dear,' says Mrs. Perfitt. 'The colour has returned to your cheeks, I think.'

'I hope so, Mama. I am sorry.'

'Don't be silly, my dear. Whatever for?'

───※───

Mrs. Perfitt and her daughter remain alone together in the drawing-room for a good hour. Mrs. Perfitt abandons her letters and allows her daughter the opportunity of playing the pianoforte. As she sits back and listens, Mrs. Perfitt cannot but think that Rose plays rather unevenly, without her usual deftness of touch. Her thoughts, however, are interrupted by the sound of the door-bell.

'Now who might that be?' asks Mrs. Perfitt, as Rose comes to a stop.

The appearance of Richards with the visiting-card of Mrs. Bertha Featherstone quickly resolves the question.

'Mrs. Featherstone?' says Caroline Perfitt, with something of a sigh. 'Really. I sometimes think we may as well rent that woman a room and be done with it.'

'Tell her we aren't at home, Mama,' says Rose, rather emphatically.

'Rose! For one thing, she will have heard you playing. For another, I told her at the ball that she would be welcome today, if she cared to call. Richards – if you please.'

Rose waits until Richards departs, before turning

to her mother. 'Mama, I do not feel quite so well again.'

'Nonsense, my dear. You are much improved.'

Rose does not dare contradict her mother and waits patiently, until Mrs. Featherstone walks into the room. And yet, as the clergyman's wife greets her hostess and daughter, it seems that Rose cannot quite bring herself to meet her gaze.

'Miss Perfitt,' asks Mrs. Featherstone, 'are you well? Again, I feel you look a little pale.'

'My daughter has been a little tired today,' interjects Caroline Perfitt.

'Ma'am, you do not surprise me. I expect it is the ball. The Reverend and I never saw a young lady dance with such vigour.'

'Our physician said much the same, ma'am,' replies Mrs. Perfitt.

'The Reverend does not object to dancing, I trust,' says Rose, finally raising her eyes to meet those of Mrs. Featherstone.

'Rose!' exclaims Mrs. Perfitt, rather shocked by her daughter's almost bellicose tone. Mrs. Featherstone, however, chooses not to take offence.

'Not when it is done in an organised and respectable fashion, Miss Perfitt,' continues the clergyman's wife. 'But there are certain places of evil resort – I need not name them – where dancing is of a most wanton kind, and best avoided. And one often finds that decent persons who visit such places – who should know better – do not know the difference and may need to be reminded, lest they lose their virtue and their good name.'

'Quite,' remarks Mrs. Perfitt, although she appears a little perplexed by the homily, and altogether rather desirous of changing the subject. 'And how is the Reverend?'

Mrs. Featherstone, her gaze decidedly fixed upon Rose, turns to face her hostess.

'Thank you, ma'am, he is very well. He is publishing a collected edition of his most recent pamphlets. I wonder – might you care to have a copy, when it is ready?'

Mrs. Perfitt smiles through gritted teeth.

'I am sure we will take two copies.'

'Your generosity, ma'am . . .'

'Please, I should be delighted,' replies Mrs. Perfitt.

'Well, I see Miss Perfitt is still feeling tired. I won't trouble you any further.'

'I am a little,' replies Rose, rather sullenly.

'You must forgive my daughter, ma'am,' says Mrs. Perfitt, darting a glance at Rose. 'Are you sure you will not have some tea?'

Mrs. Featherstone shakes her head. 'No thank you, ma'am. I must be on my way. The Reverend is expecting me.'

———

It is about five o'clock when Mrs. Bertha Featherstone leaves Edith Grove. She makes her way back to St. Mark's College, where she oversees her husband's dinner. Her rather voluminous proportions fill up the small kitchen allotted to the needs of the teaching staff, and the college's cook is, in truth, a little annoyed at her close superintendence.

At seven, the Reverend Featherstone departs for a parish meeting. He warns his wife that it may run long into the night. She, in turn, tells him that he need not worry, and that she is quite all right upon her own; that the Lord shall keep and preserve her.

At nine, Mrs. Featherstone completes an hour of reading from her Bible, and makes several notes in her commonplace book, as is her custom. The night is so mild that she almost has a mind to go for a walk in the grounds.

Then there is a knock at the door.

At a quarter past nine, Mrs. Bertha Featherstone lies dead upon the floor, her life blood pooled around her black bombazine gown, a sharp pair of scissors projecting from her neck.

PART THREE

CHAPTER THIRTY

A single public morgue, with space for no more than a dozen bodies, serves the parish of Chelsea. The building itself is a practical, economical affair, situated in the shadow of the parish's workhouse infirmary, little bigger than a working man's cottage, and not dissimilar in appearance. It lacks, however, the minor comforts and consolations of such a residence. No fire burns at its heart; no rug conceals the paving of the cold stone floor. Its windows are both high and narrow and curtains kept drawn. Indeed, the Chelsea dead-house is kept cold and quiet as any tomb; such is the atmosphere best suited to the wants of its occasional tenants.

Decimus Webb cannot help but shiver in the chill air. If he appears a little awkward as he lifts the white cloth that has been respectfully draped across the corpse of Mrs. Bertha Featherstone, it is not from any morbid sensibility. He has seen a surfeit of such things in his time. Rather, he merely feels somewhat self-conscious, watched by his sergeant who stands near by, as though he is a cheap conjuror pulling back a curtain.

It is not a pleasant sight. Webb peers at the marks of violence upon Mrs. Featherstone's neck. The skin is utterly white, drained of blood, but the rough wounds are clear enough. He directs his gaze to her face. The eyelids have already been closed by some kindly soul, but the mouth seems fixed open, in a permanent rictus of surprise.

'Well, Sergeant?' says Webb, beckoning Bartleby to step forward and take a closer look.

'At least three distinct wounds, sir,' replies the sergeant, obeying, albeit with a grimace. 'I'd say one severed the jugular, another the throat.'

'Good,' replies Webb, letting the cloth fall back over the body. 'I have taught you something of practical value, at least. Where were you this morning, in any case?'

'Robbery in Peckham, sir. I was on the duty roster. Inspector Pierce was short of men.'

'Hmm. I am sorry to impinge upon your valuable time.'

'No trouble, sir,' replies Bartleby, turning away from the corpse and taking a deep breath.

Webb shakes his head. 'Come now, Sergeant. I thought we had overcome your squeamishness. I brought you here this afternoon for a purpose; I had hoped it might prove instructive. You've seen the body and know the circumstances. What about our murderer now? What does this tell us?'

'About The Cutter?'

'No, Sergeant, not about The Cutter,' replies Webb, his impatience audible in every syllable. 'For pity's sake, man, forget this wretched phantom of yours, whoever he may be.'

'But the scissors, sir?'

'Damn the scissors,' says Webb. 'Look at the women he chooses as victims. Every other female your blessed Cutter has attacked has been a pretty girl in the full bloom of youth. In every case he has slashed at her hair or clothing. Then consider Jane Budge, burnt to death, and Mrs. Featherstone, with her throat cut. Both killed in the same location; both known to each other. Neither a young maiden, by any means. And you persist with the idea that they are all the work of the same man?'

Bartleby does not reply; he knows better.

'As for the scissors,' continues Webb, 'why should this fellow leave them behind? He has never done so before.'

'Maybe they were lodged in the neck, sir? He's never actually done for one before, not like this.'

'But that is precisely it, Sergeant – not like this. Besides, I removed the scissors with my own hands and they came out as easily as a knife from butter. If anything, I rather suspect they were placed there after the event, for dramatic effect.'

'So we'd think it was The Cutter?'

'Yes. A very deliberate attempt at misdirection. And so we must now simply ask ourselves who might want Jane Budge and her mistress dead. That is the long and short of it.'

'It was the Reverend who found her?' asks the sergeant.

'Indeed. Now, at least, you are applying your mind. Yes, the Reverend. In a case like this, one must consider wife-murder. The only difficulty is that he was with me outside Cremorne Gardens when Jane Budge was killed; and last night it appears he was at a parish meeting until midnight. From the temperature of the body, it seems likely she was killed much earlier in the evening.'

'Perhaps he did it earlier, then "found" her when he got back?'

Webb nods. 'Not a bad idea, Sergeant. But Mrs. Featherstone was seen by at least three people in the chapel, a hour or more after Reverend quit the grounds. Besides – what might be his motive?'

'The gate-keepers didn't see any strangers come in to the college?' asks Bartleby.

'Not a soul,' replies Webb.

'Then it must have been someone that lives there – one of the pupil-teachers or staff.'

'Yes, I had rather come to that conclusion myself,' says Webb. 'In the case of Miss Budge, I wondered if it might have been an intruder. But now, short of discovering it is your confounded phantom, I fear we must presume otherwise.'

'There's more than sixty of them in the college,' says Bartleby, with weary resignation. 'I've already seen them, sir, last time round. Not one had a bad thing to say against Jane Budge. No obvious motive. Nothing queer at all, in fact.'

Webb frowns. 'Perhaps Mrs. Featherstone will be a different matter. In any case, speak to them again. We must find out Mrs. Featherstone's movements yesterday. It is possible we have been looking in the wrong places. See what you can discover about the Featherstones' history; where he last worked. I will have another word with the Reverend myself.'

Bartleby nods. 'How did he take it, sir? Finding her like that?'

'He seemed quite stoical,' replies Webb. 'Gone to a better place, and so forth. A remarkable thing, to have such faith.'

'You have to wonder, though, sir,' says Bartleby. 'Someone's done for the servant, for his wife . . .'

'Whether he will be next?' replies Webb. 'It did cross my mind. Of course, Mr. Boon is the only party we know who bears him a grudge. I would not have thought Boon capable of such brutality, however – not over their petty squabble about Cremorne.'

'Still, maybe the Gardens are at the root of it, sir,' replies Bartleby, unable to resist the pun, as he opens the door that leads out of the morgue.

Decimus Webb does not dignify him with a response.

'What about George Nelson?' asks the sergeant, as they step outside into the daylight.

'Ah, yes. Well, it seems he was working at Cremorne the whole night; Constable Dawes kept an eye on his movements.'

'So he's not our villain, then, sir?'

'He is a bad piece of work, I am sure of that,' replies Webb, 'but not our murderer. In fact, I have relieved Dawes of his duty; we have few enough men available as it is.'

'Then we best get cracking, sir,' says Bartleby, with renewed vigour.

⌒

The Reverend Augustus Featherstone sits alone in the chapel of St. Mark's College, facing the altar. His eyes are closed, his head bowed in the posture of prayer. To all external appearances there is nothing to distinguish him from any other supplicant before the Almighty, his shoulders slumped in pious resignation, the words of a psalm muttered gently under his breath.

And yet, appearances can be deceptive. For there is no-one to look a little closer; no-one to observe the clergyman's hands; how tightly his fingers are clenched together; how the whites of his knuckles seem to bulge and buckle under the force of his anger, as if in protest at being covered by a mere layer of skin.

CHAPTER THIRTY-ONE

'Mama!'

Rose Perfitt stands by the drawing-room window in Edith Grove and calls out to her mother.

'Mama! There is a landau coming. It's him. It's Mr. Sedgecombe.'

Mrs. Perfitt gets up from her seat, unconsciously toying with the buttons of her polonaise. 'Rose, come away at once. Play something at the piano.'

Rose Perfitt pouts. 'He will be here in just a moment, Mama.'

'Then at least take a seat, dear. For heaven's sake, we do not want Mr. Sedgecombe to think we have been waiting on tenterhooks all morning.'

Rose reluctantly takes a seat by the window. Despite her mother's entreaties, she peers back over her shoulder, looking out onto the road. Her view is obscured by the Swiss lace curtains, tied back on either side of the window-frame, but nonetheless she can make out the figure of Richard Sedgecombe descending onto the street, removing his gloves, and strolling up the house's front steps.

A bell rings in the hall.

'Mama,' says Rose in a confidential whisper, still peering at the carriage outside, 'there's a driver and a footman.'

'Hush!' replies Mrs. Perfitt. 'I gave instructions to Richards to bring Mr. Sedgecombe directly up, Rose – you really must compose yourself.'

Rose Perfitt is not entirely sure how to comply with such a request. Nonetheless, with some further instruction, she smoothes down the linen of her promenade dress, and straightens her back, whilst her mother stands poised to greet her guest.

Mr. Sedgecombe is announced. Dressed in a black frock coat of the garden party variety, with a waistcoat of snow-white silk, he presents as handsome a picture of a young man, no more than twenty-four or -five years old, as anyone might wish. In particular, Mrs. Perfitt is distinctly gratified to find him quite as respectable-looking and presentable in the light of day as in the garish gas-light of the ball-room. So much so, that, despite their slight acquaintance, she offers him her hand in greeting and he responds in kind. To Rose, of course, in keeping with the customs of polite society, he merely offers a slight bow.

'You have a delightful home, ma'am,' he says, addressing Mrs. Perfitt. 'Quite charming. I must compliment you upon the refinement of your taste.'

'You are too kind, sir,' replies Mrs. Perfitt. 'I must confess, it is very gratifying to find a gentleman with an eye for such things.'

'I gather Mr. Perfitt is not at home?'

'I regret he had some small matter of business to attend to,' replies Mrs. Perfitt. Rose almost smiles at this; for the implication that her father is generally a member of the leisured classes is somewhat misleading.

Still, if she has an impulse to correct any misapprehension as to her father's occupation, she restrains it. Mr. Sedgecombe, in turn, bows once more, and addresses her. 'So pleasant to see you again, Miss Perfitt. A fine day, is it not?'

'Very fine,' replies Rose, feeling a little too strongly the watchful gaze of her mother, a brief nervous smile flickering upon her lips. 'I am very much looking forward to the race.'

Mr. Sedgecombe nods. 'Yes, well, it should be quite an event for the sporting fraternity. I only hope members of the fairer sex present find it of some small interest. It is very good of you to be my guests.'

'Would you care for some tea, Mr. Sedgecombe?' asks Mrs. Perfitt. 'Please, do take a seat.'

Mr. Sedgecombe hesitates, pulling out his pocket-watch, a gleaming time-piece on a sturdy-looking gold chain. 'In fact, ma'am – forgive me – I fear we – or rather, I should say myself – well, we are a little late. If Miss Perfitt cares to see the start of the race, then I think we had better depart. There is a delightful refreshment bar at the Club.'

'Oh, I am sure we should like to see the start,' replies Mrs. Perfitt, glancing at her daughter, then ringing the servants' bell. 'It is so good of you to invite us, Mr. Sedgecombe. The Prince's Club is so charming an institution.'

'Well, it is good for cricket and rackets, ma'am,' replies Mr. Sedgecombe, 'but I prefer to depend upon, may I say,' – and here he pauses – 'charming company.'

Mrs. Perfitt smiles, as Richards appears to open the door.

'Quite so,' she replies. 'Rose, was I not only saying

the same thing earlier today? The company one keeps is so important.'

'Yes, Mama,' replies Rose.

———

As they travel through Brompton, Mr. Richard Sedgecombe hesitantly broaches various topics of conversation before settling upon the subject of cricket. In truth, it is a rather one-sided discussion, but any unease this provokes in the minds of Mr. Sedgecombe's two companions is more than compensated for by the many fine qualities of his conveyance. For Mr. Sedgecombe's carriage not only boasts the crest of his family emblazoned upon the door, but is drawn by two of his father's finest mares, and possesses springs that seem to transfer not a single jolt or hint of discomfort to the passenger, whatever the irregularities of the macadam below. As they approach Hans Place, however, Mr. Sedgecombe, having finished remarking upon the astonishing turns of fortune in a particular match once played at the Prince's by old boys of Eton and Harrow, tries another tack.

'Ever seen a bicycle race before, Miss Perfitt?' asks Mr. Sedgecombe, after a distinct silence.

'No, sir, I have not,' replies Rose, as the cab draws round the central oval, into the drive of the Prince's Club. 'Will it be upon the lawn?'

Mr. Sedgecombe smiles indulgently. 'Upon the grass? I should hope not. The groundsman wouldn't thank them for that, Miss Perfitt. No, we have a little track – the fellows use it to run laps in the summer. Now, mark my words, Mr. Stanton's the chap to watch today. They say he did a fifty-mile stretch in three and a quarter hours last season.'

'Do they?' replies Rose, as the carriage finally draws up outside the Pavilion. 'Is that good?'

'It is capital, Miss Perfitt,' replies Mr. Sedgecombe, climbing down out of the carriage and holding out his arm. 'I'd wager my life, you won't see a man that can beat him.'

Rose steps down from the landau, allowing her host to support her elbow, though in truth it makes little difference to her descent onto the gravel. She grants Mr. Sedgecombe a thankful smile, which seems to please him. Her mother follows, and they make their way to the back of the Pavilion, where a crowd of members and guests gather in anticipation of the race. Mr. Sedgecombe undertakes to return with the best lemonade in London, leaving mother and daughter briefly unaccompanied.

'How do you like him?' whispers Mrs. Perfitt, when Mr. Sedgecombe is out of earshot. 'He is a pleasant young man, my dear.'

'I suppose so,' replies Rose. 'If a little dull.'

Mrs. Perfitt takes a deep breath. 'Rose, at least try and make yourself agreeable. If nothing else,' she says, looking round the assembled crowd, 'one does not know who one might meet.'

———

The bicycle race begins at three o'clock, on a marked-out track of rough ground, a good distance from the Prince's Club cricket pitch. Mr. Sedgecombe vouch-safes that it is a five-mile handicap between four gentlemen of great renown in the bicycling fraternity. Certainly, thinks Rose Perfitt, they look the part, dressed in the sportsman's uniform of loose-fitting breeches, covered by stockings and stout boots, a rough jersey and a cap of matching cloth. Each, moreover, is surrounded by a cordon of enthusiastic young gentlemen, who liberally make various oaths and exhortations, whilst slapping their respective contenders upon the back. Naturally, a photograph is taken. Then, at length, the four sportsmen line up beside their vehicles. The crowd watches closely as the competitors ascend the wooden mounting blocks and then swing themselves up above the tall front wheels, at least five feet in height, onto leather saddles. A flag is waved; the crowd cheers; and the race begins.

To the novice, unfamiliar with the sport, it goes gingerly at first, each rider balanced precariously upon his steel-framed steed, seemingly in utter contradiction to the laws of gravity; but then they pick up pace, and wheels, spokes, men all fly past at a remarkable rate. Mr. Sedgecombe's preference for the famous Stanton does not prove misguided. Three miles into the distance, the latter is sufficiently ahead to make the occasional nod to the crowd and, better still, remove one hand from the handlebars and tip his cap. Indeed, each completed circuit is greeted with applause and hurrahs from many of the Prince's Club members, who, Mr. Sedgecombe quietly confides in Mrs. Perfitt's ear, have 'invested a pound or two' upon his success.

None of the spectators, however, intent upon the matter in hand, notices the approach of a certain gentleman in a tweed suit, who walks slowly across the Prince's Club lawn, until he stands near Mrs. Perfitt.

'Good afternoon, ma'am,' says Decimus Webb.

Mrs. Perfitt looks rather surprised as she turns to notice Decimus Webb. But she regains her composure quickly enough. 'Why, it is Inspector Webb, is it not?'

Webb assents. 'Enjoying the race, ma'am?'

'Yes, of course,' replies Mrs. Perfitt. 'Inspector – this is my daughter, Rose. And this is Mr. Richard Sedgecombe.'

'My pleasure,' replies Webb, whose attention seems momentarily distracted by the spectacle of Mr. Stanton lapping a rival. 'Remarkable machine, the bicycle. Used to have an old boneshaker myself, when I was a younger man. Doubt that I could master one of these modern articles, mind you. I'd never get on the saddle.'

'Indeed?' replies Mrs. Perfitt with an air of perfect condescension.

'Are you here for the race, Inspector?' inquires Mr. Sedgecombe, a little puzzled by the peculiar interruption.

'No, sir, I am afraid not. In fact, I fear I must deprive you of your company,' replies Webb. 'I have to speak in private with Mrs. Perfitt and her daughter.'

'Inspector,' says Mrs. Perfitt, 'I am sure there can be nothing so urgent that it cannot wait until a more convenient moment?'

'I had hoped to be a little more discreet, ma'am, but since you ask, yes, when it is a matter of murder, ma'am, it cannot wait.'

'I am sorry, Inspector, but much as I have great sympathy for that poor girl, there is no excuse for—'

'Forgive me, ma'am,' interrupts Webb, 'but it is not Jane Budge. I understand you saw Mrs. Bertha Featherstone yesterday evening – am I correct?'

'Yes, I did,' replies Mrs. Perfitt. 'She regularly calls upon us.'

'Mrs. Featherstone was murdered last night, ma'am,' says Webb. 'And, short of her husband, my inquiries suggest that you and your daughter may well be the last persons to have talked to her when she was alive.'

Mrs. Perfitt blanches. But, before she can reply, there is a soft moan from the lips of her daughter, as Rose Perfitt slips into unconsciousness and tumbles to the ground.

CHAPTER THIRTY-TWO

'Fainted!'

'Please, Charles, calm yourself. It was the shock, nothing more. She has a delicate system.'

Seated in their drawing-room in Edith Grove, Caroline Perfitt reaches up and clasps her husband's hands.

'Please stop pacing about, Charles.'

Mr. Perfitt reluctantly complies and sits down, facing his wife. Nevertheless, his eyes do not meet hers, but dart about the hearth-rug, unable to rest upon one spot.

'And is she quite all right?' he says at last.

'Perfectly. I have insisted she rest. There is nothing to worry about.'

'Perhaps we should have Malcolm visit again.'

Mrs. Perfitt shakes her head. 'There is no need, Charles, none at all. It is that odious little man who is to blame. I swear, he quite terrified her – coming out with such a thing, without any warning. I have half a mind to write to the Commissioner and complain.'

'Webb? I expect the fellow was only doing his job,' replies Mr. Perfitt.

'His job, Charles? If that is his job, to frighten girls

out of their wits, then he had better find another employment. And I cannot imagine for a moment what Mr. Sedgecombe made of the whole business. I doubt we shall ever hear from him again.'

'You think not?' replies Mr. Perfitt, rather mechanically, as if preoccupied with other thoughts.

'I do not imagine, Charles, that the son of a viscount wishes to find himself in the society of police inspectors or hear talk of murders, not for an instant.'

'No. No, I suppose not.'

Mrs. Perfitt tuts. 'Charles, you are not listening to a word I am saying.'

Mr. Perfitt looks up at his wife. 'I am sorry, my dear. I was thinking about poor Mrs. Featherstone.'

Mrs. Perfitt frowns and does not speak for a moment. 'You would be better off thinking what we can do for your daughter. It will do nothing for our reputation, if we are constantly to be hounded by the police in such a manner.'

'It is hardly that bad, Caroline.'

'It does not have to be,' replies Mrs. Perfitt, with a sigh. 'There will be talk, mark my words.'

Silence falls between the pair of them. For a few moments, only the ticking of the clock upon the mantelpiece can be heard.

'The papers blame "The Cutter",' says Mr. Perfitt, at last.

'Well, precisely! I imagine they are right,' replies Mrs. Perfitt.

'It is just . . . I went to see Nelson, a few days ago. To give him fair warning, to keep away—'

'Charles!' exclaims Mrs. Perfitt. 'You did not say anything!'

'I can handle the man, Caroline,' replies Mr. Perfitt, though perhaps not with complete conviction. 'In fact, he promised me he would steer clear, in his own brutish way. But I cannot help but wonder, even if the police say they are watching him, if he is not mixed up in this awful business. First Jane Budge, now this. Would it not be better for Rose if we should leave Chelsea? Put the whole dismal episode behind us, once and for all. A fresh start?'

'Charles, I thought we agreed?' says Mrs. Perfitt.

Mr. Perfitt looks back at his wife. 'You want to stay?'

'Charles! For Rose's sake, not mine. I promise you, I would gladly be rid of George Nelson. Please God we never see that man again.'

'I am not sure what to do for the best.'

'Then go and kiss your daughter good night,' says Mrs. Perfitt calmly. 'She will be glad to see you. And then sleep upon it.'

'Yes, I suppose you're right,' replies Mr. Perfitt. 'As always.'

———

'Still here, sir?' asks Sergeant Bartleby, finding Decimus Webb in his office, the gas turned down low.

'So it seems,' replies Webb.

'Nothing to report, I'm afraid, sir,' says Bartleby. 'We've had a few words with everyone at the college. No-one saw anything. Got the impression that Mrs. Featherstone was a nuisance to some of the servants; stuck her nose into this and that, rather particular. Bit of a martinet. Could have told you that myself, mind you, having met her.'

'Is that it?'

'Pretty much, sir,' says Bartleby, rather wistfully. 'I wouldn't say there's anything that makes you think one of them would stick a pair of scissors in her neck.'

Webb puts his fingers to his temple. 'What would do it, then, Sergeant? Why should anyone kill Jane Budge and Bertha Featherstone?'

'Well, assuming it's not a lunatic, sir . . .'

'You may say "The Cutter" if you like.'

'Assuming it's not The Cutter, then . . .' says Bartleby, coming to a halt. 'Lord, I've no idea, sir.'

'There is no connection between them, after all, save that of employer and servant; and there is nothing in Mrs. Featherstone's past to connect them – I assume you have found nothing?'

Bartleby nods. 'Not yet, sir. The Reverend had a parish in Bromley, that's all I know at present.'

'Then what might it be, eh?' says Webb. 'Something they knew? Some secret of which we have no inkling whatsoever?'

'I really couldn't say, sir. Honest to God.'

A pause.

'Neither could I, Sergeant,' says Webb, getting up from his chair, and reaching for his hat from the nearby stand. 'But there will be someone who knows the truth of the matter.'

'Simple matter of finding them,' says Bartleby.

'Yes,' says Webb, ruefully. 'Quite straightforward.'

⁂

Margaret Budge walks along Sheepgut Lane in the black of night. It is a difficult journey, since the lane is built upon rather marshy ground, moist and water-logged earth that swiftly turns to mud, churned up by passing waggons and carriages. Thus, she is obliged to walk slowly and cautiously, trudging along, her boots sinking into the mire, patiently measuring her steps. Past the lane, she carries on into the brick fields, along a half-built road, where the only landmarks are the squat, ill-proportioned brick-kilns to either side, a testimony to the grand ambitions of local landowners. Terraces will follow; Mrs. Budge is certain of that, until there is nothing in Battersea but bricks and mortar. She shakes her head and holds a little tighter the small bundle of linen that she carries in her arms.

Finally, she comes to the gas-lit Battersea Road. It seems to her particularly rowdy; that there are too many men with money to spend on liquor. It is not yet ten o'clock and all along the pavement that leads up to Battersea Bridge, even ignoring her fellow pedestrians, the noise of the various public houses spills out into the road: a piano in the Red Cow, playing 'Come Home, Father' accompanied by a raucous chorus of drunks; the sound of a glass shattering upon the floor in the Marquis of Granby; the chatter of a gaggle of women in the Mason's Arms. Mrs. Budge walks hurriedly past them all.

She does not, however, proceed to the bridge. Rather, she turns down the dingy, unlit side road that leads to the nearby timber yards by the water's edge on the eastern side. There, a hundred yards on, she seeks out a particular spot, where an old causeway, long since abandoned, projects arthritically into the stream of the Thames. She walks a few feet along, kneels down upon the mouldering wood and, hesitating for a moment, peels back a fold of the linen bundle. The child's face hidden within – for it is an infant of no more than four or five months – is as pale as bone china, quite drained of all life.

She sighs, and throws the bundle into the silt brown waters. She stays for a moment or two, watching it sink into the darkness, then hurries back to the road, as fast as she is able. She starts a little, however, when she sees a man standing there, watching her.

'Little Moses,' says Mr. Budge, in the ruminative, inebriate manner that is his wont.

'Hush, you old sot,' replies his wife, sighing with relief. 'What are you doing here? Someone will see us.'

'I saw you. Saw you on the road. Old Bill chucked us out, see? Said I owes him money.'

'Then I expect you do,' replies Mrs. Budge, taking her husband's arm like that of a wayward child, and swiftly leading him up towards the bridge.

'Another of 'em gone, then?' says Mr. Budge, looking back at the river.

'No fault of mine,' replies Mrs. Budge, defensively. 'Gathered up to his Maker; poor little thing.'

Mr. Budge takes off his cap in tribute, almost dropping it in the process.

'Can you spare us something, Maggie?' he says, at last. 'A couple of bob would do us. Just to square Bill.'

'Lord, I ain't got nothing for you, Alfred Budge. I'm still saving up for Janey. You remember her, do you? Your own daughter? Dead and gone and lying cold in a box in your back parlour.'

Mr. Budge looks painfully forlorn; he avows that he does remember his daughter; that he would like to see her buried proper; that there is nothing else upon his mind. Until a thought strikes him. 'You can get another little 'un, now, though, eh?'

'Shame on you!' exclaims his wife, swatting him about the shoulders with her free hand. 'Shame! As if a body ain't got feelings. As if I can have another little angel without a thought. With Janey not even cold in the ground.'

Mr. Budge slurs something quite inaudible in drunken apology.

'Besides,' continues Mrs. Budge, 'I know a lady who has an account to settle. Who'll give us twelve sovereigns straight off, if I press her. Reckon I've left that long enough.'

Mr. Budge keeps silent; he cannot quite muster the strength to speak and walk the length of Battersea Road. Nonetheless, the expression upon his face suggests he finds the prospect of his wife renewing an acquaintance with such a liberal person to be a very promising development.

'Silk hats and crape. Best black feathers,' says Mrs. Budge. 'Twelve sovereigns and she'll have a good send-off. It's only right, after what she suffered.'

Mr. Budge nods. 'And there'll be some to spare, Maggie? Some to spare?'

Mrs. Budge lets go of her husband's arm and slaps him about the head.

CHAPTER THIRTY-THREE

Decimus Webb quits Scotland Yard at half-past ten, bidding goodbye to Bartleby and walking out through the old cobbled courtyard of the police station, down to the Embankment. He does not turn his steps homewards, but follows the grand gas-lit avenue westwards, walking by the stone abutments that conceal the river shore. Upon occasion, he casts his eye over the pavement's iron benches, set upon raised flagstones at regular intervals between the plane trees, where solitary vagrants sleep in uneasy anticipation of the steps of a police constable. But, for the most part, Webb pays no particular attention to his surroundings, his thoughts intent upon other matters. Thus, he skirts the Houses of Parliament without an upwards glance to the clock tower; ignores the Gothic pretensions of Lambeth Palace upon the far shore; barely notices the grim brick walls around the turrets of Millbank Prison, the gaol's diseased yellow stones illuminated by the gas-light from the riverside lamps. He goes past bridges and boat-yards, past the black shadows of coal-barges, moored along the shore in solemn rows. Indeed, he simply follows the lazy serpentine twists of the Thames – a far longer route to Chelsea than cutting through the back streets of Pimlico –

until he comes to Battersea Bridge, and then down a little further, to the water-gate side of Cremorne Gardens.

It is almost eleven but there are still small parties arriving by boat, queuing for tickets. Webb, however, does not need to pay for entry – a young constable from T Division, stationed at the entrance, recognises the Scotland Yard detective – and it is not long before he finds himself within Cremorne's sylvan groves.

It is hard to say whether he has a particular purpose in mind; he certainly seems quite content to stroll along the principal path, in the glow of the lanterns, each a different colour, which are suspended cleverly between the trees. In the end, in solitary contemplation, he turns his steps towards the famous Crystal Platform, where the sound of the orchestra can be clearly heard.

'On your own, sir?'

The words are whispered by a woman, thirty-five years old or so, coming in the opposite direction. She wears a walking dress of almond-coloured Mikado silk, an imitation of a better class of material; she smiles as she draws near, touching the fashionable collar of silver medallions that adorns her pale neck with one hand, whilst in the other she swings a folded tussore sun-shade, though there is little call for such an article in Cremorne's half-light.

'So it seems,' replies Webb. He casts his eye over her face; she has a brunette complexion, fine hazel eyes, large and bright.

'Would you care for company, sir?' she says, turning, and keeping pace beside him. 'A little dance, perhaps? Or we might try the shooting gallery? I can see you have a steady hand.'

'No, I think not,' says Webb, though he allows the

woman to take his arm and walk with him. 'Tell me, though, you take a chance, to come here alone at night.'

'I do all right, sir,' she replies, a little puzzled by his response.

'You might fall foul of that man they are talking about, The Cutter.'

'I'm sure you'd protect me,' she replies, squeezing his arm.

'How do you know I am not the fellow myself?'

The woman pauses for a moment. 'No, you're a straight one, sir. I can see that, clear as anything. I can tell by your hat.'

Webb self-consciously straightens the brim of his billycock, and coughs. 'I see.'

'Better than feeling a man's head for bumps,' she replies, as they draw nearer to the Crystal Platform, the sight of couples gaily waltzing visible through the trees. 'You're a copper, ain't you?'

'Another deduction based upon my hat?'

'It's crawling with your lot round here; I should have known better.'

Webb releases his arm from his companion. 'Perhaps you should.'

'They say he's killed some vicar's wife now?' says the woman.

'We are not sure of that.'

The woman looks thoughtfully at Webb. 'Do you want my opinion, Mr. . . .?'

'Webb. Inspector Webb.'

'Oh, I beg your pardon, Inspector,' she says sardonically, curtseying for effect. 'Well, do you?'

'If you like,' replies Webb.

'I know his sort, sir. They like giving a scare to the girls; makes 'em feel they're manly – if you get my meaning. They want to see the look in your eyes; put the fear of God in you. I've known one or two of 'em in my time, pulled a knife on me. It's like a little game for 'em.'

'I expect you are right.'

'Sir!' shouts a man's voice, before Webb can speak any further. It is the police constable, T 49 from the water-gate, running along the path towards them. 'Sorry, sir,' he continues, looking at Webb's companion, 'I didn't know you were . . .'

'I was what?' says Webb impatiently. 'What is it, man?'

'There's some trouble, sir. We're glad you're here, to tell the truth.'

'Whatever is it?' asks Webb.

'Fireworks, sir.'

The woman smiles and saunters off.

'Nice to meet you, Inspector.'

———

The Gardens' Firework Gallery is an outdoor theatre, concealed at one extremity by a faux Moorish façade, that skilfully hides it from the view of those enjoying Cremorne's terpsichorean delights. Quite worthy of the finest workmanship of Granada, the exterior is adorned by four tall minarets, decorated in arabesque style, that poke above the Gardens' oaks and elms. The open interior contains space for five or six hundred persons, an orchestra and then a large stage. And last of all, behind the stage, a raised tower, itself some forty feet high, again in the style of the Moors, from which fireworks are launched every other evening, to the accompaniment of a stirring score.

At first, it seems to Webb that there is nothing much amiss. But then he hears the jeers from odd members of the crowd and notices the sullen silence of the orchestra. The constable points upwards to the tower's summit, where a man stands, gesturing wildly, an oil-lamp in one hand, a book in the other.

'Who on earth is that?' asks Webb, peering down the length of the gas-lit ground. 'I can't make him out.'

'I'll tell you who it is,' says a familiar voice, coming up behind them. Webb instantly recognises it as belonging to John Boon. 'Your friend Featherstone. Gone quite off his head.'

Decimus Webb looks coolly at Cremorne's proprietor. 'I will judge that for myself, sir.'

'Judge all you like, Inspector,' says Boon, hands firmly in his waistcoat pockets. 'The man's positively deranged. I've always said so.'

Webb walks briskly down the length of the Gallery, through the crowd, most of whom seem rather mystified by the spectacle of the black-robed clergyman. As he draws closer to the firework tower, Webb can make out that the book in the Reverend Featherstone's hands is a Bible; and his words something of a sermon.

'"Then the Lord rained upon Sodom and upon Gomorrah brimstone and fire from the Lord out of heaven! And he overthrew those cities, and all the plain, and all the inhabitants of the cities, and that which grew upon the ground,"' intones the clergyman.

'Sling yer hook!' shouts a baser member of the audience. 'Here, maestro – start up the band, why don't yer? I didn't pay two bob for this.'

Boon, meanwhile, catches up with Webb. 'You must do something, Inspector.'

['And is this not truly the New Sodom?' proclaims Reverend Featherstone.]

'You did not invite him to preach, I take it?' says Webb.

219

'The man is a lunatic,' replies Boon. 'Quite mad.'

Webb sighs. 'He has just lost his wife, sir. One must make allowances; I expect it has shattered his nerves.'

['And are we not wretched sinners?']

Boon shakes his head. 'You do not understand, Webb. Apart from this embarrassing interruption to my business, he is waving that lamp directly above the blessed fireworks. If he should set light to them all together, he will have his fire and brimstone, all right – in this life, not the next.'

'Will he not come down? He has made his point.'

Boon pushes his hands deeper into his waistcoat pockets. 'If you care to go up there, you can ask him.'

Webb hesitates for a moment. 'How did he get up there in the first place?'

'There is a ladder at the back,' replies Boon.

Webb looks up at the clergyman and reluctantly finds a path through the orchestra, most of whom are already on their feet, alternately indignant or amused by the unexpected prayer-meeting, oblivious to any danger. He finds that the rear of the tower belies the Moorish façade, a plain iron scaffold with a series of steep ladders ascending to a wooden terrace behind the crenellated summit. Two stagehands stand at the base, looking upwards.

'Can we not go up and get him?' asks Webb.

One stagehand looks at his companion and laughs derisively. 'We? If that lamp spills you'll be blown sky high, guv'nor. I'd like to hold on to my 'stremities, if you don't mind.'

If Webb is inclined to remonstrate with the two men, he glances upwards and changes his mind. Instead, he tentatively sets foot on the first ladder, and begins to climb the scaffold.

'Reverend? Can you hear me?' shouts Webb. No

reply, however, is forthcoming, except the sound of the clergyman's voice, declaiming against the debaucheries of mankind.

Webb reluctantly climbs up to one deck, then another, until he is no more than a half dozen feet below the trap-door that leads to the tower's terrace. He can make out the brass loading-tubes that already contain a quintet of rockets, and the neatly laid-out store of shells, comets and squibs all waiting to be projected into the night air; and, although it may be his imagination, there seems to be a faint hint of gunpowder in the air.

'Featherstone! Stop one moment, sir!' shouts Webb.

The clergyman does pause, looking down through the trap-door. 'Inspector? Whatever are you doing there?'

'Sir, I beg you, extinguish the lamp and come down.'

'No, Inspector,' replies Featherstone, his words fast and almost garbled. 'These sinners must hear the Word, if we are to save them their fate. I have been too blinkered to see it. I must beard the lion in his den!'

'Sir, extinguish the lamp. There is enough explosive here to blow us both to smithereens.'

'Explosive?' asks the clergyman, seemingly perplexed.

'The fireworks!' exclaims Webb. 'Sir, please, think what you are about. This is not Exeter Hall.'

'The path that leads to life is straight and narrow, Inspector. There is little time for these poor souls; most are already at the devil's mercy. They must hear me.'

'They will not hear you if you are blown to kingdom come, sir. Come, be reasonable.'

Featherstone hesitates. 'My wife, Inspector . . . I owe it to her . . .'

'I understand, sir,' replies Webb. 'But she would not wish you to cause a tragedy here, would she?'

Featherstone stops quite still, as if lost in thought; his posture seems to sag a little. 'No, no. I suppose not, Inspector.'

And, with that, he puts down his Bible, cups his hand above the lamp's brass chimney, and blows out the flame. Webb, in turn, breathes a deep sigh of relief.

It is only when the clergyman begins his descent down the ladder that Webb realises quite how tightly his own hands are clasped around the wood.

⁓

Mr. John Boon stands by the King's Road entrance to Cremorne, with Decimus Webb and the Reverend Featherstone, rather stooped and defeated, before him. The face of Cremorne's proprietor is a particular shade of infuriated pink, which lends little charm to his countenance.

'I cannot believe it, Inspector – you must charge this madman!' exclaims Boon.

'I think, sir,' Webb replies, 'that if one considers the Reverend's personal circumstances; and that, in the end, no great harm was done, I am inclined to let the matter rest.'

'Let it rest! Yes, well, that does not surprise me, coming from you, Inspector. Not at all!'

'There is no need to be abusive, sir. The Reverend has given me his word that he will not return to your premises, or the immediate vicinity. That is enough for you, surely?'

'I shall believe that when I see it,' says Boon.

'May I go, Inspector?' interjects the Reverend Featherstone in a low whisper. 'I should like to return home, if I may.'

'Yes, sir. You take care.'

Boon snorts contemptuously, but the two men watch as the clergyman walks out through the gates, and along the King's Road, his shoulders still slumped and weary.

'That is an end to your ridiculous feud, I hope,' says Webb, at last. 'Surely you can see the man has been quite broken.'

'The man is a menace, sir,' says Boon, emphatically. 'And if this is how you are prosecuting your search for The Cutter, then God help us all.'

'The Reverend Featherstone is quite harmless, Mr. Boon. He is the least of my worries.'

———

The Reverend Featherstone returns to his rooms in St. Mark's to find them dark and unwelcoming. No-one has lit the gas; there is no supper ready upon the dining table; his correspondence lies unopened upon the bureau. It takes him a little while to find the matches in the bureau drawer; and then there is the chore of going round the burners. At length, however, when the room has some light, he takes the day's letters and sits down at his writing desk, not far from where he found the corpse of his wife.

He reaches down to the bottom drawer of the desk, and pulls out a silver paper-knife, cutting open the folds of each envelope one by one. When he is done, he methodically returns the knife to the drawer, where it lies, inconspicuous and unseen, hidden from the world, beside a sharp pair of household scissors.

CHAPTER THIRTY-FOUR

It is gone three o'clock in the afternoon when Rose Perfitt hears her mother's footsteps upon the stairs. Rose hastily places the book she is reading out of sight, stuffing it under the bed sheets, and resumes the languid pose of an invalid, lolling on the pillows propped up against the headboard. She answers her mother's knock upon the door with a faint voice, calculated to sound as miserable as possible.

'Rose, how are you feeling?' asks Mrs. Perfitt, as she opens the door.

'I'm still a little low, Mama.'

'Did Richards bring you that soup?' continues her mother, who walks over to the bed, and lightly touches her daughter's forehead with her hand. 'You do not have a temperature, at least.'

'I might try and get up later.'

'I should hope so. You cannot stay in bed all day, my dear,' says Mrs. Perfitt, straightening the sheets as she talks, 'there is no virtue in that, even if you feel seedy. I promised your father that you would be up and about by the time he comes home.'

'I was thinking about Mr. Sedgecombe. Has he called?'

Mrs. Perfitt sighs. 'You know full well he has not, Rose. You can hear the bell as well as anyone.'

'I might have been asleep,' protests Rose.

'He has neither called nor left his card,' replies Mrs. Perfitt, wearily.

'I'm sorry, Mama.'

Mrs. Perfitt manages a forced smile. 'Never mind, my dear. There will be other young men.'

'I suppose.'

'And he was an awful bore, wasn't he?' says Mrs. Perfitt, a hint of a smile playing on her lips. 'I never knew there was so much to be said about cricket.'

Rose laughs. 'Mama!'

'Well, never mind that. Now, I am going to visit your Aunt Elspeth again. She knows you are sickly, mind you. Why she cannot manage for herself, I do not know. I do believe she craves the attention. I do not suppose you would care to come and pay your respects?'

'No, Mama. But do send her my love.'

'I shall. I should be back before you father is home. And do not run Richards ragged, either, if you can help it. She has quite enough to do.'

'I'm sure I will get up soon, Mama. In an hour or so.'

Mrs. Perfitt accedes to this, and leaves her daughter alone, closing the bedroom door behind her.

Rose, in turn, waits until she can hear her mother going downstairs. Then she gets up, pulling her dressing-gown around her, and tiptoes towards her bedroom window, peering out along the street.

❧

An hour later, and Rose Perfitt is up from her bed and dressed. Quite still, standing by her bedroom curtains, she suddenly catches sight of something upon Edith Grove that sends her dashing from the window. Without the slightest hesitation, she rushes down the hall stairs, her feet barely touching the carpet. She does not pause for breath until she descends the final flight, down into the basement kitchen, her soft slippers sliding on the stone floor. Outside in the narrow well of the area, the railed sunken court in front of the house, she can make out a pair of boots, coming down the whitewashed steps. She hurries to the kitchen door and carefully undoes the latch. Then, with a quick glance up to the street, she swiftly ushers George Nelson indoors.

'I thought you'd never come,' she says, her tone more one of relief than chastisement.

'I should be working,' replies Nelson, looking around the kitchen. 'Told them I had a belly ache.'

'Well, do hurry up and kiss me then.'

George Nelson, a good foot taller than Rose, smiles at this, reaches out and cups her face in his hands. He leans down and kisses her, his lips lingering on hers for what seems to Rose an eternity. He grins as he pulls back, lightly touching her face with his rough hand.

'Where are they, then?'

'Papa is at work and Mama has gone to see Aunt Elspeth.'

'And?'

Rose sighs in mock vexation. 'Cook will not come for an hour yet; and I sent Richards on an errand.'

'She knows I'm here, though, don't she? I bet she does.'

'George, don't be such a goose!' she exclaims. 'Of course she does. I gave her my best ring, remember? I told you. She won't say a word.'

Nelson frowns a little. Rose, however, ignores the little show of displeasure and takes his hand; she tugs at it, moving back towards the hall stairs.

'Come on,' she says, a mischievous look upon her face. 'Come with me.'

'Where?' he replies, almost warily.

'Come on. I'll show you my room. Wipe your feet.'

George Nelson seems to hold back at first. But, in the end, he wipes his feet upon the mat by the door and allows himself to be led, like some wary animal, out of the kitchen and up into the hall. He looks quite incongruous in his working clothes, dodging the china plate displayed upon shelves on the first-floor landing, his heavy boots thudding upon the stairs. But Rose pulls him onwards with almost child-like enthusiasm, until they come to her bedroom door.

'Here we are then,' she says, proudly, bringing him inside.

Nelson surveys the room. 'I can see that,' he replies, casually casting his eye over the bed, the marble wash-stand, the lace curtains.

'Here is my little desk, where I wrote you all those letters,' says Rose, 'the ones I told you about. You will have to read them.'

'I will. Not now, eh?'

'And that's my bed,' she says.

'I can see that too. Is that where you dream about me, then?'

'Sometimes.'

'What sort of dreams?'

Rose blushes. 'Just dreams.'

'What's that?' asks Nelson, looking in the direction of the armchair by the hearth, where a tumble of white silk lies draped over one arm.

Rose follows his gaze; it takes her a moment to see what he might mean. 'My night things. I had to stay in bed to put off Mama.'

'You needn't have dressed for me,' he replies.

She laughs, nervously.

'Put them on again,' he says, picking up the night-dress, the soft white material so fine that it flows between his fingers like water. 'Put them on for me, Rosie. Let me see you.'

Rose blushes once more. 'I don't like to,' she replies, hesitantly. 'We don't have long. They'll all be back soon.'

'Go on,' he says, sitting down in the armchair. 'You will when we're married; you'll do it for me then. Why not now, eh?'

'Married? Don't tease,' she says, her voice suddenly abrupt. 'You know Papa will never—'

'Hang your bloody father. We'll find someone who'll do it; I know a fellow who can write out the neatest Alfie-Davy you ever saw. We'll have your Papa swearing a blinding oath to anything we like. You said you'd like to be my wife, Rosie.'

Rose walks over to where George Nelson sits, clasping his hand and dropping to her knees. 'Oh, I would. More than anything!'

'Well then, just you think about that. Why don't you go and close those curtains?'

Rose gets up, and does as she is told, drawing the curtains shut, leaving the room in a darkened half-light. She pauses for a moment, then walks back towards the hearth. Turning her back to him, she undoes the line of brown buttons at the front of her day dress, until it hangs loose about her shoulders. She carefully peels the cotton free of her skin, letting it drop to the floor under its own weight, revealing her bare arms and the corset of burgundy satin, which tightly moulds her waist into the perfect shape. She looks back over her shoulder.

'Undo me then,' she says, in a whisper.

CHAPTER THIRTY-FIVE

'Evening, sir. I see you're working late again. How are things with you?'

Decimus Webb finds his sergeant waiting for him, standing by his desk, as he walks into his office.

'Tolerable. The Assistant Commissioner would like to see me strung from a lamp-post at the earliest opportunity, but apart from that I am quite well.'

'Gave you a dressing down, did he, sir? About The Cutter?'

Webb pauses. 'Sergeant, you have the annoying ebullience that characterises that rare occasion when you stumble upon some useful information. Can I suggest you impart it to me forthwith? Or must I play some wretched game of forfeits before you deign to honour me with whatever fascinating revelation awaits me?'

'Here, sir,' says Bartleby, pulling a crumpled newspaper from behind his back. 'Police report in *The Times*, three years old. I had to bribe Sergeant Walker to let me take it out of the library. Have a look at that.'

Webb creases his brow, and peers at the article to which Bartleby directs him.

WOOLWICH. On Wednesday evening, a tall, respectable-looking man, about fifty-five years of

231

age, dressed in a silk suit which placed him well above the middle rank of life, was brought up by a constable of the K Division, and placed at the bar before Mr. BUTCHER, on the charge of having in a most indecent and disgusting manner exposed his person to a young female in Greenwich Park, a short distance from the Royal Observatory.

'I hope this is worth my trouble, Sergeant,' says Webb.
'Oh, it is, sir. You just read on.'

The prisoner at the bar seemed highly conscious of the degrading situation in which he was placed, and objected to giving his name and address, as he also had done at the station-house. The requisite information was, however, elicited by an officer of the court who, on looking into the prisoner's hat, discovered the lining bore the words – 'The Rev. Augustus Featherstone, No. 14, Cherry Tree Lane, Bromley.'

Webb looks at his sergeant, his eyebrows raised.
'Puts an interesting complexion on things, doesn't it, sir?' says Bartleby.
'How did you come by this?' asks Webb.
'One of the men at Bromley recalled the case, sir. Sent me a note this afternoon.'
Webb nods and reads on.

The prisoner, unattended by any legal adviser, had been brought up instanter by the constable and elected to represent himself.
Mary Davies, residing at No. 35, Barking Lane, Ilford, was then examined and deposed as

follows:- This afternoon, at about four o'clock, I was passing by the shrubbery near the Observatory in Greenwich Park. I saw the prisoner there and when he turned himself round, he exposed to me his person. I then walked briskly in another direction, and was again insulted by him in a similar manner.

Mr. BUTCHER – Were you alone?

Mrs. Davies – No, sir; I had two children with me. I went and gave information directly to a parkkeeper, who caused the man to be apprehended.

Albert Springett, 62 K, said, As I was on duty near the park gate, I was called upon by one of the keepers who pointed out the man and begged me to keep an eye on him, while he went in search of the lady who had complained of him. I waited until the lady was found, and took the prisoner in charge, telling him it was for exposing himself in a public place.

Mr. BUTCHER – Did he make any reply?

Witness. – He said, if he had done so, he was not aware of doing it. He said he was relieving himself.

Mr. BUTCHER (to Mrs. Davies) – When the prisoner exposed himself to you, was he making water?

Mrs. Davies – He was not; he acted towards me in an infamous way and followed me for five minutes or more, creeping and crawling about behind us.

Mr. BUTCHER – You must describe more particularly what he did.

Mrs. Davies – He opened his trousers in front, and in that way exposed himself, sir. I turned my back on him, and walked to a bench with the children. When I looked around, he was there in the same shameful situation.

Mr. BUTCHER – Did he say anything to you, during this time?

Mrs. Davies – Not a word, your worship.

Mr. BUTCHER – Does the prisoner have anything to say?

Prisoner (with much emotion) – Your worship, I am placed in the most distressing situation that might be imagined. I am convinced that the defendant in such cases has but little chance, as a prejudice will be excited against him from the first. I can only hope you might consider the character of this witness, and not judge too hastily. I might, perhaps, have obeyed the call of nature in a spot not set apart for that purpose, but I had no intention of insulting or offending this female.

Mr. BUTCHER – Constable, have you established the character of this witness?

Constable – No, sir.

Mr. BUTCHER – Then I shall remand this gentleman until to-morrow, in order that such evidence may be procured.

Prisoner was remanded back to the police-station.

'There is no more?' asks Webb.

'I telegraphed back straightaway, sir. The constable says he recalls he was acquitted. Doesn't think there was more in the press.'

'Acquitted?' says Webb, musing.

'I've got a cab waiting, sir. If you want to go down to Chelsea?'

'You've heard about the incident at Cremorne last

234

night, I suppose,' says Webb, his brow still furrowed in thought.

'Yes, sir.'

'This does not make him a murderer, Sergeant. In particular, if he was found not guilty.'

'Only the girl's word against his, I suppose,' replies Bartleby. 'But it makes a person think, doesn't it?'

Webb folds the newspaper and tucks it under his arm. 'Very well, let us go and show this to Featherstone. Though I am far from certain we will get any sense out of him.'

Bartleby nods, but hesitates. 'I swore blind to Sergeant Walker I wouldn't take that out of the Yard, sir,' he says, gesturing to the newspaper.

'Then I am about to make you a liar, Sergeant,' replies Webb.

~

The journey to Chelsea goes swiftly, and it is a little past nine o'clock when the two policemen find themselves once more at St. Mark's College. There is, however, no answer when Webb knocks upon the door to Augustus Featherstone's rooms. Bartleby is despatched to the chapel and school house; Webb makes inquiries in the Masters' Common Room; further questions are directed to the men at the gates upon the King's Road and Fulham Road. But, when they return to the Reverend Featherstone's door, a good hour later, neither Webb nor Bartleby is any the wiser as to his whereabouts.

'No-one's seen him since last night, as far as I can make out, sir,' suggests the sergeant.

'So it seems,' mutters Webb. He tries the door-handle. 'He appears to have left his door open, in any case. Rather careless.'

'Do you think we should—'

But before Bartleby can finish the sentence, his superior has already opened the door and gone inside.

The study itself is dark and gloomy, the heavy drapes drawn across the windows left closed from the previous night. Webb strikes a match, and lights the gas above the fire-place.

'Reverend?' says Webb.

There is no reply.

'Check the other rooms, Sergeant,' says Webb.

Bartleby obliges and returns a minute or so later. 'Nothing, sir. No sign of him. Do you think he's legged it?'

'It seems he was supposed to be teaching in the school this afternoon, but did not put in an appearance,' replies Webb. 'But then, I do not think he is quite himself, if last night is anything to go by.'

'What do you think we should do, sir?'

Webb takes a long, deep breath. 'Search the rooms, Sergeant. Thoroughly and carefully. Try not to disturb anything; we are not strictly within our rights, after all.'

'We already did that when they found his better half, sir.'

'You looked everywhere?'

'Well, mainly here in the study, sir. The Reverend said there wasn't anything missing, so I wouldn't say we—'

'Every room, Sergeant. I have complete faith in you.'

Bartleby nods. 'Yes, sir. And what will you be doing?'

'I'll shall be taking a walk in the grounds.'

'And if anyone comes and asks what I'm up to, sir?'

'You had better hope that they do not.'

'Sir!'

Webb extinguishes his pipe, turning to see the figure of Sergeant Bartleby running towards him, across the gas-lit quadrangle.

'Keep your voice down, man, for pity's sake,' says Webb, as Bartleby jogs to a halt. 'I assume you have found something? You have been long enough about it.'

'Have a look at this, sir,' says Bartleby, eagerly, handing over a plain envelope.

Webb opens the envelope and peers inside, his eyes straining to make anything out in the dim light of the gas. For a moment, he cannot quite make sense of it, and pokes the contents with his finger. Then he realises that it is a half dozen or more locks of hair.

'Found the envelope at the back of his dresser, sir. Like little trophies. We've got him! Featherstone's The Cutter!'

'The fear of God,' mutters Webb. 'I should have known.'

'Sir?'

'Nothing. Something that someone said to me last night. I suppose this would explain why he was not overly concerned by those schoolboy threats. He knew that they were just that, and no more.'

'This'll be one in the eye for the Assistant Commissioner, sir.'

'We haven't got our man yet, Sergeant. Unless you know where we might find him?'

'I'm thinking we should try the Gardens,' replies Bartleby. 'He's drawn to the place.'

'I suppose we must. For one thing, it appears I owe Boon an apology.'

'We'll soon find him now, sir.'

Webb frowns.

'I am still not convinced, Sergeant, that it is that simple.'

———

In Battersea, Margaret Budge opens to the door to her back parlour, a candle in her hand. The air in the room is rather damp and foetid. Before her, in the dim light, three small wooden cots are laid out upon the stone floor and, beside them, laid out upon an old oak table, is a plain coffin. It is a parish affair, with no handles or brass, merely half a dozen panels of bare rough elm. There is nothing to distinguish its occupant, save a series of scratches upon the side, which approximate to the name *Jane Budge*, the work of some ill-paid functionary of the parish of Chelsea.

Mrs. Budge looks at the box for a moment, then peers down, checking inside each cot. There is little vital spark in the small creatures that nestle inside the three cribs. Each is an infant less than six months old, with a listless, languid appearance, and eyes that do not seem quite able to open wide. Their meagre bodies, wrapped in dirty off-white swaddling clothes, likewise seem to have little natural childish energy, and each one is, in truth, disproportionately small for their age. One of the three, however, wriggles a little in the glow of the candlelight, reaching up with its tiny hands, clutching at nothing. Mrs. Budge puts the candle to one side and picks the child up, cradling it in her arms.

'How are you, little 'un, eh?' whispers the old woman.

The child, however, perhaps exhausted by its exertion, does not respond. After a minute or so, Mrs. Budge replaces it in the cot, picks up her candle, and returns to the front parlour of Budge's Dairy. Taking her regular seat before the hearth, though the fire is not lit, she pauses to contemplate an opened purse upon the nearby table. Its contents – a dozen gold sovereigns – lie piled in a small heap, as if eagerly tipped out and counted; whilst beside it stands a bottle of expensive-looking brandy.

· Mrs. Budge reaches for the bottle, pulls out the stopper, and takes a swig of the brown liquor.

'Best black feathers, now, Janey,' mutters the old woman to herself. 'Best black feathers, first thing in the mornin'.'

Mrs. Budge takes another swig.

CHAPTER THIRTY-SIX

Charles Perfitt hears footsteps and turns round to see his daughter enter the dining-room.

'Rose, your Mama told me you were feeling better when she came back. Will you have dinner with us?'

'Yes, Papa,' says Rose, bending down to kiss her father upon the cheek. 'If I may.'

'Rose, dear,' says Mrs. Perfitt, as her daughter takes a seat, 'I hardly think you need ask permission.'

Mr. Perfitt smiles as Rose kisses him, but then glances rather nervously at his wife. 'Rose, there is something I would like to tell you. I would have come up and spoken to you this evening but, since you are feeling better, we may as well discuss it now.'

'Papa?'

'I have talked to your mother, and to Dr. Malcolm, about your constitution. Malcolm believes we are over-taxing you; that a rest might do you good. Indeed, it might do us all good. So I have made arrangements for a holiday.'

'A holiday?' says Rose, turning to her mother. 'Mama! We cannot go on holiday during the Season. Beatrice says we may be invited to the Prince's again; and there is a garden party at the Boscombes' – we are sure to go, Mama, you said so.'

'Yes, I know, my dear,' replies Mrs. Perfitt, sympathetically, 'but your father is only thinking of your best interests.'

'But how long shall we be away?' ask Rose.

'I thought two months,' replies Mr. Perfitt. 'I have rented a cottage near Broadstairs; it is a good spot – if the firm has any need of me, I can easily catch the train back, as required.'

'But, Papa, we can't just go,' says Rose, with obvious anxiety in her voice. 'I shall miss everything.'

Mr. Perfitt shakes his head. 'We are leaving on Saturday, my dear. That is an end to it. Now, where is Richards with that soup?'

'I do not want to go to Broadstairs, Papa,' says Rose, rather too emphatically.

'My dear!' exclaims Mrs. Perfitt. 'For heaven's sake, do not make such a fuss. You must do as your father says. We shall come back in time for the end of the Season, I am sure.'

Rose gets up hurriedly from her chair, which scrapes the rug as she pushes it backwards.

'I am sorry,' she says, 'I do not think I am hungry.'

With that, Rose quits the room, turning her back on her parents before either has an opportunity to speak.

'Good Lord,' exclaims Mr. Perfitt, under his breath. 'I knew she would not be happy, Caroline, but this is quite remarkable. Whatever has got into her?'

'I shall talk to her when she has calmed down,' says Mrs. Perfitt. 'She will have to apologise.'

'I swear, I do not understand her moods.'

Mrs. Perfitt frowns. 'Neither do I, Charles. Neither do I.'

⌒

Rose Perfitt apologises to her father at ten o'clock, having been prevailed upon by her mother. At eleven, she follows her parents in retiring to her bed. At a few minutes before midnight she sneaks down into the kitchen and lets herself out onto the street. On this occasion, she wears one of her own dresses, though it is not a particularly expensive or showy article. It is covered, moreover, as to its upper portion, by a dark green hooded mantle that all but conceals her face from any passer-by. And, in one hand, she carries a capacious leather bag, a piece of travelling luggage, of the sort that commonly accompanies young women in railway carriages. Thus attired, she makes her way along Edith Grove, across the King's Road, and down to the gates of Cremorne Gardens.

'What you selling, darlin'?' exclaims one waggish gentleman, not of the highest class, gesturing at her rather battered bag as he climbs into a waiting hansom. Rose, however, does not reply but merely draws her hood further over her face, pays for her admission and hurries into the grounds.

But once inside, she hesitates. For her elopement from Edith Grove is an impromptu one, and she has no idea where in particular to find George Nelson, nor quite how to go about it. At length, she decides to follow the nearest path from the main avenue, which, as a fingerpost makes plain, leads directly to the Gardens' Marionette Theatre. It is a rather shabby-looking venue, a Grecian building of two storeys, boasting a colonnade of stunted columns, made from some indeterminate and insubstantial material, akin to papier mâché. She walks over to the ticket window, which, she discovers, houses a short young man of slumped posture and poor manners.

'I'm sorry,' she says, 'can you tell me, do you know George Nelson? He is a labourer here.'

The young man shrugs. 'Can't say as I do. Can't say as I don't. Maybe he's inside, like.'

'What do you mean?'

'I mean, go and have a look if you like,' says the young man, disinterestedly. 'Up to you.'

Rose hesitates, looking at the twin doors that form the entrance to the theatre; she can hear the boisterous sound of a brass band from inside the small auditorium. Just as she determines to follow the young man's suggestion, he calls out to her.

'Tuppence, mind.'

Rose stops, and impatiently rifles through her purse for the change. Once inside, however, she despairs of making any progress. The stalls are quite full to bursting, with men and women standing in the aisles, and a pall of tobacco smoke heavy in the air. The evening's final attraction is one of the Gardens' most demanded acts, The Beckwith Frogs, their name emblazoned upon a giant piece of card at the front of the stage. Performing within a transparent tank of water, almost too large for the theatre, the submersible family – father, mother, son and daughter – are engaged in a watery family meal, to the accompaniment of trumpet and tuba. Mr. Beckwith sips from his tea-cup – to much applause. Master Beckwith gets down from his chair and swims round the head of his mother – to greater applause. All rise for air, then sink to their subaqueous abode once more; the table is cleared and a game of cards begins – to positively thunderous applause.

Rose peers about her. There is no possible way to get behind the scenes; nor, she realises, any certainty of finding George Nelson when she gets there. Her eyes meets those of a blue-uniformed police constable, stationed upon the other side of the theatre. He looks at her pointedly. It is the same glance that members of Her Majesty's Police reserve for any solitary woman in a crowded theatre; the same unfortunate suspicion that attaches to all lone females in resorts of dubious reputation. But Rose herself is not so certain; she imagines her father has already notified the authorities; that a search is under way, to prevent her reaching her lover. And so she turns and runs, back outside.

She pointedly ignores the ticket clerk and returns to the path. A voice calls out to her, a hand touching her sleeve.

'Miss Perfitt? I thought it was you. Whatever do you have there?'

Rose jumps in surprise, almost dropping her bag.

'Oh,' she says, taking a deep breath, 'Reverend! You startled me.'

CHAPTER THIRTY-SEVEN

'I confess, Miss Perfitt,' says the Reverend Featherstone, 'I am saddened to find you here, in this wretched place, at such a late hour. Here, please, take my arm.'

Rose Perfitt, rather dumb-founded, obeys. The clergyman begins to walk her back along the path towards the central avenue.

'I – I have to see someone,' she says, stumbling over her words.

'I do not suppose your father knows that you are here?' asks Featherstone.

Rose hesitates. She looks up at the clergyman's implacable, stony expression and despairs of lying. 'No, sir.'

'It is some young man, I suppose.'

Rose says nothing but the Reverend clasps his hand upon her arm.

'I have seen unsuspecting innocence beguiled and corrupted too many times, Miss Perfitt, for me not to read the signs. You intend to elope with this young man, am I right?'

'Please, do not tell my father, sir,' says Rose, after a pause for thought. 'I love George and he will marry me, I know it.'

'George?' says Featherstone. 'And, tell me, Miss

Perfitt, is he the fellow whom I saw creeping into your house, like some area sneak, this very afternoon?'

Rose's mouth drops open. 'You saw him?'

Reverend Featherstone smiles, not the friendliest of smiles. His hand still tightly holds his companion's arm, as they stroll down the gas-lit path.

'I have kept my eye upon you, Miss Perfitt. Do you think me a fool? I have seen you outside the Gardens, time and again, loitering about. Then Mrs. Featherstone – God rest her soul – informed me that she actually observed you come through the gates, quite unaccompanied. It was the night before she died; before she fell prey to . . . well, that is another matter . . . the devil is abroad, Miss Perfitt; there is no other explanation for it. But do you recall? She said you ran away. You had some shame left, then, at least.'

Rose bows her head, perhaps reasoning that if she does not speak, she cannot tell a lie.

'I thought Mrs. Featherstone must be mistaken. I told her as much,' continues Featherstone, with a sigh. 'But now it seems I was the one who was wrong.'

Rose bows her head. 'Please don't tell Papa. He will be so angry.'

'You should have thought of that before you embarked upon such a terrible course, Miss Perfitt,' continues Featherstone. 'Long before.'

Rose looks up at the clergyman once more, her eyes pleading with him, welling up with tears. She fancies that, as she glances at him, something softens in his expression.

'Tell me more about this "George", then,' says Featherstone, guiding Rose further along the path.

⁓

Decimus Webb and Sergeant Bartleby reach the King's Road gate of Cremorne Gardens. The entrance is still busy with carriages collecting and disgorging the Gardens' nocturnal habitués, with the result that it takes the two policemen some time to fight their way through the milling crowd.

'I shall go and inquire after Mr. Boon,' says Webb, 'in case he has heard anything from Featherstone.'

'Are you worried about his safety, sir?' asks the sergeant.

'I no longer feel quite as certain as I once did about Featherstone's state of mind, I confess,' replies Webb. 'In any case, speak to all the men on duty. If anyone so much as glimpses Featherstone, they must detain him.'

'Shall I tell them on what grounds, sir?'

'Just tell them to watch out for sharp objects, Sergeant.'

———

'Do you know what they think of you, Miss Perfitt?' asks Featherstone, as they come towards the river esplanade, where the last steamboat of the night is moored by the pier. 'Do you know what they imagine, these men and women that we pass, as they watch the pair of us here, strolling in the moonlight?'

'No, sir,' replies Rose.

'They believe you to be a whore, Miss Perfitt. They believe that you have sold your virtue to an ageing old man. And are they far from wrong?'

Rose blushes, uncertain how she might answer.

'Ah,' says Featherstone, as they continue by the riverside, 'here is the maze. As twisted and crooked as the path upon which you have been walking.'

'I promise, I will make amends,' says Rose, pleadingly, 'just do not speak to Papa before I do. I will tell him about George and everything, I promise.'

'Come,' says Featherstone, 'let us go inside.'

'Into the maze?' says Rose, puzzled.

'Yes,' replies Featherstone, all but dragging Rose along, 'I think it is quite apt.'

—

'You are telling me, sir,' says John Boon, 'that I have a certified lunatic running around the Gardens, and his name is Featherstone?'

Webb grimaces. 'I believe it is possible.'

'Well, this is news,' says Boon with heavy sarcasm. 'You startle me, sir. You positively astound me.'

'We now have reason to suspect the Reverend is The Cutter, sir, that is the point. I am just a little concerned he may have come back here. Your man on the gates has not seem him, but if he has proved adept at getting in and out unnoticed before . . .'

'Quite,' replies Boon. 'You know, I will be writing to the Commissioner about your conduct, Inspector. You could have arrested the infernal fellow days ago.'

'On what grounds, sir? We require some evidence, you must appreciate that.'

Boon snorts. 'I hope whatever poor woman he next assaults may appreciate it too.'

—

The Reverend Featherstone comes to a halt in the centre of the maze, a clearing about ten feet square. Lit by lanterns, suspended from iron supports that arch above it, the clearing contains two stone benches and reveals four exits back into the neatly crafted corridors between the tall yew hedges.

250

'You know the maze rather well, Miss Perfitt?' he remarks.

'I used to come and play here, as a child, sir.'

Featherstone scowls. 'I see. An unfortunate cradling.'

'We did nothing wrong, sir. I am sure respectable people have always come here, during the day at least.'

Featherstone shakes his head, grabbing Rose by the arms, and setting her down on one of the benches. 'Respectable people? What respectability is there, wretched girl, in imbibing spirituous liquor? In coarse dances and crude entertainments? What respectability is there, when decent girls of tender years squander their virtue? When they are seduced by some cold-blooded villain? What then?'

'I do not know, sir,' replies Rose. 'Please, you are hurting me.'

'I am trying to make you understand, Miss Perfitt. To comprehend the nature of your sin. If you might only show some true contrition—'

'But I love him, sir. Can that be wrong?'

'You are in love with the devil, Miss Perfitt. Who do you imagine lies behind such seduction, eh? The Great Enemy that lurks in the heart of every man.'

Rose squirms in Featherstone's grip. 'What are you doing?' she exclaims, her voice a mixture of anger and, all of a sudden, a tremor of fear.

'I am sorry, Miss Perfitt. If you will not repent, I fear you must become an object lesson,' says Featherstone emphatically, holding her arm with one hand, whilst the other reaches into his coat pocket, pulling out a gleaming pair of scissors.

'Any luck, Sergeant?' asks Webb, finding Bartleby by the Crystal Platform.

'I've passed word round, sir. I'm not that sure he's here. There was a constable that saw an elderly gentlemen – in regular get-up, not a clergyman – with a young woman, near the esplanade. He thought the fellow was a bit old for . . . well, for Cremorne. I had a quick look round, couldn't see anything, sir. I don't think that was him – doesn't normally keep company with the girls before he goes for them, does he?'

Webb sighs. 'Do you think I have made a mess of this whole business, Bartleby?'

'Not if we can catch him, sir,' replies Bartleby.

'Thank you for your loyalty, Sergeant,' says Webb, wearily. 'Still, I think we are done for the night.'

———

Rose Perfitt's gaze is transfixed by the shining blades. If she suddenly understands the danger of her situation, it is only through a deep sinking sensation in the very pit of her stomach, rather than from any rational assessment. Instinctively, she tries to struggle free, but Featherstone slaps her fiercely across the face, enough to disorientate her, sending her stumbling across the bench.

'Listen to me, Miss Perfitt,' says Featherstone, grabbing at his victim's hair, ignoring the careful pinning that holds it in place. 'Listen,' he says in a hoarse whisper, roughly chopping at the roots with the scissors, drawing blood as he does so. 'Only when men see what lies behind the fresh cheeks and curls of girls like you, will they understand the corruption in this place . . .'

Rose Perfitt does not listen. Instead, she screams –

an incoherent cry that resembles no spoken word –
and kicks out with her legs. More through chance
than design, her boot lands squarely upon her
attacker's shin, causing him to stumble and loosen his
grip. She squirms loose and dashes towards the nearest
opening in the hedge. But even before she has gone
a yard, she can feel something tugging at the base of
her skirts, and the sound of a blade ripping through
the material. She glances over her shoulder, to see the
clergyman, having fallen on his knees, grabbing her
dress, slashing wildly at her legs, cutting at her exposed
petticoats. She reaches back and pulls sharply at the
cloth, desperately willing it to tear. And, after what
seems to her like an age – though it can only be an
instant – it obliges.

A strange feeling of exultancy overwhelms her as
she runs headlong into the maze, her hair cropped
like some prisoner in Newgate, her legs half exposed.
Everything seems a mad blur as she runs through the
labyrinth, with hardly a thought to her direction.
And, although she knows each twist and turn perfectly
well when she is in her right senses, Rose soon becomes
lost.

She slows down, trying to find her bearings; but it
proves impossible; each turning is much like another.
Nonetheless, she keeps going, until, confounded, she
comes to a dead end.

Finally, she stops and turns around, her heart still
pounding. Then she hears the sound of footsteps on
the gravel path.

'Miss Perfitt?'

It is the clergyman's voice. Desperately, she tries to
find some opening in the hedge; but she finds it is as
solid as any brick wall and she only succeeds in
scratching her hands.

The black-suited figure of Featherstone turns the corner.

'I am afraid, Miss Perfitt, you cannot escape me.'

She stays perfectly still as the clergyman approaches, more cautious this time, the scissors raised before him. There is something almost perversely mesmerising in the fixed look in his eyes, the grim determination in his face.

Then a voice breaks the silence. 'Rose!'

Rose Perfitt, however, can hardly find the strength to speak.

'Rose!' exclaims George Nelson, running up behind Featherstone. 'Was that you? I saw you come—'

Nelson stops in mid-sentence. He is quick enough to see the scissors as Featherstone turns and lunges towards him. He should be, moreover, younger and stronger than the clergyman. But there is something frenzied and frantic in Featherstone's assault that catches him off guard, the cold metal inches from his arm, even as he tries to throw his assailant to one side.

Rose watches, rooted to the spot, as the two men struggle, Featherstone pushing Nelson into the hedge. It becomes difficult to make out who has the upper hand until, without warning, something in the clergyman seems to give way, and he falls back, clutching his stomach. Rose watches, mute, as a sickly choking sound emerges from Featherstone's throat, and he collapses to the ground, blood soaking through his fingers, his hands vainly trying to stem a crimson flood from his belly.

As for George Nelson, he drops the blood-stained scissors, his face quite gaunt.

And then comes the sound of footsteps once more,

and two police constables of T Division, truncheons raised, appear in the narrow corridor.

'Bloody hell!' exclaims one to the other. 'We've only got him, Charlie. We've got The Cutter!'

CHAPTER THIRTY-EIGHT

Decimus Webb looks on as the steamboat shudders noisily into life, chugging away from Cremorne pier, gliding into the darkness until only its red warning lamp is visible. The light becomes smaller and smaller, fading as the boat passes Battersea Bridge, as if drowning in the murky river. Webb turns to his sergeant.

'Is that the last?' he asks.

'The Gardens should be empty now, sir,' says Bartleby.

'Except for Miss Rose Perfitt,' replies Webb.

'What do you make of it, sir?'

'I don't know,' replies Webb. 'It cannot be a coincidence. I do not believe it. From what the constable told me . . . well, let us go and speak to her; at all events, she cannot stay here all night.'

Bartleby nods his assent. The two policemen walk back along the esplanade and into the Gardens. Their route takes them past the Crystal Platform, past the twin tiers of supper-boxes that surround it and along another path that leads to the Cremorne Hotel, an old waterside mansion adjoining the pleasure grounds.

In fact, the building itself, though constructed in a grand style, is a little run-down and shabby. Once famous for its Sunday table d'hôte and The Cremorne Sherry, it is common knowledge that the hotel now possesses a rather dubious reputation. For even the greatest supporters of Cremorne have occasionally questioned what goes on behind the muslin curtains of its four private rooms – known by the romantic names of the *Gem, Star, Rose* and *Pearl* – whilst others have openly speculated upon the character of the women who frequent its crush bar. But none of this matters to Decimus Webb, who is merely content to find Rose Perfitt seated indoors, in the empty space of the hotel's ground-floor saloon. Her dress is still in tatters but a blanket lies about her shoulders, and a glass of warm negus is clutched in her hands.

'Miss Perfitt?' says Webb, stepping tentatively into the room, nodding to the policeman who stands watch near by.

Rose Perfitt looks up. Her face is red and flushed, her eyes bloodshot and verging upon tearful.

'Yes,' she replies, quietly.

'You remember me, perhaps?'

'You're the policeman,' she replies.

'That is correct. My name is Webb. Forgive me, Miss Perfitt, but this is a serious business, and I have no time to waste on pleasantries. Are you capable of discussing what transpired this evening?'

Rose Perfitt seems to hesitate for a moment, but assents. Webb, in turn, pulls up one of the saloon's chairs, and sits down in front of her.

'Can you tell me first, Miss Perfitt, how you came to be in the Gardens?'

'I was running away, Inspector,' says Rose, in a matter of fact tone.

'I see,' replies Webb, a little non-plussed. 'From whom?'

'Papa said he was going to take me away from Chelsea; I don't know why. I would have missed the Season! I said I would not leave. We had an argument.'

'And so you thought you would run away to Cremorne Gardens? Forgive me, Miss, I don't quite follow.'

'I . . . I suppose I was not thinking, Inspector. You must consider me very foolish.'

Webb tilts his head. 'I reserve judgment on that score, Miss. And so you went into the Gardens alone?'

'Yes.'

'Have you been there before?'

A pause.

'Not at night, no.'

'I see,' says Webb. 'Please, continue.'

I was walking by the Marionette Theatre, and Reverend Featherstone found me there. He took my arm; told me I was, well, that I should go back to my parents. The Reverend – is he . . . dead?'

'Yes, I'm afraid so, Miss. Did you know him well?' asks Webb.

'His wife used to call upon Mama, Inspector. And we went to hear his sermons on occasion. I cannot say I knew him well. If I had known the truth about him, I would have . . . well, I do not know.'

'The truth being . . .?'

'Inspector,' says Rose, firmly, 'don't you see? He was The Cutter! That is why he dragged me into the wretched maze; he meant to kill me.'

'Rest assured, I can see you have been through the wars, Miss. So he took you into the maze?'

'Yes,' replies Rose, wearily. 'He attacked me like a lunatic. I ran but I lost my way. Then . . . then a man followed us. He must have heard me scream.'

'This man, did you recognise him?'

Rose hesitates once more, but only for an instant. 'No.'

'And then?' prompts Webb.

'I think that scared him. He seemed to go wild, Inspector. He took the scissors and he went and . . . he cut himself . . . I am sorry, I cannot . . .'

Rose Perfitt shuts her eyes, rubbing them with her hand.

'Let me be quite clear, Miss Perfitt,' says Webb, steadily. 'Are you saying that Featherstone killed himself? That it was suicide?'

Rose Perfitt nods, her lips trembling.

'The fellow who came up to you, Miss Perfitt, is a ticket-of-leave man, known to the police. A convict by the name of Nelson. We have him under arrest – so you are quite safe from him. Now, are you telling me that Nelson had nothing to do with the Reverend's death?'

'Yes,' says Rose, looking up again. 'Reverend Featherstone must have known that he had been discovered; that he could not get away. I suppose that is why . . . why he did it. If you had seen his eyes, Inspector. He was demented.'

'Very well,' says Webb. 'That will be all, for the moment, I think.'

'May I go now, Inspector? I suppose I must go home.'

'Finish your drink, Miss Perfitt. I had better accompany you. I won't be too long.'

Webb finds George Nelson seated in a private room, not far from the saloon, his hands handcuffed behind his back, and two policemen at his side.

'Mr. Nelson, we meet once more,' says Webb.

'Oh, it's you, is it?' replies Nelson.

'Yes, sir. Aren't you fortunate? Now, perhaps you'd care to tell me what happened.'

'And maybe,' replies Nelson, 'you might have your bully boys here take these blasted cuffs off.'

Webb ponders for a moment then nods. One of the constables retrieves a key, and releases the metal bonds.

'I'm obliged,' says Nelson, without much sincerity.

'I should think you'd be used to it,' says Bartleby, 'down Pentonville.'

Nelson smirks. 'Nah, they have proper heavy iron there, old man. None of your daisy chains.'

'Now, why did you kill him, eh?' asks Webb bluntly, without further preliminaries.

'Kill who?'

'The clergyman. You gutted him, did you not, with those scissors? A nice piece of work for a reformed man.'

Nelson chuckles to himself. 'You'd like that, wouldn't you? Who says so?'

'Never mind that,' says Webb.

'I never killed no-one. And I'll lay odds you know it, too.'

'How should I?' replies Webb.

'Well, you've got a witness, ain't you?'

Webb shrugs. 'Perhaps. If you are so innocent, tell me, then, why were you in the maze?'

'I was clearing the grounds, looking for stragglers, like we do every night. I heard a girl shouting; sounded like she was in trouble. I went and had a look, to see if I could do anything.'

'Very valiant of you,' remarks Bartleby.

'Thank'ee,' replies Nelson, tipping an imaginary hat in acknowledgement.

'So you went into the maze?' asks Webb. 'You found her pretty quickly, it seems.'

'I know the grounds, don't I? I found her all right – and that old devil, too. Good thing I came along, I reckon. I probably deserve a medal.'

'And what happened then?'

'The old man lost his nerve, I suppose. Did for himself.'

'Simple as that?' asks Webb. 'Plunged the blades into his own belly?'

'I reckon so,' replies George Nelson.

'You had blood on your hands.'

'I tried to help him. It was too late.'

'How convenient for you. The constable here,' says Webb, nodding in the direction of the nearest policeman, 'has you down for the Cremorne Cutter, Mr. Nelson, not the old man.'

Nelson shrugs. 'Then he's an idiot.'

The policeman in question visibly bristles.

'Still,' continues Webb, 'I think we better have you down the station house, just to be safe. We shall let the Coroner decide. Put the cuffs back on him, Constable.'

The constable readily obeys with a certain degree of vigour that has George Nelson regret his remark. But the convict does not complain, allowing himself to be shackled.

'Bring him this way, if you will,' says Webb, quitting the room, and walking down the hotel corridor, in the direction of the saloon. Bartleby follows, with Nelson in the custody of the two policemen, one holding each arm. When Webb comes up to the saloon, rather than proceeding directly to the hotel lobby, he opens the double doors that lead inside.

Rose Perfitt immediately rises from her seat, a look of surprise on her face.

'Inspector! Whatever are you doing? I told you – he . . . that man . . . he is quite innocent.'

'Just routine, Miss. Nothing to worry about,' replies Webb. 'We'll soon have you home.'

Rose, speechless, sits down. But not before a glance passes between her and George Nelson, who slightly shakes his head in disapproval, as if to say 'no, don't say a word'.

It is just a glance; it lasts the briefest of moments. Still, it does not escape Decimus Webb's notice and, when they have left the room, he allows himself a brief smile before he calls over Bartleby.

'Take him to the station house, Sergeant. Release him in an hour or two.'

'Sir?'

'I have seen all I need to see.'

CHAPTER THIRTY-NINE

It is two o'clock in the morning by the time Decimus Webb returns Rose Perfitt to Edith Grove. With unusual tact, mindful of prying neighbours, he descends to the area and rings the tradesman's bell outside the kitchen door, keeping Rose by his side. Unsurprisingly, given the hour, it takes repeated efforts to rouse the Perfitts' maid-servant from her sleep. Nonetheless, Webb perseveres and, after a minute or two, when Richards appears, he has the consolation of knowing the whole household must also have been awakened. The theory is swiftly proven by the appearance of Mr. Perfitt, in his dressing-gown, a protective poker in hand, treading carefully down the kitchen steps, a few seconds after his maid-servant.

'What the devil is this?' he exclaims, as the maid lets them in. 'Good Lord, Rose!'

'The good news, sir,' says Webb, shepherding Rose Perfitt into the kitchen, 'is that your daughter is virtually unharmed, despite appearances.'

'But what in heaven's name does this mean?' asks Mr. Perfitt.

'Well, we found your daughter in Cremorne Gardens, sir. Apparently she was in the process of running away from home. As for the condition of her clothes and hair, as I say, I believe she is unharmed. It is something of a long story.'

Mr. Perfitt nods, although his expression is one more of disbelief than anything else. 'Rose, are you quite all right?'

'Yes, Papa,' replies Rose, quietly.

'Then I think you had best go to your room, while I talk to Inspector Webb. Richards – you had best help her.'

Rose readily assents and quits the room with the maid, leaving the two men alone.

'I think we should talk, sir,' says Webb, 'but, in this instance, I would rather your wife were present.'

⁓

'I fear we have been foolish, Inspector,' says Charles Perfitt, having heard an abbreviated explanation of the night's events.

Webb raises his eyebrows, turning his gaze from the drawing-room mantelpiece to his reluctant host and hostess.

'How so, sir?'

'Rose has always had an unfortunate interest in the goings on at the Gardens,' interjects Mrs. Perfitt. 'Such places, to a fanciful young girl, may possess an unfortunate fascination.'

'We should have removed her from their influence long ago,' continues Mr. Perfitt. 'But we thought she was quite cured of it.'

'You make it sound like she has some disease, sir,' says Webb. 'Cremorne Fever, perhaps.'

'You may find this amusing, Inspector,' replies Mr. Perfitt. 'I assuredly do not.'

'No,' says Webb. 'Quite. However, you might consider it was not so much the Gardens as Reverend

Featherstone who is to blame for your daughter's condition – at least, as far as this evening goes.'

'And you are convinced Reverend Featherstone was The Cutter?' asks Mrs. Perfitt.

'It seems rather likely. We have some additional evidence – it will all come out at the inquest.'

'Inquest?'

'Why, there must be a Coroner's inquest, ma'am, suicide or not. Your daughter will be the principal witness. I should have thought that would be obvious.'

Mrs. Perfitt looks aghast. 'Must this all come out? Think of the scandal, Inspector!'

'It can and it must, ma'am,' replies Webb emphatically. 'And, as for the scandal, I fear your daughter has only herself to blame.'

'But Inspector!' protests Mrs. Perfitt. 'She is not well. You saw how fragile she is when you came to the Prince's Ground. If our good name is to be dragged through the papers – frankly, I am not sure she can bear it!'

Mr. Perfitt, however, touches his wife lightly on the arm. 'Enough, Caroline. Please.'

'I am only thinking of Rose, Charles,' says Mrs. Perfitt. 'You might do the same.'

'I think, my dear, we must be grateful she is still with us at all. Our position in society is not everything. We must live with what Rose has done. Besides, it is clearly not the inspector's fault.'

Mrs. Perfitt bows to her husband's will, albeit reluctantly, and falls silent.

'Is there anything else, Inspector?' asks Mr. Perfitt.

'Ah, yes,' replies Webb. 'I neglected to mention the man who found her. Saved her life, most likely.'

'Who?' asks Mr. Perfitt. 'I should be happy to thank him for it.'

267

'George Nelson,' says Webb, observing the Perfitts' faces closely. Both seem suitably shocked and a silence descends upon the room.

'Nelson? An odd coincidence,' says Mr. Perfitt at last.

'Is it, sir? I do not suppose that your daughter has ever been acquainted with Mr. Nelson?'

Mr. Perfitt reddens a little. 'Are you insinuating something, Inspector? If so, I'd rather you came out with it.'

'No, sir. It's just I rather formed an impression that they knew each other.'

'Did Rose tell you this?' asks Mrs. Perfitt.

'No, ma'am. Quite the opposite.'

'Well then,' replies Mrs. Perfitt. 'There is your answer.'

Webb shrugs. 'I have been wrong before, ma'am. Well, I had best leave you be. We will notify you about the inquest directly – but it will be tomorrow or the day after.'

'So you believe he killed poor Jane Budge, and his own wife?' says Mrs. Perfitt, as Webb gets up to leave.

'Who, ma'am?'

'Reverend Featherstone, Inspector! Who else?'

'You would think so, ma'am,' replies Webb, as if still musing over the question in his own mind, 'wouldn't you?'

~

Mrs. Perfitt walks into her daughter's room without knocking, her head held high. She finds Rose seated on her bed, dressed in her nightgown once more, staring into the corner of the room. An oil-lamp burns on the nearby dresser, and the glow of the flame seems to emphasise her puffy, swollen eyes and red cheeks. Rose gets up as her mother enters.

'Mama, I'm sorry, truly I am.'

'It's him, isn't it?' says Mrs. Perfitt, her voice a flat, controlled monotone. 'Nelson?'

Rose nods her head.

'I should have seen the signs. What a fool I was.'

'I'm sorry, Mama, I love him; I always have done. I can't help it. You see, he wants to marry me.'

'Marry?' says Mrs. Perfitt, incredulous.

'I know Papa won't agree, not yet. But if you were to talk to him . . .'

The stiff resolve in Mrs. Perfitt's stance seems to suddenly ebb away. She takes a step backwards, leaning against the door, taking a deep breath. For a second, she closes her eyes, as if to rally her strength. When she opens them again, the look she gives her daughter is somewhere between pity and contempt.

'You stupid, stupid, little girl,' she says, spitting out the words. 'After all we have done for you. How could you!'

'Mama!' protests Rose, her tears welling up once more.

But Mrs. Perfitt does not answer. She merely turns on her heel, quits the room and slams the door behind her.

And then there is the sound of a key being turned in the lock.

CHAPTER FORTY

The Coroner's inquest upon the death of Augustus J. Featherstone is convened in the Cremorne Hotel, being the nearest public building to the place of his demise. The venue is the hotel's modest ball-room. Decimus Webb, amongst the first to arrive, looks over the efforts of John Boon's staff in creating the temporary court. A substantial desk has, it appears, been moved from one of the private rooms, to accommodate the literary requirements of the Coroner; a trestle-table, likewise, has been laid on for the benefit of his officers. As for the jury and general public, chairs from the saloon and lesser bars, requisitioned for the purposes of justice, lie arranged in neat rows, in a good approximation to the plan of the Old Bailey. Decimus Webb sits down next to Bartleby, in the seats reserved for witnesses, and wonders to himself where a distinct smell of liquor is coming from. Then he realises – the chairs still carry with them the spirituous, tobacco-heavy scent of the saloon.

The room soon fills up. Such is the interest in the deceased clergyman that all the seats are quickly taken and, after a short interval, the walls are all but obscured by curious members of the public. Some are the usual habitués of such public spectacles; others

271

Webb recognises as members of St. Mark's College. Many of those seated are respectable female residents of Edith Grove and its environs. Almost without exception, they turn their gaze to Rose Perfitt and her parents as the three of them enter the room from a side door, and take their place amongst the witnesses. Webb himself watches Rose closely, not least to see whether she turns her head towards George Nelson, seated a few feet away. But she keeps her gaze directly ahead, rather unnaturally rigid in her posture.

'Nerves, do you think?' says Bartleby, observing his interest.

'I should imagine,' replies Webb. 'She is about to confess before all her friends and neighbours that she was caught wandering about the Gardens, unaccompanied, at midnight. I am sure some will consider that a greater scandal than anything Featherstone might have done. He was,' continues Webb in a sardonic tone, 'a man of the cloth, after all.'

'Why do you think he did it?' whispers Bartleby.

'It was his scheme to close the Gardens, Sergeant; or, at least, to teach Chelsea's loose women a lesson. He even told me that he thought people might "learn" from it. I should have paid closer attention; I fear, looking back, he was almost taunting me. I wonder what he thought when he received those schoolboy threats; he must have found it rather amusing.'

'A queer business, sir.'

'Quite. I can only imagine the attacks became some kind of morbid compulsion with him. That is why he could not help himself at the ball.'

'And what about Jane Budge, and his wife? Do you think that's why he did for them? They discovered his secret?'

Webb bites his lip. 'You are getting carried away again, Sergeant.'

'Sir?'

'For the last time. Featherstone was with me outside Cremorne when Budge died. Likewise, it seems unlikely he killed his wife whilst he was simultaneously at a parish meeting.'

'You don't think he could have arranged it?' says Bartleby. 'So he had an alibi?'

'That, Sergeant, would require an accomplice. And I doubt that very much.'

'Still, someone must have done it, if it wasn't him. '

'Your mental faculties are as alert as ever, Bartleby. Yes, for all his madness, I do not think Featherstone was a killer. There is a murderer still out there, I am quite certain of it. Of course, whether we choose to make that clear to the Coroner is another matter. Now, hush. Here comes our man.'

The Coroner, it turns out, is a rather pragmatic individual, not given to the speechifying of some of his colleagues in the metropolis. Thus, he goes through the preliminaries of the proceedings at a brisk pace, briefly outlining the duties of the jury and keeping all else to a minimum. The customary visit to the scene of the tragedy is denied the jurymen – principally to avoid the possibility of the entire court becoming lost in Cremorne's maze – and instead the novel expedient is discovered of drawing a chalk sketch upon the ball-room floor, outlining the dimensions of the particular dead end where the Reverend Featherstone met his Maker. All in all, for a Coroner's inquiry, the hearing begins quite swiftly and, once the Coroner has made his opening remarks, witnesses are called. The first is Rose Perfitt, who takes the appointed seat.

'Miss Rose Perfitt, resident at 37, Edith Grove, Chelsea?'

'Yes, sir.'

'You witnessed the death of the Reverend Featherstone?'

'Yes, sir.'

'Can you tell the court how you came to be in Cremorne Gardens on the night in question?'

'I had had an argument with my father, sir. I decided to run away from home.'

The sound of excited whispers, exchanged between respectable parties, echoes round the room.

'And so you proceeded, by yourself, to Cremorne Gardens?'

'Yes, sir.'

'To what purpose?'

A couple of the gentlemen of the press smirk to themselves.

'I do not know, sir. I did not think there was any harm in it.'

There is an audible guffaw from the back of the room. The Coroner looks sternly in that direction, whilst Rose Perfitt blushes.

'And how did you come across Reverend Featherstone?'

As Rose Perfitt answers the question, Bartleby whispers to Webb. 'She's taking it better than I thought she would, sir. Quite composed, all things considered.'

Webb frowns. 'Yes, she is.'

———

'You are George Nelson, resident in lodgings at 14, Albion Terrace.'

'Yes I am, sir.'

'You are by profession a labourer at Cremorne Gardens.'

'Yes, sir.'

'And on ticket-of-leave, is that correct? From Pentonville gaol?'

'Yes, sir.'

A murmur of concern in the court. The Coroner raises his hand.

'I would ask the jury to be conscious that whilst Mr. Nelson is a convicted felon, he is an important witness in this inquiry.'

'Thank you, sir,' adds Nelson. 'And I should like to say that I have served my time and I have the greatest respect for Her Majesty's justice.'

———

The inquest lasts for a good three hours. At last, an intermission of a half-hour is called, during which the jury may elect a foreman and deliberate upon their decision. The majority of the crowd decamp to the saloon, where the bar has cannily been opened for the sale of sandwiches and refreshments, albeit of a temperance variety. Webb once more watches Rose Perfitt, as she gets up, for any sign that may pass between her and George Nelson. Her mother, however, swiftly ushers her away.

'Care for a drink, sir?' asks Bartleby.

Webb does not reply, distracted, as George Nelson walks by.

'Morning, Inspector,' says Nelson, with a smirk.

'You do not fool me, Mr. Nelson,' replies Webb.

'I don't need to,' says Nelson, as he walks in the direction of the saloon. 'I ain't done nothing wrong. I got my ticket to think of.'

Webb takes a deep breath as Nelson walks off.

'Rose Perfitt went to Cremorne to meet him, Sergeant. I would swear an oath on it.'

'You didn't though, did you, sir? You could have mentioned it, to his worship over there.'

'I think it better they both think we do not suspect them. I am just not sure what it all means.'

'You think he killed Featherstone, then, sir? And she's lying to protect him?'

'It had crossed my mind. But, you see, Featherstone was The Cutter, I am sure of that. The business in Greenwich Park, the hair, everything we know about him. What possible motive is there?'

'Perhaps he found out about them, threatened to expose them. Sir! What if that's it?'

'But you see, Sergeant, if Rose Perfitt was quite willing to elope with Nelson, regardless, what sense does it make? None.'

Bartleby frowns, puzzled. He does not get an opportunity to reply, since he is interrupted by the sound of a loud, repeated banging, coming from the nearby hall.

'What the blazes is that?' asks Webb, as the two policemen walk briskly from the room. They find a small circle of people has gathered round a nearby door. Outside the door stands Charles Perfitt, repeatedly banging his fists against the wood panels.

'Rose!'

Webb steps forward.

'Sir, whatever is the matter?'

'Inspector!' replies Perfitt, breathless. 'You must do something! Rose . . . she went to use the convenience . . . she must have fainted.'

Webb looks over his shoulder, beckoning Bartleby towards the door. 'Break it down, Sergeant.'

Sergeant Bartleby appears not overly enthusiastic

276

to put his physical prowess to the test. Nonetheless, he barges at the door, with his shoulder braced, twice, then three times, until the latch inside gives way and it flies open.

Mr. and Mrs. Perfitt come up behind Webb and Bartleby, as they look around the small room, which contains merely a water-closet, a mirror and a sink. Rose Perfitt, however, is nowhere to be seen – though there is an impressive view of the lawn outside, through the open window.

CHAPTER FORTY-ONE

'There is little further I can say regarding the distressing nature of this case. It seems beyond any doubt that his wife's death unbalanced the mind of Augustus Featherstone and there can be no doubt that the verdict of the jury – suicide whilst in a state of temporary mental derangement – is correct and proper. The evidence presented by Inspector Webb of Scotland Yard has been of great assistance, but it is not the place of this court to pass any additional judgment . . .'

The voice of the Coroner resounds through the ballroom. Neither Decimus Webb nor the Perfitts are there to hear it. Instead, they stand outside the hotel, looking out across the Gardens.

'Perhaps you had better take your wife home, sir,' suggests Webb.

'I am quite all right, Inspector,' replies Mrs. Perfitt, though her expression is rather bloodless.

'As you wish, ma'am, although I am not sure there is much to be done here. Ah, here is Bartleby.'

Sergeant Bartleby, in fact, comes jogging briskly down the nearest path.

'Nowhere to be found, sir,' he says, breathlessly. 'I've left the men on it, but we can't find her anywhere in the Gardens.'

'And Nelson?'

'Vanished, sir.'

Mrs. Perfitt seems to grow visibly paler. 'Take me home, Charles,' she says at last.

'Yes, my dear. I think that is best,' replies Mr. Perfitt. But before he can take his wife's arm, Webb interrupts him.

'I think we may as well drop the pretence, sir. All things considered.'

'Pretence?' says Mr. Perfitt.

'Your daughter's plan was to elope with George Nelson, was it not? That was why she came to the Gardens. And now she has accomplished her purpose, albeit in a rather melodramatic manner. I assume you have been keeping a close watch upon her at home?'

Mrs. Perfitt exchanges an anxious look with her husband.

'I think,' says Mr. Perfitt, 'it might be best if you came home with us, Inspector. We might have some privacy there, at least.'

───

'It began five years ago, Inspector,' says Charles Perfitt, pacing in front of the hearth in his drawing-room. 'Rose made the acquaintance of George Nelson through Jane Budge. I believe they met him in the Gardens.'

'The Gardens?' asks Webb, incredulously.

'During daylight, naturally,' replies Mrs. Perfitt. 'Jane and I used to take Rose on walks around the grounds. The place was more respectable in those days.'

'And they formed a close bond? '

'I would not say that,' replies Mrs. Perfitt. 'His interest—'

'His interest lay elsewhere, Inspector,' interjects Mr. Perfitt. 'You already know the facts of the matter. He would visit Jane Budge, in secret, just as we told you. But, in the end, we discovered Rose had been let in on their secret and had developed a girlish infatuation with him. Young girls of that age are given to such things. Rose has always had a foolish romantic nature; and I suppose he was a handsome young man. I expect it flattered him to have such a beautiful and tender young girl interested in him.'

'And now, how do things stand?'

'Now, Inspector,' says Charles Perfitt, 'he is using her to punish me. He believes it was my fault he went to gaol and so he has rekindled this unfortunate passion in her. He wishes to rob me of my daughter and see me suffer.'

'It doesn't look like she was kidnapped, though, sir,' says Bartleby. 'You don't think he . . . well, that they . . .?'

Mrs. Perfitt casts a withering glance towards the sergeant. 'If you mean that my daughter went of her own free will, I am sure she believes that she did. But he is a vicious criminal, Sergeant. Good Lord, why are we here talking? You must do something. Inspector – now you know the whole wretched business, will you not act?'

'I might be more inclined if you had told me all this before, instead of lying, ma'am,' says Webb, warily.

'That my daughter should have been infatuated with a common criminal is hardly something I care to make public knowledge, Inspector.'

'A little late for such discretion now, ma'am, at all events. Still, as for doing something, I am not sure there is much we can do in cases of seduction, if the girl appears complicit.'

'Surely the law is on our side?' says Mr. Perfitt, desperation in his voice.

'Up to a point, sir. The girl is below the age of discretion, and I suppose she belongs in legal possession of her father. But whether a magistrate would be willing to have her moved back here by force – well, I would not be quite sure of it, not if she protests.'

'We could demand it, Inspector, surely? She is mine by law, as you say.'

Webb shrugs. 'That would be your prerogative, sir. If you think it best. As for Nelson, if she has left voluntarily, then there is no crime committed. Not yet, at least. A marriage would be a different matter, if, say, he were to give misleading particulars as to your consent.'

'Marriage!' exclaims Mrs. Perfitt. 'God forbid! Charles – we must do something!'

'We will try and find her, ma'am, rest assured,' says Webb. 'If nothing else, I still have a couple of questions I should like to ask her. And perhaps you may persuade her to see sense, without recourse to the law.'

'Questions?' asks Mrs. Perfitt.

'Oh, I'm sorry, ma'am. Nothing to trouble yourself with. It's merely this Cutter business. You see, I have the feeling, ma'am,' says Webb, 'there's something that I'm missing. Like a desiccated puzzle that's lost one of its pieces.'

'The only thing missing, Inspector, is my daughter. If you are done, perhaps you might expend your mental energies in locating her, rather than upon ridiculous metaphor. As for myself, if that is everything, I'm afraid you must excuse me; I fear I have something of a headache coming on.'

Mrs. Perfitt gets up and, with a brief nod to her husband, hastily leaves the room.

Mr. Perfitt, meanwhile, looks at Webb. 'Forgive my wife, Inspector. This business with Nelson is a terrible strain. You will try to help us get Rose back? You know what sort of man Nelson is.'

'I will do my best, sir.'

—

'You weren't wrong, sir,' says Bartleby, as the two policemen walk back along Edith Grove.

'Thank you, Sergeant,' replies Webb. 'I do appreciate credit where credit is due. Now, may I have some suggestions for how we locate Rose Perfitt and her wretched paramour.'

'I was wondering about cabs. We weren't far behind them but they made a clean break of it. If I was them, I'd grab a ride, quick as I could.'

'A good idea, Sergeant. Make that your task for this afternoon.'

Bartleby agrees. Webb, in turn, falls silent for a few moments, lost in thought.

'They're still hiding something, Sergeant,' he says at last. 'I can almost taste it. This business with Jane Budge, Nelson and the girl. There's something there. I know there is.'

'I suppose they don't much fancy him as a prospective son-in-law.'

'He can't marry her until she's twenty-one, not without some measure of fraud, and that would breach his licence. He has been quite meticulous about that so far; I don't think he would make such a stupid mistake. No that is not it. It's something we haven't uncovered; something important. It may be the key to this whole affair.'

'I thought you didn't believe in instinct, sir,' says Bartleby.

'It is not instinct when every inquiry leads to the same place, Sergeant, however mysterious it all seems. Rose Perfitt is at the centre of this, I swear.'

'Centre of what, sir?'

'Yes, well, quite. That is the question. What are we missing, eh?'

CHAPTER FORTY-TWO

Alfred Budge keeps odd hours. His position as potman at the Old King's Head is, in fact, something of a sinecure, a repayment of sorts for the sheer volume of liquor consumed during a lifetime of dedicated imbibing. Thus he is at liberty to come and go much as he pleases and it is not unusual to see him quit his post and totter homewards along the Battersea Road at any hour of the night, whenever the fancy takes him. Indeed, such instances balance out the occasions when he remains in the warm luxury of the public bar from sunset to sunrise, blissfully unconscious of the world around him; with such dedication to his workplace, it is generally considered only fair that he should exercise himself when the mood takes him.

Tonight, after an absence of several nights in a row, he stumbles along the muddy track of Sheepgut Lane at a little past ten o'clock. It is difficult to say what precise obligation draws him back to Budge's Dairy; perhaps some dim recollection of his marriage vows; or the gut desire for a home-cooked meal, rather than the cheap pies and puddings, sold by itinerant merchants, upon which he generally relies for sustenance. Without a doubt, he expects the sharp end of his wife's tongue upon his arrival and, in the dim corner of his drink-addled mind that once stored his capacity for sound judgment, he is probably conscious that he thoroughly deserves to be castigated. Hence, he creeps cautiously up the path to the dairy's front door.

It is a drunk's caution, mind you. A pantomime of tiptoe footsteps, that is twice as clumsy and noisy as the approach of any normal individual. But, for all his mental confusion, Alfred Budge is still surprised to find that the door is not on the latch, but falls open as he knocks upon it.

'Maggie?'

No answer. Inside, the room is as black as pitch, only the shape of his wife visible, sitting in her chair in front of the hearth.

Alfred Budge fumbles for the lucifers in his coat pocket, and strikes one. The tiny spluttering light seems puny in the blackness of the room, and a shiver runs down his spine, as he steps a little closer to the fireplace. Then the smell strikes him; the stink of loose bowels, a rotting lingering stench he associates with the privy at the Old King's Head.

The match singes his fingers and he swears to himself as he blows it out, flicking it to the floor. He is close enough to Margaret Budge now to shake her. But instead he lights another match and looks at her face. He knows in his heart what he will find as he touches her cheek, and her head lolls to one side.

But he can only truly believe it when he sees her dead, lifeless eyes.

—◦—

'You're used to better,' says George Nelson, more as a statement of fact than an apology, leading Rose Perfitt by the hand into a small room.

Rose looks around. Situated above a fishmonger's, a short distance from the Lambeth Road, the room possesses a bed, covered with a grey-looking mattress and sheets, a fire-place with a cracked mirror, suspended above the mantel, and a simple deal table and twin chairs. The floor is bare boards, except for a frayed piece of red drugget that lies beside the bed. And throughout, there is the distinct scent of the ocean.

Rose Perfitt is indeed used to much better. And yet, she clasps hold of George Nelson's arm with earnest enthusiasm.

'Our own room!'

'It stinks but it's all I could get. We'll find something better once your father sees sense.'

Rose nods but already she seems preoccupied by her surroundings. 'I will get some flowers; that will help. And some proper curtains.'

'I told you, Rosie, we won't have money. Not at first.'

'They'll understand in the end,' says Rose, peering through the single sash window that looks onto the street below. 'Mama will, anyway. When we're married. She always says she only wants me to be happy.'

'I'd have liked to have seen their faces.'

'Don't say that,' says Rose, turning to look at him, slightly annoyed.

'No,' says Nelson, smiling. 'You're right. A man shouldn't bear a grudge. Now come here, why don't you, you silly little bitch? You know I love you.'

Rose Perfitt grins.

—

Alfred Budge is not sure what to do.

The lamp. He begins with lighting the lamp. He

fancies that when he lights it, everything will be better. But, when he holds it up, it only shines upon the corpse of his wife, slumped before the empty fireplace, as if waiting for coals to be brought in, for a fire to be started. He stumbles as he sees her, inadvertently leaning against the nearby table, sending a heavy bottle of brandy crashing to the ground. He barely seems to notice it, walking over the broken glass in a daze, crunching it into the floor beneath his boots.

What next?

He checks the back parlour. The room is as cold and damp as ever, and the air almost sobers him up. Death is here too, he can sense it. Not just the coffin of his daughter – though that is still there; he had forgotten about that. The funeral. He must arrange the funeral. Best black feathers. And three little ones, here they are, lying in their cots; he touches the cheek of each infant; cold, dead porcelain.

Something, he thinks, must be done. The police. They will come. They are bound to come.

He goes off in search of a blanket.

~

'Do you really love me, George?'

'You know I do. I said it, didn't I?'

Rose Perfitt stretches out on the bed, content.

'I know, I just like to hear you tell me.'

~

It is almost half-past eleven when Alfred Budge returns to the Battersea Road. He passes by several public houses without a glance to see whether they are open or closed and walks briskly along. Occasionally, he looks over his shoulder. Even when he slips on the pavement, he keeps going, gripping tightly the large bundle of coarse cloth he holds to his chest. He only slows down when he comes to the bridge, treading cautiously down the side road that descends in a steep slope down to the river. Once he is by the wharves he walks purposefully along a familiar stretch of causeway, the timbers creaking beneath his feet. At the end, he drops the bundle and stoops down. He feels a little faint as he bends down, and he has to steady himself with his hand. Distracted, he does not notice the footsteps behind him.

'What's this then?'

Alfred Budge turns his head, to find a cloaked police constable standing over him. He looks down at the bundle, the blanket having fallen open.

'Three little Moses,' says Budge, his voice slurred and indistinct.

The police constable blinks. 'God help us,' he says at last. 'What's your game?'

'God help us,' echoes Alfred Budge.

CHAPTER FORTY-THREE

'Damn me!' exclaims Bartleby, as he enters the front parlour of Budge's Dairy. Webb, likewise, winces and swiftly pulls out a pocket handkerchief, putting it to his mouth.

'Go and open the window, for pity's sake,' mutters Webb, swatting ineffectually at the dozen flies that buzz noisily about the room. 'No wonder that blasted constable stayed outside. If that is what passes for humour in V Division, I am not laughing. Take his number when we leave.'

'Yes, sir,' coughs Bartleby, struggling with the latch on the front window, finally managing to lever it open. He leans his head outside, and takes a deep breath.

Webb, meanwhile, walks over to the corpse of Margaret Budge, the body still seated on the armchair in front of the fire. He notices the broken glass on the floor near by, and briefly bends down to peer at the remains of the bottle. When finished, he motions towards his sergeant.

'Over here,' says Webb imperiously. Bartleby reluctantly obeys.

'You cannot hold your breath for ever, man,' says Webb. 'You may as well train yourself to bear it. Now, tell me, look at her, what is the cause of death?'

Bartleby casts his eyes over the body. 'She's not long

dead, is she, sir? I thought she must be, what with this stink in the place.'

'Correct. A day or two, maybe three at most, I'd hazard. Have a good look, Sergeant, she won't bite.'

Bartleby swallows hard and walks around the chair, gingerly moving Mrs. Budge's arms and legs, tilting her head. Then something on the floor catches his eye.

'Ah. Vomit, sir, dried on the floor here.'

'And on her sleeve, Sergeant. Anything else?'

Bartleby coughs. 'I'd say she soiled herself, sir.'

'Right again. What does this tell us?'

'Well, it's either stomach fever or poison, sir,' replies Bartleby.

'Stomach fever? You are a trusting soul, Sergeant.'

'Just considering the possibilities, sir.'

'There is no sign of convulsions or rictus, so we may eliminate *nux vomica*,' continues Webb. 'My guess would be arsenic.'

Bartleby nods, and coughs once more.

'Very well, Sergeant. The autopsy will tell us. Let us have a look in the back. Perhaps the air will be a little fresher.'

Bartleby willingly agrees and the two men proceed to the back parlour. It is untouched since the previous night, the coffin and empty cots being the principal items of furniture.

'Jane Budge,' says Webb, reading the name upon the wood. 'You had best be grateful they did a decent job of sealing her in, Sergeant, or the odour would be considerably worse.'

'No money to bury her?' suggests Bartleby.

'I wonder. They found a dozen gold sovereigns in Budge's pocket,' remarks Webb, looking at the cots, turning over the dirty linen in each.

'Can he account for it?' asks Bartleby.

292

'The man can barely account for anything, Sergeant. The doctor says it will take him two days to sober up, if the process does not damage him irrevocably. She was his wife, that much seems certain. Kept her business secret, as well she might.'

Bartleby looks down at the empty cots. 'Poor little beggars. She should have been registered.'

'I think you will find, Sergeant, that her kind do not care over much for the finer points of the law. And, I suspect, despite the Act, still no-one much cares to inquire about unwanted infants. They are too much trouble all round.'

'Do you think he killed her?'

'Budge?' Webb allows himself a wry laugh. 'That man could not muster the wits to kill a fly. Not unless it drowned in his beer. And even if he could, I doubt he would choose poison. Tell me, did you notice the broken bottle?'

'In the front, sir?'

'Yes. Brandy. Have a look at the label. It is an excellent name, not the sort of thing one finds in a tuppenny beer-shop or low public. There's an empty purse upon the table too; again, good quality silk. A lady's purse.'

'Stolen?'

'Or payment, for services rendered. What is the price for adoption, these days? Twelve sovereigns sounds plausible. As for the bottle of brandy, I suspect that is payment of a different sort. '

'You've lost me, sir.'

'Yes, well, I am afraid that may be because I am stumbling in the dark myself. Search the house. See if you can find anything of interest. I fear I need a breath of fresh air.'

Bartleby emerges from the house an hour later and finds Webb waiting outside, standing in the lane beside the cab that brought them, reading a piece of note-paper.

'Nothing in there, sir,' says Bartleby. 'Some baby linen, a few knick-knacks. Nothing to help us at all.'

'Hmm?'

'I didn't find anything in the house, sir.'

'Never mind, Sergeant,' says Webb, getting into the cab as he speaks. 'I believe our luck has turned.'

'Sir?'

'Get in, man,' says Webb impatiently, waving the note-paper at his sergeant. 'The Yard's found the cab that Rose Perfitt used – you were right. Dropped her and Nelson on the Lambeth Road. You used to have a beat in Lambeth, did you not?'

'Yes, sir, as it happens.'

'Then I am sure it will be a simple matter to find them.'

———

'George, is that you?'

'Who were you expecting?'

Rose Perfitt smiles. 'Only you. Was there anything?'

'A letter from your mother. She says she'll come and see us, just like I said.'

Rose walks over and throws her arms around her lover's neck. 'I knew she would, George. And I know we can make her understand; she only needs to see how much I love you. Then she can change Papa's mind.'

'I'll go on my own, mind,' says Nelson.

'On your own?'

'Could be a trick, your father might try and get you back. And we wouldn't want that, would we?'

Rose looks thoughtful. 'No, you're right.'

Nelson leans down and kisses her upon the forehead.

'Good girl.'

CHAPTER FORTY-FOUR

'Here?'

Decimus Webb looks rather incredulously at the shoddy fishmonger's, whose mackerel and haddock lie in serried rows upon wooden blocks.

'There's a room above it, sir,' says Bartleby. 'Up these stairs. Fellow on the corner reckons he saw the pair of them going up there yesterday. Recollects the girl's dress; said you don't see much of that quality around here.'

'More than likely. Very well, Sergeant. After you.'

Bartleby readily leads the way, up the wooden steps beside the shop, until they come to a landing upon the first floor.

'Shall we knock, sir?'

Webb demurs and opens the door. Inside, Rose Perfitt is busying herself, straightening the frayed cloth that covers the room's small dining-table. Her appearance still has a good deal of Edith Grove about it, and seems in stark contrast to the dowdy realities of the Lambeth Road. When she sees the two policemen, she jumps in fright.

'Inspector!'

'I am sorry, Miss Perfitt,' says Webb. 'I did not mean to alarm you.'

Rose takes a deep breath. 'I am afraid you did.'

'I see you have fallen on your feet,' says Webb, looking around the room.

'It is just until we are settled,' replies Rose, nervously.

'How cosy,' says Webb.

There is a silence. Rose, at last, steels herself to speak.

'I expect you have come to take me back home. Well, I shall not go.'

'Sergeant,' says Webb, 'go downstairs and watch the door in case Mr. Nelson returns. I should like to talk to Miss Perfitt alone.'

Bartleby obliges, whilst Webb takes a chair and offers one to Rose Perfitt. She sits down, facing him, uncertain quite what to make of the situation.

'Are you familiar with the practice of what the newspapers like to call baby-farming, Miss Perfitt?' asks Webb.

'I suppose so.'

'Yes, I supposed so too. Tell me, how long have you known George Nelson? Be honest with me, now, Miss Perfitt. You no longer need to keep your little secrets, after all.'

'If you like. Five years, I should say.'

'You met him when you were, what, thirteen years of age?'

'Yes.'

'Did you have intimate relations with him then?'

Rose Perfitt blushes bright crimson. 'That is none of your business.'

'I rather regret it is police business, Miss Perfitt. Rest assured I take no pleasure in discomforting you.'

'I did not, Inspector,' says Rose Perfitt, proudly. 'But even if I had . . . well . . . I am not a criminal.'

'You would have been of an age to consent to your own seduction. I am aware of that, Miss Perfitt. That is the law of the land and I have neither time nor inclination to quibble with it. But, you see, that is where it all started, is it not? The root of this whole wretched business.'

'What "business"?'

'The murder of Jane Budge, Mrs. Featherstone and, of course, Margaret Budge. She was the last one on your list, unless we still have others to find.'

Rose Perfitt puts her hand to her lips, but cannot stifle a nervous giggle. 'Murder?'

'I do not find it amusing, Miss Perfitt. I am missing only the fine detail. At thirteen years old, you found yourself with child, did you not? Your parents hid you away in Leamington Spa, so that Dr. Malcolm might discretely attend the birth. As for the infant, it was placed in the care of Margaret Budge. Doubtless you were persuaded it was for the best.'

Rose shakes her head, her face miming disbelief.

'The child,' continues Webb, 'died. As any poor creature would die in the hands of such a woman. Starved. Frozen to death. Or perhaps a sudden fever. No matter. The child died and you thought that was the end of it. Your secret was safe.'

'I have no "secret", Inspector,' protests Rose Perfitt. 'You are quite deluded.'

Webb shakes his head. 'It was George Nelson's return that did it. Jane Budge had put him away. He wanted revenge. Tell me, does he know about the child? Was that what persuaded you to help him kill her? Is that why you have stuck with him?'

Rose Perfitt's mouth drops open. 'You are mad, Inspector. What do you take me for?'

Webb does not answer. 'Mrs. Featherstone had

discovered something, I imagine? Perhaps Jane Budge had spoken out of turn? And, finally, Mrs. Budge herself. Was that to indulge Nelson's grudge or yours?'

'Inspector,' replies Rose, 'this is making me dizzy. What are you talking about?'

'I think you know, Miss Perfitt. Although, there is another possibility, of course. That you did it all yourself, to protect your little secret. You all but murdered Nelson's child, after all. He might not take that so kindly. Or did you never plan to elope with him? Did you hope for a respectable marriage, to an agreeable young man? Any hint of an illegitimate child might be rather unfortunate.'

'This is nonsense – all of it!' declares Rose.

Webb shrugs. 'I have little proof as yet, but I can find it and I will. No-one can kill three people without a trace, Miss Perfitt. And you are foolish to deny the child, at least. A doctor would know and, if you force my hand, I can propose to a magistrate to have you examined.'

Rose Perfitt freezes. For a second or two she says nothing. At last, when she speaks, a certain steely determination is in her eyes. 'Very well. Send for a doctor.'

Webb blinks. 'You are bluffing, Miss Perfitt.'

'Send for your blessed doctor and be done with it. If that is the indignity required of me, Inspector, then I will submit to it.'

'I think, first, we shall speak to Mr. Nelson. Where can I find him?'

Rose instinctively looks at a piece of paper that lies on the table. Before she can reply, Webb has it in his hands.

'Ah, I see. He appears to be going to meet your mother. At the Prince of Orange public house? How salubrious. Tell me, Miss Perfitt, is blackmail the next stage in your game? He will take good care of you, at a price?'

'I have no "game", Inspector, I keep telling you.'

'Then why would you attach yourself to such a man, Miss Perfitt, so beneath your own station in life?'

'Because,' replies Rose, tears of frustration in her eyes, 'I love him.'

Decimus Webb sighs. 'I can have Dr. Malcolm swear on oath, Miss Perfitt. He will have to admit to it. You will have to explain how you disposed of the child.'

'Dr. Malcolm?'

'Come now. Your parents sent you to his establishment in Leamington Spa after your first dalliance with Nelson. Except that it was not to treat your "nerves", was it?'

'Oh, this is madness!' exclaims Rose in desperation, wiping her eyes. 'I have never even been there! Mama was there, I think, when she was not well. I stayed with my sister. Where does all this come from?'

Decimus Webb opens his mouth, but does not speak. He stays stock still, then, at length, closes his eyes and sighs.

'Bartleby!'

'Sir?' say Bartleby, running back up the stairs.

Webb gets up from his chair and walks hastily towards the door.

'I have been an utter idiot. Watch Miss Perfitt, Sergeant.'

'Where are you going, sir?'

Webb does not answer, but hurries down the stairs. In a second or two, however, he reappears at the door.

'Tell me, Sergeant, where do I find the Prince of Orange?'

CHAPTER FORTY-FIVE

George Nelson opens the door into the private room. It is a little-used, dusty place, upon the first floor of the Prince of Orange, reserved for the likes of commercial travellers or unaccompanied females, anyone who does not wish to be pestered in the public bar. He finds Caroline Perfitt already seated at the table, her hat placed neatly upon it and, in the middle, a bottle of brandy and two glasses, with the liquor already poured.

'I wasn't sure that you'd come, Missus,' says Nelson, taking the seat opposite, grinning to himself.

'I had to,' replies Mrs. Perfitt, 'for Rose's sake.'

'Did you tell your husband?'

'He thinks my sister is ill.'

'Does he?' replies Nelson. 'How is the old man, anyhow?'

'You have kidnapped his daughter. How do you think?'

Nelson wags his finger. 'I know the law, Missus. There's nothing wrong for my part if a girl comes willing. And she is willing, I'll give her that. Tries really hard to please a fellow.'

Mrs. Perfitt visibly winces.

'Don't you like that, Missus? Don't you want to

hear how much she loves me, your little Rose? Of course, you were better. But she'll learn, give her time; I can teach her a few tricks.'

'Why, for God's sake? Why are you doing this? You know she has no money. Not even when she is twenty-one.'

Nelson shakes his head, and slams his fist upon the table. Mrs. Perfitt glances anxiously at the brandy, the bottle rattling with the motion.

'You don't know?' he says, anger in his voice. 'You think you can put a man away for five bastard years, and he'll just brush it off? You try five years in that hell-hole, with just a bloody number for your name, and see how you like it. I swore I'd pay him back. And I have, because I've got the one thing that's most precious to him in all the world, and he can't do a bloody thing about it. I've got my ticket, you see. I stick to the rules.'

'What about me? She is my daughter.'

Nelson shrugs. 'I expect you do as your old man tells you. It makes no odds to me.'

Mrs. Perfitt falls silent.

'Have some pity,' she says at last.

Nelson snorts in derision. 'Like you did?'

'What if I were to tell you that there was a child?'

'What child?'

'I had a child, from our union, a boy; it was yours.'

Nelson laughs. 'Bloody hell. Did *he* know it?'

'Yes.'

Nelson slaps the table once more, this time with sheer delight on his face. 'Now that, Missus, is sweet as anything. What became of it?'

'It . . . he died.'

'Pity,' says Nelson, still with a smirk upon his face.

'Please – George – for my sake, give Rose up. You

have made your point. We have all suffered for what we did.'

'"George" now, is it? What's it worth to you, Missus?'

'We have money. I am sure if I ask Charles—'

'To blazes with Charlie-boy. I'm talking about you.'

'What do you mean?' asks Mrs. Perfitt.

'You might persuade me, if you liked. Now I look at you, you're still not so bad, for your age; I admire that. You've always made the best of yourself, ain't you?'

Caroline Perfitt looks down at the ground.

'You will leave Rose alone?' she says at last.

'I'll think about it,' replies Nelson. 'Funny. We only did it the once. But I reckon I wouldn't mind another go.'

'Very well,' she says softly. Nelson grins once more, a smug contented smile spreading across his face.

'Now, that's more like it, Missus,' he says.

'Have a drink with me, first,' she says, reaching forward for the brandy.

George Nelson shrugs. 'If you like,' he says, taking a glass.

Caroline Perfitt watches him as he raises it to his lips. Perhaps she watches too closely, for he hesitates a little, frowning, perplexed by her close scrutiny. And in the same moment, the door to the room is flung wide open.

'It rather pains me to say it, Mr. Nelson,' says Decimus Webb, breathless, standing in the doorway, 'but I would not drink that if I were you.'

Nelson looks up in disbelief. 'What?'

'I am afraid I am in deadly earnest.'

Nelsons frowns, but lowers the glass, placing it carefully back upon the table.

'Inspector,' says Mrs. Perfitt, haughtily, 'whatever do you mean by—'

'I know the truth, ma'am. I went round the houses to get there, but I know the truth. Please – do not get up – there is nowhere to run and I have a constable not far behind me. You had a child by this man, am I right? You may as well confess it. I am sure we can persuade Dr. Malcolm to tell us, when he knows what you have done to keep it hidden.'

Mrs. Perfitt does not reply. But she makes no denial. Webb continues.

'Jane Budge arranged for its adoption, if that is the word. Her mother was quite willing to look after it . . . for a month or two at least. But then, a couple of weeks ago, she threatened you; she wanted money, perhaps. She threatened to expose your little secret, just as you were trying to bring your daughter into society. In any case, whatever the reason, you met with her at St. Mark's and you killed her.'

'It was not like that,' replies Mrs. Perfitt quietly.

'No?'

'They told me he was still alive, my boy. I paid them . . . well, I paid them when I could, from the housekeeping. I was a fool. But I found them out in the end.'

'Ah, I see,' says Webb.

'I didn't kill her. It was an accident, Inspector. I told her I knew the boy was dead and she threatened me, just as you say. I knocked over the lamp. It was an accident, you see?'

'An accident that you left her there and locked the door behind you?'

'I am sorry for that.'

'An accident, when you had doubtless heard about the threat to "roast" Mr. Featherstone – from his wife,

306

I assume? A convenient mishap. And what of Mrs. Featherstone? Another accident?'

'She came to us that afternoon; she knew something, I do not know what. She was dropping heavy hints about the Gardens. I thought perhaps Budge had said something to her.'

'And so you killed her too? How did you get into the college?'

Mrs. Perfitt sighs. 'I had a key for the old servants' gate in the Fulham Road. They no longer use it; Budge gave it to me, so I could meet her in secret.'

'I see,' says Webb. 'And "The Cutter" helped again, did he not? You thought, with the scissors, he'd get the blame. How ironic that it proved to be Featherstone.'

'Inspector, I had to do something. It would have ruined us if it came out. Rose could never have married. Don't you see?'

'Which brings us to Mrs. Budge,' says Webb. 'When was it? Two days ago? Three? Why so late? You might have killed her before.'

'If you must know, she wrote to me demanding money; she did not realise I had deduced that the boy was dead.'

'I still do not follow,' says Webb.

'I did not know where she lived. She would always meet me at some public place of her choosing.'

'Ah, of course. So you had to wait until a meeting was arranged; and her death could not be in public. The brandy was a clever touch – was it arsenic?'

'Rat poison. We always keep some about the house. You need not mourn for her, Inspector, I promise you. She was a wretched creature.'

George Nelson looks in astonishment at the drink before him.

'Nelson, get out,' says Webb. 'Wait downstairs with the constable.'

Nelson begins to argue but Webb's expression convinces him it might be wiser to obey; reluctantly, looking back at Mrs. Perfitt, he quits the room.

'Why, ma'am?' asks Webb. 'All this just to hide some sordid affair?'

'It was not even that, Inspector. It was one moment of weakness, that is all.'

'With George Nelson?'

'I met him at Cremorne, through Jane Budge; and one day, to my shame, I let him seduce me. It was only meant to be the once; that is what I told myself. A moment of madness. But Charles caught us. I was an utter fool. Thankfully, my husband forgave me; I love him for that.'

'So why all this?'

'I did it for my daughter, Inspector! So that she would have a decent start in life and not pay the penalty for my crime. The child, you see, made it so much worse. There was proof. Letters I had written. If Budge had spoken out, it would have been the end for Rose.'

Webb sighs. 'Your daughter seems to have other ideas, in any case, ma'am. I am sorry to say she appears genuinely besotted with Mr. Nelson. And now she must lose her mother, too.'

Mrs. Perfitt pauses, and takes a deep breath.

'Yes, I know,' she says at last. 'I realise that, Inspector. I should, at least, very much like to spare her the trial.'

She glances down at the table. Webb's eyes seem to follow hers, though he remains standing by the door.

'Thank you, Inspector,' she says, snatching up the glass before her and downing the brandy in one long gulp. Webb merely bows his head.

'You didn't stop me?' she says, looking at him.

'No, ma'am, I didn't.'

⬩

George Nelson looks on in disbelief as Decimus Webb descends the stairs into the public house entirely on his own.

'Don't tell me you ain't putting her away,' exclaims Nelson.

'Be quiet,' says Webb, turning to address the constable who stands by Nelson's side. 'I am afraid Mrs. Perfitt is dead. Leave the room alone; no-one goes in until I come back. Understood?'

'Yes, sir.'

'And if you are incompetent enough to let anyone go in, on no account let them touch the brandy.'

'Sir.'

'As for you, Mr. Nelson, I suggest you come with me.'

George Nelson shrugs, but accompanies the policeman out into the street.

'She's dead?' he says, a little perplexed.

'In a few minutes, I expect she will be. I stayed with her as long as I could stomach it.'

'She drank the brandy?'

'Yes, Mr. Nelson, she drank the brandy that she had intended for you. Though why I saved your worthless neck remains a mystery to me. Now perhaps you will explain to me the one thing I do not understand in this almighty mess.'

'What?'

'Why you have gone to such lengths to humiliate the Perfitts. You do not love the girl, surely?'

'She ain't bad.'

'No, you have done it to punish them; that much

309

is clear. Is it merely because Perfitt gave evidence against you?'

'You're not much of a detective, are you, Webb, eh?' says Nelson.

'Then enlighten me,' says Webb.

'I never laid a finger on Jane Budge,' says Nelson. 'Leastways, not unless she wanted it. The whole thing was to put me away, pay me back for doing his wife. Perfitt arranged it all.'

'You are certain? You did not touch her? I read a report of the trial – she was not unharmed.'

'I touched her all right. She started to kick and scream like a banshee; I had to do something. I thought she was having a fit. Then Perfitt comes down the stairs, flattens me with a poker. Next thing I knew, I was in Pentonville.'

'You said nothing of this in court,' says Webb.

'And who would have believed me, eh? His word against mine. No, I knew I was beat. I bided my time.'

'I see. And so you planned it out; you stole their daughter?'

'She always had a soft spot for me. Used to come and play in the Gardens. That's how I met them. Besides, it ain't "stealing". I know my ticket. I don't want to go back to gaol.'

'What about Rose? Does she know all this? That you and her mother . . . and Jane Budge . . .'

'I ain't told her. Believe it or not, I don't reckon they did either.'

Webb stops in his tracks. 'It has all been for revenge, then?'

'All legal and above board.'

Webb shakes his head. 'Legal, perhaps. Tell me, Mr. Nelson, have you had your fill now?'

'How do you mean?' asks Nelson.

310

'What will become of Rose Perfitt? Her mother is dead; a murderess. In a few days she will be quite infamous for her crimes. Mr. Perfitt has lost his daughter, his wife . . .'

'I don't give a damn about him. He deserves everything he gets.'

'Very well. What about his daughter?'

'She'll stick with me, I reckon.'

'But she does not belong with you; you must know that. Do you have any love for her at all?'

Nelson says nothing.

'Well, do you?' asks Webb.

EPILOGUE

Charles Perfitt sits in his drawing-room, dressed in mourning. Decimus Webb sits opposite, observing Mr. Perfitt's expressionless face.

'The inquest is done with, at least,' says Perfitt. 'I am glad it is over.'

'Yes, sir.'

'I have found a plot for her. For Caroline.'

'I am glad to hear it,' says Webb.

'Unconsecrated ground, of course. They tell me it must only be the name on the headstone, nothing more.'

Webb says nothing.

'I swear, I did not know about the child – that she thought it was still alive. They all told me it had died, you understand? I think that was the thing, that is what played upon her nerves.'

'I expect so, sir.'

'I forgave her, Inspector, I promise you. The night I found her with that man. It pained me to do it, but I forgave her.'

'She told me as much, sir. She was grateful for that.'

'Tell me, Webb, I never asked – did she suffer much, at the end?'

Webb shifts uncomfortably in his chair. 'No, not much. It was a quick business.'

Neither man speaks for a moment.

'I still cannot forgive him, mark you,' says Perfitt, reflectively, breaking the silence.

'Nelson did not deserve five years in gaol,' says Webb, quietly, 'however much you loved your wife.'

Mr. Perfitt shakes his head. 'Look what he has done to Rose – degraded her, for sheer spite. You have seen the sort of man he is.'

'I have,' replies Webb. 'I hope you are still willing, though, sir? I can see no other way. Besides, the law is the law.'

'Is that your motto, Webb?'

'I find it suffices, in most cases.'

'And our arrangement? Is that simply "the law"? Is that what you told Nelson when you cooked this up between you.'

'Have a care, sir. I would have taken you in, regardless. This way, at least, Mr. Nelson thinks he is getting a bargain.'

Perfitt shakes his head. 'It will be much easier for you if I plead guilty.'

'Easier on Miss Perfitt, too.'

'It will break her heart to find out what I did, Inspector. Although I am sure it is shattered already.'

'If you leave her with Mr. Nelson, I'd hazard he'll break her heart again and crush her spirit for good measure.'

Mr. Perfitt falls silent for a moment.

'Very well, you have me. Take me to the magistrate.'

—

'I can't fathom it, sir,' says Bartleby, putting down his copy of *The Times*.

'What, Sergeant?'

'Perfitt – why he's just come out and confessed to giving false witness at Nelson's trial. His wife had a child by some fellow; killed three poor souls to keep it quiet. You'd think he'd want to keep his head down.'

'Perhaps he felt guilty.'

Bartleby shakes his head. 'He's managed for five years; what changed his mind? He's looking at two years inside.'

'Perhaps he felt he had nothing left to lose. Perhaps he wanted to atone for his sins. How on earth should I know?'

'The daughter, too,' continues Bartleby, puzzled. 'She goes to all that trouble to elope with George Nelson – finds her father put him away in the first place – then she's off to live with her sister in Edinburgh.'

'Apparently Mr. Nelson simply grew tired of her.'

'Did he though? I've been wondering, sir. It's almost like they did some sort of deal. He goes inside; the girl goes free.'

'Don't be ridiculous, Sergeant. I swear, you are constantly at the mercy of your imagination.'

Bartleby gives up on his train of thought.

'Are you going to answer that telegram from Mr. Boon, sir?'

'I suppose we must allow the Gardens to re-open,' says Webb. 'Tell him the day after tomorrow, depending on our review and the magistrate's decision.'

'With respect, sir, that's what you said yesterday.'

Webb smiles. 'Really, is that so? Poor Mr. Boon. My heart goes out to him.'

Sergeant Bartleby puts the telegram to one side.